THE SILENT VOW

JAIMIE L. VERMETTE

BLACKTOP
PUBLISHING

Book Cover by GetCovers

Chapter art by Jaimie L. Vermette

First edition 2025

ISBNs:

Hardcover: 979-8-9996385-5-7

Paperback: 979-8-9996385-4-0

eBook: 979-8-9996385-6-4

Printed in The United States of America

For what was certain before the words were ever spoken.

Chapter 1: Life After Death

"From the last rider's fall shall rise the war that wakes the realm." —Fragment of the Lost Chronicle

There was no sky.

Only darkness, hot and close, like smoke in her lungs.

Her body ached—an ache too heavy, too rooted, to belong to the living. The stone beneath her was warm as coals, but her skin burned and shivered all at once. Her blood moved like tar through narrow veins, thick and stubborn, every heartbeat dragging her farther from air.

"She stirs."

The voice was not loud—just near. It carried the weight of stone, as if a mountain itself had decided to speak in a man's throat.

Eliryn's breath caught. Her eyes flew open. The dark didn't shift. It didn't soften. No shapes, no edges, nothing to separate one shadow from another.

"Vaeronth?" she rasped.

I am here.

His voice bloomed in her mind like a flare in a cavern—warm, familiar, steady. The sound of home.

But it didn't slow her breathing.

"Why can't I see?"

You bled too long, Little Flame. You crossed the line between realms. When they pulled you back... you were changed.

"They?"

The Kin. The ones who guard this place.

Her throat tightened. *Kin* was the wrong word for the voices circling her cot. They did not sound like family. They sounded like ages—like rain carving a canyon, like winter breaking a peak. She flinched at the scrape of footfalls—stone on stone, slow and certain.

The air moved, and she felt it: a shadow passing overhead. Wings. The sense of immensity. Not

Vaeronth. This was closer. Living bodies surrounded her, each one radiating a steady heat like sun-warmed granite.

"Do not crowd her," another voice said, the command quiet but ironclad.

Hands—rough, ridged like weathered rock—slid beneath her arms and lifted her upright. The contact was startlingly warm. Her ribs screamed. She tasted iron as she bit down against the pain and confusion swirling inside her.

"Easy." A breath, measured. "She's held."

Held? She swallowed against a dry throat. "Where am I?" Her voice scraped like chalk.

You are safe, Vaeronth answered, his mind-voice low and even. *In the Fold. In their place of healing.*

The Fold. Hearth-tales and whispered lore. A sanctuary high in the mountains where the last gargoyles had vanished when the dragons had fallen. She had thought them statues abandoned in ruined cathedrals, wings furred in moss, mouths choked with ivy. Not... this. Not voices that breathed. Not warmth at her back and the careful way those rough hands steadied her as if she might shatter.

"They called me back?" she whispered. "From—"

You were gone for mere moments, Vaeronth interrupted.

Memory cracked open. The press of the crowd. The power of the Flame she never wanted, too heavy on her heart. The heat that wasn't heat but *atten-*

tion, hundreds of eyes pinning her in place. The rebellion's roar surging like a tide. And then—his voice, the one that had murmured her name like a prayer and a threat: *I'll make it quick.* Cold iron sliding through her side. The whole realm tilting. Vaeronth's scream tearing the sky. The wind, and then nothing at all.

Her mouth tasted of ash. "I died."

For mere moments.

Her fingers moved—slow, shaky—to her ribs. Thick bandages pulled taut beneath her touch. Stitches tugged at bruised skin.

They carried you to their med wing, Vaeronth said. *Their healers bound you and poured strength into your blood. Old rites. Old magic. Dangerous, but needed.*

Low murmurs rippled around her bed.

"She should not live."

"Yet she has returned."

Eliryn stiffened. "Stop talking about me like I'm not here."

Silence fell. Not empty—weighted. The air itself seemed to hold its breath.

The words echoed back at her, too sharp, too alive in the hush. She swallowed hard, pulse thudding against her bandages. "I'm sorry," she said quickly, the heat draining from her voice. "I've been doing the same—talking to someone you can't hear."

Her fingers clenched in the blanket. "My name is Eliryn. I've been... communicating with my dragon,

Vaeronth. He says I'm among the guardians of the old tales—that you are the Kin?"

The silence shifted, less brittle now, like stone considering whether to move.

You are more myth than girl to them, Vaeronth murmured against the inside of her skull. *They revere what you are. They do not know what to do with what you have become.*

What I've become, she echoed, her throat tight. *Still blind. Maybe powerless.*

You are a Dragonrider, he said simply. *That is enough.*

The cot shifted as someone—something—leaned closer. The heat of a body large as a doorway eddied over her, baking away her sweat-chill.

"She breathes steady," a voice said, nearer. "The bandages hold."

"She is marked," another answered, wary. "But the Flame is quiet."

A third voice cut through the murmurs—deeper, rough-edged like stone dragged against stone. The air itself seemed to tighten around it.

"Enough," he said. "Do not speak of her as though she is not present. Show respect. She bears the bond-marks of the last Dragonrider."

Silence followed—thick, chastened. Even the fire seemed to lower its crackle.

Eliryn's fingers traced the grooves along her forearm, the raised lines of rune and script seared into her skin when she and Vaeronth had bonded in the Trials of Sovereignty. The marks pulsed faintly, answering her touch like a sleeping beast turning toward warmth.

"The Flame left me," she said, pulse stuttering. "That's what you're discussing?"

For a breath, no one spoke. The silence weighed like a hand on the back of her neck.

Perhaps it passed on, Vaeronth offered gently. *Perhaps it waits. But it is not alive inside you.*

She could not see their faces, but she could *feel* attention pivot, prickle across her skin. She lifted her chin. "How long?"

A different set of hands, cooler, more careful, touched the edges of her bandages. Fingers checked knots, pressed lightly for seepage. She hissed when they found a tender spot.

"Nearly eight days," the first voice said. "You drifted in and out. Fever took you once, then broke."

Eliryn swallowed, her throat raw. "Eight days... and all that time, you cared for me?"

"We watched over you," came the answer. "You would not wake. Your dragon remained a steady presence outside."

A faint vibration stirred through the stone, the echo of distant wings. *I remained near,* Vaeronth murmured in her mind. *Though they insisted the roof was not built for me.*

One of the Kin gave a low, grinding sound that might have been laughter. "He circled the cliffs above the Fold," the voice said. "Three days and nights he kept to the skies. When storms gathered, he roared them apart. When we entered this chamber, his shadow covered the walls."

Eliryn blinked hard, emotion tightening her chest. "I'm surprised he let you near me at all."

A pause—and then the deeper, steady voice, the one that carried command like bedrock, answered her. "All dragons know the Kin. They remember the old vows, even when mortals forget. We were shaped to guard your kind—to heal and to serve the bond between flame and flesh. No hand here would have harmed you."

The truth in his voice was unyielding, and she felt it settle over her like a weight and a promise both. "Then I owe you my life," she whispered.

"Not owed," he said. "Only honored."

Warmth pressed at the edges of her thoughts again—Vaeronth's voice, steady as the heartbeat of the mountain.

Even in death, our bond could not be broken. The gods chose well, Little Flame. You are living proof—the prophecy walking, breath returned from ash.

The words reverberated through her chest until she couldn't tell where her pulse ended and his began. She drew in a slow, shaking breath, feeling the truth of it settle deep, where her fear had been.

The realm steadied, piece by piece. She inhaled through her teeth and forced her legs to move beneath the blanket. They felt like someone else's. Lead-heavy. Trembling.

"Where exactly is the 'med wing'?" she asked, needing the shape of the room to anchor herself. "Because this doesn't smell like herbs and linens."

"Hearth cavern," a voice answered. "The mountain's heart keeps this place warm. Pools lie beyond the curtain—healing springs. The healers keep their tools here."

A pause, the faintest ripple of dry humor. "You bled on most of them."

Eliryn huffed out something between a laugh and a groan. "Apologies," she said, voice rough but wry.

The air shifted—less solemn now, almost companionable.

Let me help you see, Vaeronth said.

"How?"

I will anchor you with our power.

It had never been so deliberate between them. On the road to the trials, sight had come and gone in flashes—moments of clarity like flint sparks in dark grass. In her moments before the attack, she had learned to borrow Vaeronth's sight as her own. Now, as she steadied her breathing and opened that soft place in her chest where their bond lived, she felt his presence swell like a tide. Warmth slid behind her eyes.

The dark didn't lift so much as... bend. Not *her* sight. *His.* The room emerged in impressions, at first hazy, then sharpening: a vaulted space ribbed with natural arches, firelight blooming along wet stone. Rivulets ran in the walls like veins of silver. Curtains hung from iron rods—hide and woven wool. Basins glinted. Hooks held bone-handled tools, careful and clean. The air lay thick with the scent of boiled linen, crushed root, and old smoke.

And beyond her bed—three figures.

They were not statues.

Wings folded tight to their backs, they stood like living fortresses, their skin a marbled grey that caught firelight and threw it back in dull glints. Talons curled where toes should be; their hands were massive and ridged, knuckled like river-worn rock. Their faces were not monstrous, just... old. Etched. Eroded by time into something that refused to be anything but itself. Eyes glowed with a steady ember-light, not bright or showy, simply present.

Her breath hitched.

Can you see through me as well? she asked, the thought barely formed.

When you allow it, he said.

Her lips parted. "Gods," she whispered. "This will never seem normal."

A low warmth curled through her—his amusement, content to be small and private, a coal banked against the cold.

"You see us now," one of the gargoyles said. It wasn't a question.

"I... guess we can call it that," Eliryn said.

"She borrows from the dragon," another murmured. "She is not without gifts."

"No," the first agreed. "She is not."

They watched her. Not with hostility—just with the patience of mountains watching weather.

Eliryn smoothed the blanket over her lap, grounding herself in the warmth beneath her fingers. "I know you are all guardians," she said softly. "Protectors of dragons and their bonded. So that's why you pulled me back into the land of the living. It's your duty."

A low sound passed through the air—agreement, edged with something older than words.

"It is the purpose for which we were made," said the deep, steady voice of the leader. "We were carved from the gods themselves, shaped to guard what was sacred—the dragons, and those bound to them."

She drew a careful breath. "Then you must know about the Sightless Prophecy."

The silence that followed felt alive. The warmth of the hearth deepened, shadows stretching long across the walls.

"We know," one of the gargoyles said, rough with age. "It was spoken before the rot touched magic. Before the gifted were outcast. Before the dragons fell from the skies and the realm forgot its own light."

A third continued, softer: "We have guarded its words through the ages, waiting for the sign."

"The blind dragonborne," murmured one. "The one who would fall and rise again. Sightless, yet chosen to reignite what was lost."

Eliryn's breath caught. The air itself seemed to still.

Then the leader spoke, his voice low and absolute. "We knew the moment we saw you. You are the one the prophecy foretold."

Heat pricked behind her eyes, sharp and unbidden. She blinked hard, swallowing the ache before it could become something else.

Beyond the bed, carved into the rock wall, a band of runes caught her eye. She turned toward them without thinking. Lines of script cut with deliberate care, each stroke shallow and precise. One rune—angular, flanked by two curling marks—pulsed faintly, a heartbeat of emberlight. It tugged at her with the same inexorable pull as the marks on her skin.

Ignoring the pain rippling through her, she rose without thought, her body unaware of her mind's intention. She reached out her hand.

Careful, Vaeronth warned, but did not stop her.

Her fingers brushed stone.

The rune flared—not bright, but deep, as if waking from a long sleep. Sound rolled through the chamber in a single low note, a hum that set her teeth on edge and eased a knot in her spine at the same time. Her forearm tingled. The script along her skin warmed and answered.

"She is more heavily marked than we could have imagined," one of the gargoyles breathed. Softer now. Almost reverent.

Eliryn pressed her palm flat against the rune until its light softened to a pulse that matched her heartbeat. When she drew back, warmth lingered in her hand, then slid down to pool low in her chest.

"I'm more than that," she murmured. "Or I was."

No one contradicted her.

The exhaustion hit like a wave—all the pain she'd been holding at bay rushing back in, all the questions crowding her ribs. She exhaled shakily, pressing a hand to her temple. "I have so many questions," she admitted, voice low but steady. "But maybe we should start with names."

A pause—then the largest of the Kin stepped forward, his movement deliberate, precise. "I am Garrion," he said, the sound of his name carrying weight, carved and certain. He inclined his head toward the two beside him. "This is Brakka, and that is Zesh. They tended your wounds."

Eliryn nodded slightly, committing the names to memory. "Thank you," she said quietly. "For keeping me alive."

Brakka tilted his head, his ember-lit eyes studying Eliryn with open curiosity. "You should not have survived," he said, not unkindly. "Yet here you stand. Tell us—what do you remember of it? Of how you came to us?"

Eliryn hesitated, her throat tightening. The room seemed to tilt around her.

She staggered slightly, gripping the edge of the stone table to steady herself. The weight of their stares pressed in from all sides.

Tell them the truth you remember, Vaeronth urged gently.

Eliryn swallowed. "I remember the citadel. I remember the choosing. The Flame. And then..."

A flash.

A blade.

His voice in her ear—*forgive me.*

Her pulse lurched. Her knees nearly buckled.

"...Then it goes dark."

Brakka stepped forward slightly. "You were attacked?"

Eliryn nodded. "I think someone tried to kill me. My memories—" She exhaled through clenched teeth. "They're shattered."

Your mind is protecting you from the moment of pain, Vaeronth whispered. *Betrayal runs deep. But you must face it.*

She stared at the floor. Her jaw clenched.

It was Malric.

His name hit her like a wound reopening. She felt her balance waver again—like the room itself tilted under her feet. *Betrayal.* The word didn't do it justice. She'd trusted him. Leaned on him. Chosen him.

And he had driven the blade in. Literally.

"I need—" her voice cracked. "I need a moment. Please."

The Kin looked between one another. Garrion inclined his head. "You are safe within these walls," he said. "Take what time you need."

They left with the silence of stone.

Only when the door sealed behind them did Eliryn let her knees give out.

She sank to the floor in silence, pressing her palms to her face as if she could hold the grief back.

Her breath came shallow, sharp.

She could still feel the echo of his hands—the heat of his betrayal.

"Why..." Her voice cracked. "Why would he do that?"

No answer came.

Only silence—and the knowledge that survival hadn't spared her the pain.

It had only delayed it.

Chapter 2: The Kin

"We guard the body. The dragon guards the soul. Between us, death has no claim." —Kin Proverb

Eliryn didn't know how long she sat on the floor. Time stretched, unmeasured.

It felt like she'd been there for hours—maybe days. Maybe lifetimes.

The stone was cold against her skin, but she barely noticed. Not past the blood—dried and flaking against her legs, her arms, her ribs. It caked the torn remains of her coronation dress, now little more than rags hanging loose from her frame. Her feet were bare, filthy and bruised, toes curling against the uneven ground like a tether to what was real.

Her entire body was shaking.

Every movement pulled at the bandages cinched tightly around her waist, the pressure biting into the wound left behind by Malric's blade. It still ached. Still throbbed with shallow pain. But worse than the sharpness was the weight of it—the knowing.

She'd died.

Not metaphorically. Not in some poetic way that people whisper about later.

She had died. Taken her last breath. Faded into a state of nothingness.

And now she was here, in a place she couldn't comprehend, breathing air her lungs had no right to claim, speaking to a dragon who should've mourned her.

Eliryn let her head fall back against the stone wall and laughed.

It wasn't a good sound.

It was fractured. Cracked down the middle. The kind of laugh you choke on before it ever becomes real.

Eliryn. Vaeronth's voice slipped into her mind like wind through a broken window—soft, but steady.

Her stomach turned. "It was him," she said quietly. "Malric."

Vaeronth didn't answer right away. The silence said enough.

"I knew what he was," she went on, her voice shaking. "An assassin. The man who killed whoever he was told to. I told myself it wasn't his choice. That he didn't want that life. I thought..." She pressed a hand to her chest. "I thought I could see the part of him that still had a soul."

You believed there was good in him, Vaeronth said gently.

"I did. Gods, I did. I thought we were the same, just trying to survive what the realm made us."

Her throat closed up. "And he still did it. He put a blade in me because someone told him to."

The memory hit like a wave—his face, calm and cold; the whisper of her name; the shock of metal and heat. "He didn't even hesitate."

Her voice broke. "I bled out on your back, didn't I?"

Yes, Vaeronth said. *By the time we reached the Sanctuary, your heart had already stopped.*

Eliryn dragged in a shaky breath. "He killed me because Thalen wanted it done."

He followed his orders, Vaeronth said quietly.

She shook her head hard. "No. He *chose* it. He always had a choice."

Vaeronth didn't argue.

Her hands were shaking. She stared down at them, at the faint glow under her skin where the runes still pulsed. "I really thought he cared about me," she whispered. "That maybe someone finally saw me."

Her voice cracked again, small and sharp. "And I was wrong."

Vaeronth's presence pressed against her grief, warm and steady, the only thing holding her togeth er. *You're still here, Little Flame. That's what matters.*

But the words didn't feel like comfort. They just hung there, heavy and hollow, while she tried to remember how to breathe.

Then she barked another laugh—sharp and bitter. "I didn't even want the crown. I *never* wanted it. I was just trying to survive the trials. I never asked for any of this."

She pressed the heel of her hand to her eyes.

"But then I was chosen. And for a moment..." her voice cracked, "for just one singular moment, I thought maybe... maybe I'd done something right. Like if the Flame found me worthy, then maybe I really was meant to rule."

A long breath shuddered out of her.

"And now all of that is gone."

You were betrayed.

"I was *stupid*," she spat.

She curled forward, arms wrapping around her knees.

"I survived growing up different. I survived impossible odds in the trials. But I was too blind to see the blade coming. I *let* him in." Her voice splintered. "I let him close enough to kill me."

He hid himself from me too, with his magic.

She shook her head. "You warned me. You always warned me. And I didn't listen. I told you I could handle it. That I *knew* who he was."

Her lip trembled. "But I didn't. I *didn't*."

There was silence. Then:

You wanted to see the good in him.

"I saw what I wanted to see. That's not seeing the good in someone—that's delusion."

She stared down at her hands. Blood under her nails. Bruises blooming up her arms.

"I've died before I even got the chance to live," she whispered. "And without you, I'd be dead a dozen times over."

But you're still here.

"Because of *you*."

Eliryn tilted her head back and stared into the dark. She would be sightless without him, the black emptiness pressing in around her like smoke with no source.

"I owe you everything," she whispered.

You owe me nothing. We are one. I would carry you across a thousand lifetimes if I had to.

Her chest caved inward.

He meant it. That was the worst part.

And she had failed him. Failed herself. Failed Silas. Failed *Garic*.

"Oh gods..." Her voice broke completely. "Garic."

The name ripped something loose inside her. She saw him as clearly as if he were standing there again—broad-shouldered, scarred, steady as bedrock. Garic of Stonefell. A man who had already buried two sons and still managed to believe there was something in the realm worth fighting for.

"He found me," she whispered. "After Malric dragged me from the hall. He'd pulled me into an old wing—somewhere no one would see. Garic found me anyway."

The memory rose like a flood: Malric's hand at her throat, the scrape of steel, the shimmer of candlelight on stone. Then Garic bursting through the archway, his sword raised, shouting her name. He didn't hesitate. He'd stepped between them, knowing exactly what it would cost.

"He was fighting for me," she said, her voice shaking. "And I left him there."

The air thickened. Vaeronth's voice came low, full of quiet sorrow. *He made his choice, Little Flame. He gave you the only thing he had left to give.*

Eliryn's throat tightened. "And Malric took everything from him for it."

For a long moment, neither of them spoke.

Do you remember what I told you, before the trials ended? Vaeronth said at last. *That there was something cold about him. Ancient. Wrong.*

She nodded faintly, tears burning her eyes. "You said it felt like the air bent around him. Like shadow pretending to be a man."

That was the power I felt when he struck you, Vaeronth said. *Hidden, deep under his skin. I think now it wasn't his own. It reeked of the Thalen's hand—and the crown's corruption.*

Eliryn swallowed hard. "So he was a puppet. That magic—whatever it was—it made sure he couldn't stop, even if part of him wanted to."

Yes, Vaeronth said softly. *The crown has always demanded blood to keep its power. He was just the blade it used.*

She pressed a shaking hand to her mouth. "Garic didn't stand a chance."

None of us did, Vaeronth murmured. *Not then.*

Eliryn's voice cracked. "He should've ran."

He chose to make sure you escaped, Vaeronth said. *And that choice was something the crown couldn't control.*

She bowed her head, trembling, the weight of it all pressing against her ribs until breathing hurt.

The sob ripped from her throat like it had claws. She folded in on herself, curling as tightly as she could, trying to keep it all inside—but it wouldn't stay.

Pain like that couldn't be hidden.

It poured out.

Grief. Rage. Guilt. The crushing weight of know-ing she hadn't just been fooled—she had *let* it hap-pen.

And then—

A shift in the air.

She lifted her head, slow and wary, as the deep rumble of a voice filled the chamber.

"You burn like a dying star."

Eliryn blinked. "That's... poetic." Her voice was hoarse. "You always start conversations like that?"

A low hum, almost like the scrape of boulders rolling in the deep. "Only with those who've forgotten they still burn."

She almost laughed, but it caught somewhere be-tween her ribs and her throat. "I thought I asked for time alone."

"You did," the gargoyle said. "But solitude is not the same as being left to drown. Even stone knows when to reach."

Looking more closely at him, she realized it was the one who had introduced himself as Garrion. "You were the one who told the others to respect me."

"I told them to remember what you are," he cor-rected. "Even when what you are is... complicated."

Eliryn's mouth twisted. "That's a polite way of saying 'blind, wounded, and not what you expected.'"

He didn't deny it. "You are not what I expected," Garrion agreed, and she could almost hear the uncertainty behind his words, "but you are what was promised."

Her eyes closed shut, forcing the emotion to stay inside.

Garrion was silent for a beat, and then she heard a sound—stone folding on stone. When she realized what it was, her chest tightened.

He was lowering himself to the floor with her.

The air shifted with the sheer mass of him, the faint grit of dust settling from his movement.

"You've met death," he said. "But the Flame's choosing does not end at death. Not truly."

Her voice dropped. "It felt like it did. It's gone now."

"Feelings are for the living," Garrion said. "The Flame sees beyond them."

She almost snapped back, but stopped herself. "You speak like you've known it."

"I was one of the first protectors," he said simply. "I have seen it all."

Her breath stilled. "...All?"

His head inclined—she didn't see it, but she felt the faint shift of weight. "Until the dragons fell."

"And now?" she asked, her voice quieter.

"Now," Garrion said, "I will support you. Whether you believe in yourself or not."

Her throat tightened. "You don't even know me."

"You are bonded to the last dragon in the realm," Garrion said. "That is all I need to know."

Eliryn shifted against the cold stone, her knees drawn to her chest. "That's... honest," she admitted reluctantly, "and terrifying at the same time."

His voice rumbled low, almost like distant thunder. "Both can be true."

For a moment, there was only the muted crackle of a distant fire somewhere in the hall beyond, the faint scent of burning cedar threading through the cooler smell of mineral-rich air. The space felt vast, but not empty—its weight was in the high, vaulted ceiling she could almost feel pressing down, the slow pulse of magic in the walls, like the sanctuary itself was listening.

"I didn't even know gargoyles were real," she said finally. "I thought you were statues in old cathedrals. Or stories meant to scare children into behaving."

A sound like a quiet laugh rolled from him. "Most who have seen us think the same—right before they stop breathing."

Her lips twitched. "Comforting."

"We are not meant to comfort," Garrion said. "We are meant to protect."

She was quiet for a long moment, fingers tracing the frayed hem of her ruined dress. "And you've been waiting here all this time?"

"Yes," Garrion said. "The city of Vireth and the outer villages may have forgotten what we are, but the gods did not. The prophecy spoke of one who would come—blind, marked, the last of her kind. We were told to be ready."

Eliryn's throat tightened. "And then I arrived, dying on my dragon's back."

Garrion's reply came without hesitation. "We didn't expect to meet you in that condition."

She exhaled slowly, a half-laugh slipping out. "Well. Sorry to ruin the legend."

"I did not say you ruined it," Garrion countered. "Legends rarely look the way we imagine."

That earned a quiet huff from her. "Guess I'm not the only one with trouble seeing clearly."

For a heartbeat, she thought she heard it—the faint scrape of stone softening, a sound almost like amusement.

"Perhaps," he said.

The silence between them this time wasn't sharp—it was steady, like breath shared between two living things. Eliryn let herself settle into it, noticing what she hadn't before: the faint pulse of heat rising from the floor, the slow drip of water somewhere in the distance, the weight of centuries pressed into every stone.

She swallowed, her voice low but clear. "I owe you my life. All of you. Whatever you did... thank you."

Garrion inclined his head, the motion deliberate, solemn. "You were gone when Vaeronth brought you to us. No heartbeat. No breath. We gave what was required—blood, stone, and magic."

Her brows knit. "What does that mean, exactly?"

"It means," Garrion said, "that to restore you, we had to give a part of ourselves. Our blood bound to your own, our stone to your flesh, our magic to your spark."

She blinked at him, trying to take that in. "So I'm... what, part gargoyle now?"

A low sound rumbled in his chest—not quite a laugh, but close. "No. You are still what you were. But the line between us has thinned. If you bleed, we feel it. If you fall, we will know."

Eliryn's pulse stuttered. "You mean we're bound."

"In every way that matters," Garrion said. "Your survival is now ours. If you burn, we burn with you."

A strange shiver passed through her—not fear exactly, but something heavier.

"Does that mean you can hear my thoughts now?" she asked cautiously.

"No," Garrion said without hesitation. "That is the dragon's bond. We guard the body. He guards the soul."

For some reason, that distinction made her chest tighten further.

Her voice dropped. "I don't know what I'm supposed to do next. Everything I thought I was... is gone."

"You are still breathing," Garrion said. "That is enough for today."

She gave a soft, humorless laugh. "That sounds like something Vaeronth would say."

"Then perhaps your dragon is wiser than you think."

Her lips curved faintly despite herself.

Garrion shifted, the stone beneath him groaning faintly at his folded position. Up close, she could see the tiny fractures in his granite skin—fine lines filled with faintly glowing dust, as though he'd been carved from the heart of a mountain and still carried its molten core.

Eliryn angled her head toward him. "Do all gargoyles look like you?"

He gave her a long, measuring look. "No. Some are uglier."

She huffed, startled by the dry jab. "Noted."

The faintest twitch ghosted across his mouth, almost a smile.

Silence hung between them, thick but comfortable. The fires along the walls hissed softly, the warmth mixing with the deep chill of the mountain.

When she finally spoke, her voice was quiet. "Vaeronth told me that magic in the realm has been fading for centuries. That it's dying."

Garrion inclined his head. "It is."

"Why?" she asked. "What's killing it?"

For a long moment, he said nothing. Then: "A man who was never meant to hold it."

Eliryn straightened slightly. "Thalen."

"The Sovereign," Garrion confirmed, the title edged with stone and contempt. "He was not born of the Flame, but he found a way to bend it to his will. When he took the crown, he bound himself to its heartfire. Its power should have passed through him, feeding the realm. Instead, he drew it inward—kept it for himself."

She frowned. "He's been using the realm's magic to keep himself alive all this time."

"Alive," Garrion said, "and thriving. His body endures while the realm withers. The forests thin. Rivers grow shallow. Magic turns sour. It is the price of one man's hunger."

Eliryn's pulse quickened. "And no one stopped him?"

"There was one force that could have," Garrion said, his gaze shifting toward the far shadows of the chamber. "The dragons—and their riders."

Her stomach sank. "But they fell."

He nodded once, slow and heavy. "All but one. When the dragons died, it was as if a flame had been snuffed out across the sky. It happened within days of Thalen's coronation. No one saw the connection then. We do now."

Eliryn's hand curled into her blanket. "So he's been bleeding the realm dry for centuries. And Vaeronth... hid himself because he knew."

"Because he was told," Garrion corrected. "The last of the dragons knew of the prophecy—when the realm began to rot, Vaeronth was told to wait. Wait for the one born blind, marked, and bound to Flame."

Eliryn let out a shaky laugh, half disbelief, half dread. "And that's me."

"Yes." Garrion's eyes burned low and steady. "The realm is dying, Eliryn. And the only thing strong enough to fight what's left of its poison is standing right here."

She stared at him. "You've really just been waiting for me to fix this?"

"Yes." His answer was as blunt as stone.

Eliryn blinked. "You really didn't come up with any better strategies?"

For the first time, she could have sworn she heard him exhale—something like the ghost of a sigh through granite lungs. "We had time to consider strategy," he said. "But this is your birthright, Dragonrider."

Her gaze dropped to her torn skirts, stiff with blood. "Without Vaeronth, I'd be nothing."

"You'd be dead," Garrion corrected. "But nothing? No. That is not what I see."

The chamber smelled of stone dust and something sharper—iron, maybe, or old magic. The air was cool but heavy, the way caves get after centuries of holding their breath.

Through Vaeronth's borrowed sight, she saw shelves carved straight into the rock, laden with jars of crushed herbs, gleaming vials, rolls of linen bound tight with leather cord. Along the far wall, a brazier glowed faintly, casting thin ribbons of smoke into the air. The scent of burning sage and some bitter root clung to her skin. It reminded her of home.

She shifted slightly, feeling the scrape of grit against her bare legs where her ruined skirts had ridden up. The torn fabric stuck to her in places where blood had dried thick, cracking when she moved. Her feet were raw and darkened with soot and dirt.

"Tell me," Garrion said. "How did you win the trials?"

Her laugh was humorless. "You sound like you can't believe I did win."

"I believe it," Garrion replied. "I want to know *how*. We've heard nothing from the citadel in years—not since Thalen sent his last hunting party, and even then we didn't hear much. We stopped scouting for information decades ago; it wasn't worth the risk."

Eliryn dragged her hands over her face, feeling the grit and dried blood scratch her palms. "I survived. Barely. I made alliances where I could, fought when I had to. Most of the others were stronger, faster, more dangerous than me. But I..." Her voice caught, remembering the Flame, the way it had answered her in the end. "I had Vaeronth."

"You adapted," Garrion corrected. "That matters more than strength. Even dragons cannot win on fire alone."

True, Vaeronth's voice murmured in her mind, quiet but approving.

She tilted her head toward Garrion. "And yet I ended up here. Crowned for five minutes, and dead because I trusted the wrong person."

His expression didn't change, but the faintest crack of sympathy appeared in his voice. "The wrong person can sometimes wear the right face. Even the Kin have been deceived before."

Her chest tightened. "Malric didn't just try to kill me. He killed Silas—my guard. My friend." She swallowed, the memory hot and sharp in her throat. "And I didn't see it. Literally and figuratively. His magic cloaked his intentions from Vaeronth, and I..." She shook her head. "I thought I was clever. Thought I could keep him close without letting him *too* close."

"You think that makes you foolish," Garrion said.

"Doesn't it?"

"No." He said it simply, as if it were fact. "It makes you human. The gods don't choose those without weakness—they choose those who can turn weakness into strength."

She huffed out a breath, bitter. "Not sure that's working out so well for me right now."

"You're not finished yet." He said simply.

They sat in silence for a long moment, the brazier's smoke curling between them.

"So what exactly is it you think I'm supposed to do now?" Eliryn asked finally. "How am I supposed to fix an entire realm?"

Garrion's gaze didn't waver. "The prophecy says the last Dragonrider will break the king's hold. That the rot will end when the Flame burns in the right hands again."

Her laugh was a harsh whisper. "I don't even *have* the Flame anymore."

"Perhaps not," he said, leaning back slightly. "But you are still bonded to a dragon. And that bond is older than the Flame itself. Older than Thalen. That is not nothing."

Vaeronth's voice slid into her mind again, steady as stone. *He's right.*

Eliryn pressed her lips together, staring down at her filthy, bloodstained hands. "So you hide me here until I figure out how to kill a king who's been alive for centuries?"

Garrion's mouth curved, not into a smile, but something that hinted at it. "We don't hide our weapons. We sharpen them."

That landed somewhere deep in her chest, solid and sharp, impossible to ignore.

"I'm not a weapon," she said.

"Not yet," Garrion allowed. "But you could be. And when the time comes, you'll have to decide if you want to be."

Her pulse thudded in her ears.

The brazier popped, sending a brief flare of sparks into the air, and she thought about the way her rune had glowed against the wall, answering her touch like it had been waiting for her. Waiting just like the Kin.

Maybe she wasn't ready to think about what came next. But sitting here, under the steady, unflinching gaze of a guardian carved from the bones of the mountain, she thought... maybe she could survive the becoming.

Garrion shifted his weight, the stone of his armor-like skin catching the firelight. "You touched one of the runes earlier," he said. "It answered you."

She glanced toward the far wall, where the faint glow had long since faded. "It felt... familiar."

"It should." Garrion unfolded his massive frame from the floor, his wings spreading briefly before folding tight again. "Come."

Eliryn hesitated, then pushed herself upright with a quiet groan. Every movement tugged at her wound, a sharp reminder of how close she'd come to never standing again. She wrapped her arms around herself and followed Garrion across the chamber, her bare feet whispering against cool stone.

The brazier's light deepened as they approached the far wall. At first, it looked solid—just another stretch of carved granite. But as they drew closer, faint lines shimmered beneath the surface, like veins catching firelight.

"This is the Chronicle Wall," Garrion said. His voice dropped low, reverent. "It remembers every bond that was ever forged between dragon and rider."

She stared. Hundreds—no, thousands—of runes spiraled outward from a single point at the center. Each one was unique, carved deep into the stone and filled with a faint internal glow, like the last breath of an ember refusing to die.

"They carved their names here?" she asked softly.

"Not carved," Garrion said. "The stone itself accepted them. When a bond is formed, the wall knows. It feels the joining of flame and flesh, and it burns the mark of that pair into itself. When one dies, the mark darkens. When both fall..."

He trailed off. The meaning didn't need words.

Eliryn stepped closer. She could see now that most of the runes near the center had dimmed entirely—cold scars on the rock. "They're all gone," she whispered.

Garrion nodded once. "When Thalen took the crown, the wall went wild. Symbols flared brighter than they ever had before, and then their light went out completely. Dozens. Hundreds. It was as if the mountain itself screamed. So many bonds severed at once that the stone nearly cracked apart."

Her stomach twisted. "That was when the dragons fell."

"Yes." His gaze lingered on the darkened marks. "The power that ties dragon to rider is ancient—older than kingdoms. When that many bonds were broken at once, the realm itself faltered. Magic turned inward on itself. The realm has been unraveling ever since."

Eliryn reached out, tracing one of the cold runes with her fingertips. The stone pulsed faintly under her touch, a ghost of heat—recognition. "So this wall... it's alive?"

"In a way," Garrion said. "It's bound to the same currents that connect all dragonkind. It feels what they feel. It keeps their memory when no one else can."

She looked up, her throat tight. "And it's still adding marks?"

"Only one in recent centuries." He looked at her—steady, unreadable. "Yours."

A tremor ran through her. The brazier's glow flared, and for a heartbeat, she saw them—shapes in the light. Wings. Riders. A thousand souls etched into the mountain, watching. Waiting.

She drew in a sharp breath and pressed her palm against the stone. Warmth surged beneath her skin—soft at first, then building until it felt like the wall itself was breathing with her.

She didn't see fire this time. She saw shadows. Falling skies. The roar of dragons fading into silence.

When she pulled her hand back, the glow lingered, a pale brand against her palm.

"Why show me this?" she whispered.

Garrion's gaze never left the wall. "Because memory is power. You carry the legacy of all who came before you. Do not waste it."

Her chest ached, but this time it wasn't just grief. It was something heavier. Older.

"I don't even know where to start," she admitted.

"Then start here," Garrion said. "Learn our history. Learn *your* history. We will train you until you are ready to take it back."

Vaeronth's voice curled in her mind, warm despite the weight of the moment. *This is just the beginning.*

Chapter 3: The Key the Realm Shall Heed

The mountain keeps no secrets from those it has claimed."
—Kin Proverb

The cold met her the moment she stepped beyond the chamber.

Eliryn followed the heavy, deliberate stride of Garrion, her bare feet whispering over the runed flagstones. Every step sent a dull throb through her side where the bandages bit into her ribs, and she fought to keep her breathing even. Her legs still felt unsteady, the ache under her skin a reminder that her body hadn't caught up to the miracle of still existing.

The corridor was vast, the ceiling lost in shadow, broken only by the faint ember-glow of runes carved deep into the walls. They pulsed faintly as she passed, almost like a heartbeat—though she could not shake the feeling they were keeping time with hers.

They are watching you, Vaeronth murmured in her mind. His tone wasn't a warning, but it made her spine straighten all the same.

The runes? She thought back.

The Kin.

Somewhere far above, the soft beat of wings drifted down—a whisper against the air that could only be Vaeronth's true form cutting through the high winds. The thought settled something tight in her chest, but it didn't loosen the coil of unease building beneath her breastbone.

"This place feels..." She searched for the word. "...awake."

"It is," Garrion said without glancing back. His voice was a low rumble, each syllable weighted. "The Kin built this sanctuary before there were thrones. Magic still has a home here."

They turned a corner, and the corridor spilled into a great hall. Vaulted arches soared above them, each carved with scenes of dragons in flight, riders clasping spears, and winged warriors—gargoyles—standing sentinel over citadels swallowed by cloud. The floor was inlaid with sweeping circles of silver and obsidian, their patterns converging toward the center like a sun drawn in shadow.

"Stay close," Garrion rumbled, his voice a low vibration through the floor.

She matched her pace to his as best she could, though close for Garrion meant his strides still covered twice hers. Her side throbbed harder now, but she kept her jaw tight, unwilling to ask him to slow.

The corridor stretched ahead, lined with great pillars carved into the likeness of dragons mid-flight. Ancient runes wound down each column, faintly pulsing as they passed. The light was soft—gold from sconces that smelled faintly of resin and pine—and the whole place seemed to hum with a quiet life.

They emerged into a wide courtyard open to the sky, the wind curling cold and crisp against her borrowed vision. Peaks loomed beyond the walls, their crowns wreathed in mist. Below, on a lower terrace, more gargoyles moved—training with heavy bladed weapons, wings flaring as they vaulted across open spaces. Their movements were precise, unhurried, the kind of efficiency that came from centuries of knowing exactly how to kill.

"You train for war," she said.

"We train for what will come," Garrion replied simply. "War is only one shape the future may take."

They crossed through the courtyard into a narrower passage where the walls pressed close. Her shoulder brushed cool stone, and she caught the scent of something earthy, mineral. On her left, a channel of clear water ran along the wall, catching the glow of runes etched into its bed.

Do not let his calm mislead you, Vaeronth murmured. *The Kin have been waiting for their war longer than you have been alive.*

A shiver passed through her despite herself.

"Your powers will grow here," Garrion said after a stretch of silence. "The bond between rider and dragon is more than shared eyes."

She glanced at him, brow furrowed. "I still don't know what my gift is supposed to be."

"You already bear the markings of having power," he said. "But time will tell."

"My mother had visions," she said quietly. "She could tell what the future would hold. And she never bonded with a dragon. She thought—" Eliryn swallowed. "I hoped that maybe it would pass to me. But I've never seen anything like that."

"Perhaps your gift is yet to wake," Garrion said. "Perhaps it waits for the moment you need it most. Or perhaps..." He studied her as they walked. "...your death has changed its shape."

Her chest tightened. "So you think it's gone."

"I think," he said, "that the magic in you has been altered. And altered magic can be more dangerous—and more powerful—than anyone expects."

The ache in her ribs spiked as they climbed the broad spiral stair ahead, each step pulling at the wound. She kept her breathing slow, letting the pain sharpen her focus instead of breaking it.

They stepped into a hall lined with high, arched windows that let the mountain air spill in. Using her borrowed sight, the carvings on the frames seemed to ripple with meaning—dragons and riders flanked by protectors, a tapestry of guardianship in stone.

They passed through another set of doors, and sunlight spilled over them. The terrace jutted straight from the cliff, the drop sheer enough to make her pulse spike.

Vaeronth stood there in his true form, the sun turning the edges of his obsidian scales to molten gold. Even at rest, he was a wall of coiled power.

You've been circling us, she thought.

Watching you. And listening.

Garrion stopped beside her. "Your dragon said that you are familiar with the prophecy. But... There is more you have not heard."

Her pulse jumped. "More?"

I did not tell you because you were not ready, Vaeronth's voice murmured in her mind.

Her jaw tightened. *That wasn't your choice to make,* she snapped back through the bond, the words sharper than she meant them to be.

Garrion's wings shifted, stone on stone. "You should hear it now, Dragonrider. The mountain keeps no secrets from those it has claimed."

The wind coiled around them, tugging at the tattered edges of Eliryn's ruined dress. Below, the land stretched in jagged lines of stone and shadow, the peaks disappearing into a haze of cloud. Vaeronth's tail curled along the terrace like a living wall, sealing them into a space that suddenly felt very, very small.

Garrion's gaze held hers—steady, unflinching. "The first part, you already know."

Her mother's voice rose in her mind, clear as the night she'd first heard it by the hearth. She spoke it aloud, the words like embers on her tongue:

"When Flame withdraws its hallowed spark,
And silent skies no longer mourn,
The blood of wyrm, long cast to dark,
Shall waken creatures once forlorn.
With smoldering gaze that sees no light,
And ash-bound breath beneath her tread,
She bears the weight of oathless flight—
Of bonds betrayed, of dragons bled.
From shattered line and fire's disgrace,
The Flame shall stir, the throne unmake.
Her shadow looms where silence aches—

And ruin walks, or hope shall wake."

The last line fell into the wind and was carried away. Eliryn exhaled, the familiar ache of it pressing at her ribs.

"That's the prophecy," she said. "All that I know of it."

Garrion's voice was quiet stone. "That is the part the realm remembers. The part the king lets them remember."

Vaeronth's claws ground softly against the terrace floor. *Eliryn...*

She turned to him, the edge in her voice sharper than she intended. "You shouldn't have denied me this."

It was not time.

Her chest burned. "And now it is?"

Garrion's wings shifted, the sound like stone cracking under pressure. "When you fell," he said. "your death was not the end of the prophecy—it was the turning of it. The second verse awakened when your heart stopped."

He moved closer, his voice lowering, the words carrying an old weight:

"Yet death's embrace shall mar her purpose,
Its spark unmoored, yet not undone.
What once was whole takes other name,
And through the break, new power runs.

Where magic wanes and kingdoms bleed,
Her breath shall call the root to rise.
She is the key the realm shall heed,
And through her will the realm reprise."

The words lingered long after he fell silent, vibrating through the stone until even the air felt alive with them.

Eliryn swallowed hard. "So it's true," she said finally. "All of it. I really am what it spoke of."

Garrion's gaze held hers. "You always were," he said. "Your mortal death did not change the prophecy. The gods were waiting for you to arrive at the place they already named."

Her pulse quickened. "So everything that's happened... it was always supposed to?"

"The gods do not guess, Rider," Garrion said. "They simply know. You are not lost—you are exactly where you're supposed to be."

Eliryn let out a slow, shaky breath. "Then maybe it's time I stop fighting it."

"You were never meant to fight it," Garrion confirmed. "Only to see it through."

You are still mine, Vaeronth's voice murmured through the bond, steady and sure. *And through us, the prophecy continues to breathe.*

Her gaze fell to her hands. The runes along her skin glowed faintly, a heartbeat of light.

The key the realm shall heed.

The words sat in her ribs like a pointed blade daring her to move. She didn't know whether the second part of the prophecy terrified her... or made her want to stand taller.

The wind bit at her bare feet as Garrion folded his wings with barely a whisper of sound.

"We should walk," he said. "It will help you feel the weight of where you are."

"It feels like sacred ground," she murmured.

"It is," he replied. "But you have leave to walk anywhere among the Kin."

Vaeronth lowered his head until one molten eye filled her vision. *Go,* he said. *See the heart of the Sanctuary. I will be near.*

She hesitated. The thought of too much physical distance between them made her chest clench, but she forced herself to nod. "Don't fly too far from me."

Never.

Garrion led her down carved steps worn smooth by centuries. Every surface seemed to hum faintly—not magic exactly, but the echo of it, like the stone remembered every vow it had ever heard.

"You built all this?" she asked quietly.

"Our hands shaped it," Garrion said. "But the gods' will gave it life. The first dragonriders needed a place beyond the reach of kings, and so the Kin became their shield."

Her fingers brushed a wall that glittered faintly in the half-light. "And when the dragons fell?"

His jaw tightened. "We kept watch over an empty sky. We thought the Flame's era had ended, but we knew that with your future foretold by the gods, it wouldn't be permanent."

They passed an open colonnade that looked out over a deep valley, waterfalls veiling the cliffs below. The air smelled faintly of wet stone and something sharp—like ozone after lightning.

They turned past a training chamber where Kin sparred with heavy stone blades, their movements precise and merciless. She slowed, watching them, her mind replaying Garrion's words: *Altered. Dangerous. Key.* The Sanctuary pressed in around her—not as a prison, but as something awake, aware.

They had barely stepped into the outer court when Garrion stopped, his shadow falling long over her.

"Hold on," he said.

Before she could ask what he meant, her vision lurched. Massive, stone-carved hands closed around her waist—solid and warm despite their granite feel—and the ground dropped away in a blur of wind and motion. She barely had time to grab on to him before they were rising, the scent of stone and cold air rushing past, her stomach swooping. The flight was not long, but it was so swift she didn't register what had happened until her feet struck smooth flagstone again.

They were standing on a wide, overhanging terrace three stories above the court. The mountains yawned open beyond the railing, peaks clawing at the mist.

Garrion set her down with the same care he might place a sword on an altar. "Your wound needs more healing before you can brave the eastern stair," he said. "You've had enough movement for the day."

She blew out a sharp breath, trying to decide if her ribs hurt from the landing or from her heart trying to escape her chest. "Sure. Who needs stairs when you can give someone a heart attack instead?"

"I could have warned you," he admitted, utterly unbothered.

"You think?" she muttered under her breath, still catching up to the fact that she was no longer on the ground.

Garrion ignored her and turned toward a set of tall double doors carved with sweeping wings from floor to lintel. The faint scent of cedar and smoke drifted from within.

"This will be yours," he said.

She blinked. "Mine?"

"You've spent enough days in the Healers' Hall," Garrion rumbled. "The Kin keep their wounded there only until the stone judges them steady. You are steady enough to walk. That means you are steady enough to claim your own space."

Eliryn glanced at the doors, then back at him. "Where... exactly is here?"

"The eastern wing of the Great Hall," he said. "Close to the council chambers and the training courts. You will not be far from the heart of the Sanctuary—or from those who would answer your call."

A strange mix of gratitude and apprehension tightened her chest. "Thank you."

He tilted his head, wings rustling faintly. "No thanks are necessary, Dragonrider."

She stepped inside. The chamber beyond was larger than she expected—stone walls inlaid with faintly glowing veins, a hearth smoldering low, and a narrow balcony that looked out toward the mist-wreathed peaks. The air here was warmer, scented faintly of resin and something sharper—old magic, lingering in the mortar.

Her gaze snagged on a series of shallow carvings etched into the stone arch above the balcony doors—runes she didn't recognize. They were almost hidden in the grain, catching the light only when she moved. For a moment, she thought one of them pulsed faintly, like a heartbeat, but when she blinked the glow was gone.

Garrion remained in the doorway, his presence filling the space like a second hearth. "Rest. You will need your strength."

"For what?" she asked.

His eyes, deep as shadowed granite, didn't waver. "Prophecies are rarely gentle in their fulfillment."

The door shut softly behind her.

The room was dim, the fire low. She sat on the bed, curling her toes against the rug. Her bandages pulled tight as she leaned forward, the wound's throb keeping pace with her heartbeat.

The new lines of the prophecy whispered through her head, looping until they blurred with the old ones. *She is the key the realm shall heed... And through her will the realm reprise.*

Her chest rose on a shaky breath. The prophecy's words echoed through her mind—too vast, too heavy, too certain. She didn't know if the gods foretold the healing the realm... or her burning with it.

The quiet wasn't empty. It held its breath with her.

This feels impossible, she thought. *All of it.*

Many truths do, Vaeronth said, his voice low and warm against the edges of her mind. *Until we survive them.*

She almost smiled—almost. "I'm afraid," she whispered. "And I hate that I am."

Fear means you understand what stands before you, he said. *It does not make you weak. Only human.*

Her throat tightened. "Everything that's happened... it still doesn't feel real."

Then we will let it become real one breath at a time, Vaeronth murmured. *You and I.*

The ache in her chest eased—not gone, just quieter. The kind of quiet that came before resolve.

Rest now, he said, softer. *You are where you were always meant to be. The mountain will keep its watch—and so will I.*

Chapter 4: Eyes of The Sanctuary

"Stone does not ask for trust. It earns it by never moving."
—The Sanctuary Codex

She woke to the mountain breathing.

At first it was only a feeling—a low, steady pulse in the stone beneath her bed, like a heartbeat too deep to belong to anything living. The air was cool against her skin, thin enough that every breath scraped the edges of her ribs. Somewhere beyond the chamber, something shifted—a wing? a voice?—and the sound rippled through the rock.

Her eyes blinked open to dim light. The brazier in the corner had burned low, its coals pulsing faintly, the scent of smoke and metal sharp in the stillness. For a moment she didn't know where she was. Then the ache in her side reminded her. The Sanctuary. The Kin. The prophecy.

And then the voices.

They came softly at first, carried through the walls—low, indistinct, but steady enough that the stone itself seemed to listen.

Not loud—but the stone carried them, rolling each word into the marrow of her bones.

Her quarters opened onto a small inner hall, which in turn opened onto a wide terrace—one of the few open spaces in the Sanctuary where a dragon could stand at full height. The thick wall between her and that terrace should have muted everything. Instead, it sang with sound. The mountain was old, its veins of crystal and ore carrying voices the way rivers carry current.

Garrion's voice came first, deep and deliberate, each word set down like the weight of an axe.

"She cannot stay here like a wounded fledgling, Vaeronth. She needs to stand. Train. The longer you shelter her, the weaker she becomes."

And then—a sound Eliryn had never heard before.

Vaeronth's voice, *aloud.*

It was deeper than she'd imagined, rougher—a growl made of thunder and smoke. The sound hit the wall like a blow, bled through it, and settled low in her chest. She could feel the size of him in the cadence alone.

"She bled out on my back, Garrion. You saw it. You saw how close I was to losing her."

"I also see," Garrion countered, "how the prophecy named her. Do you think the gods choose those who cower behind walls?"

A sharp scrape of talons on stone—close, right outside the terrace's archway.

The silence that followed was so taut it felt like the whole mountain was holding its breath.

Eliryn's palms pressed flat to the cool wall, as if the stone might give her more. Through the faint grit beneath her fingers, she imagined Vaeronth looming over Garrion, molten eyes fixed, wings half-furled in warning.

When Vaeronth spoke again, his voice was colder.

"And if she breaks before she is ready? If the mountain takes her strength instead of giving it?"

"Then she was never meant to carry it," Garrion said.

The words landed like a strike to her ribs.

She stepped back from the wall, pulse quick, the ache in her side a slow throb. Garrion's voice might have been carved from the same stone he stood on, but Vaeronth's... it was heat and weight and warning all at once. Hearing it aloud—feeling it—made something primal in her shiver.

Her gaze dropped to herself. Gods.

The blanket she'd wrapped around her while sleeping had slipped to the bed, leaving her in nothing but the long strip of linen binding her ribs, and the thin scraps of her dress from the Rite.

She looked like a half-bandaged ghost—and one gust of mountain wind away from indecent.

No. Absolutely not.

She moved quickly, scanning the room. There had to be something here—something that wasn't stitched half-open or smelling faintly of dried blood. Her quarters weren't large, but the Kin had furnished them with meticulous care: a low bed carved from a single slab of stone, shelves chiseled into the walls, and a small chest at the foot of the bed bound in dark iron. She crossed to it and flipped the lid.

And froze because she noticed something was missing.

Her hand went instinctively to her throat.

Bare skin. No chain.

The breath she drew caught halfway, shallow and sharp. She pressed harder—searching for the familiar weight that wasn't there. The obsidian amulet. Her mother's heirloom. Vaeronth's vessel.

Gone.

Her heart lurched, pounding hard enough that the ache in her ribs flared in protest. The air felt too thin all at once, her pulse too loud. She dropped to her knees, shoving aside folded fabric, dragging her hands through the chest as if she might have missed it falling from her throat—tunic, belt, boots—nothing.

The memory of it haunted her fingertips: smooth stone, carved edges warm from her skin. The one thing she'd kept through every loss. Every battle. Every moment that made her who she was.

And now—

Her thoughts skidded to a stop as a low vibration rippled through the floor. Voices. Garrion's, deep and deliberate, cutting through her panic like a blade.

"She will not survive this if you keep her caged. The Sanctuary is a place of strength, not shelter."

She stilled, frozen mid-breath. The shock of loss twisted tighter in her chest, but the sound of that voice—the weight of it—dragged her back to the present.

And then Vaeronth answered.

Low. Rough. The sound of thunder breaking stone.

"You think I would let her test her magic's Well without knowing if she can even draw a full breath without pain?"

Her pulse still hammered, but her focus shifted—snapped outward, away from grief, toward the rising tension beyond the wall.

The amulet. Her mother. The loss. It all receded, pressed down beneath something sharper: the unmistakable warning in Vaeronth's voice.

Magic's Well?

Eliryn pulled the tunic over her head, wincing as the motion tugged her ribs. The fabric was blessedly warm, smelling faintly of cedar smoke and clean air. She bound the belt at her waist, the weight grounding her more than she expected.

The boots were trickier—she had to sit on the edge of the bed to lace them, fingers working quickly, straining to catch every word that filtered through the stone.

"She will not heal fully until she moves," Garrion pressed. "Until she learns the Sanctuary's paths, its strength. The gods' choice does not rest idle. The longer she waits, the harder it will be to take back what was stolen."

Stolen.

The word prickled along her skin like cold air down her spine. *Perhaps he was referencing the Flame?* She wondered.

Vaeronth didn't answer right away. The scrape of his talons on the terrace floor came again—a restless, coiled sound.

"She is not ready," he said finally. "And if you try to push her before she is, Garrion, you will answer to me."

Eliryn froze, her hand on the last lace, waiting to hear what Garrion would say to that.

For a moment, there was nothing—just the deep, aching quiet of the mountain. Then Garrion's voice came again, calm and unflinching:

"Then we had better make her ready."

That was it. That was her cue.

She stood, having yanked the last lace tight, and stormed for the door—well, *stormed* in the sense that she limped awkwardly, one hand pressed to her ribs to keep from doubling over. But it was the thought that counted.

The door swung open, spilling cold air against her face. She stepped into the inner hall, boots striking the stone harder than necessary, and made straight for the terrace.

Both of them turned toward her—Garrion's granite gaze steady, Vaeronth's molten eyes narrowing.

"Good news," she announced, raising her voice before either of them could speak. "I'm alive, I'm dressed, and I can walk. Which means you can stop deciding my fate without me like I'm a child."

Garrion's wings shifted slightly, the movement silent but somehow still commanding.

"You should be resting," he said.

"Oh, I was," Eliryn said brightly, even as her voice carried the rasp of sarcasm. "But then I overheard the two of you arguing about me like I'm a child, and I thought—*you know what?* I should join in."

Vaeronth's tail curled tighter along the terrace floor, his molten eyes narrowing. *You shouldn't be eves dropping.*

"You shouldn't be speaking about me like I'm not one slab of stone away," she shot back. "Also—you have an *outside* voice? Was I just not important enough to get that before now?"

His head lowered until his snout was almost level with her. "Among the Kin," he rumbled aloud, the sound shivering through the air, "I have no reason to hide my voice."

She blinked. "So I get the private 'voice-in-my-head' communication, but Garrion gets surround-sound dragon rumble?" She flicked her gaze to the gargoyle.

Garrion's mouth didn't so much as twitch, but something in his eyes suggested he was perilously close to amusement. "You argue well enough for someone who just came back to life."

"Of course I argue well," she said. "And I don't intend to spend the rest of my days hiding in a stone room just because one stab wound thought it could get the better of me."

Vaeronth's gaze sharpened. "It did. You *died*."

"I came back." She spread her hands. "And I refuse to give Malric the satisfaction of leaving me too broken to stand. I'm not going to play the victim while he sits somewhere congratulating himself."

"That is not the same as being ready," Vaeronth said.

"No, it's better," she said, stepping closer. "It's being stubborn enough to do something about it."

Garrion's wings shifted again, and the faintest grin ghosted over his features. "Then you will train."

Her eyes slid toward him. "I'll decide when I train."

"Decide now," Garrion said.

Her brows arched. "Pushy."

"You have a prophecy tied to your blood," he said simply. "Pushy is needed."

For a heartbeat, the three of them stood there, the wind curling around them, cold and sharp.

Finally, Eliryn crossed her arms. "Fine. Training starts tomorrow."

Vaeronth growled low in his throat. *Too soon.*

She smirked. "If I can storm out here to yell at you, I can survive a few laps around the mountain."

Garrion inclined his head, the gesture almost formal. "Dawn."

"Not *that* soon," she said. "Mid-morning."

"Dawn," he repeated.

She groaned. "I see the concept of 'negotiation' hasn't made it to the Kin."

He only turned away, wings spreading. "Mid-morning is for the unprepared."

Vaeronth's gaze tracked Garrion as he stepped off the terrace edge and dropped into the air, wings catching the wind with ease.

Eliryn watched him disappear toward the training grounds, then glanced at Vaeronth. "He's bossy."

He's right, Vaeronth said, and though his tone was dry, there was something like pride behind it.

She shook her head. "You're both impossible."

And yet, he rumbled, *we know what's best.*

She didn't answer—not out loud. But the faintest smirk tugged at her lips as she turned back toward her room, already plotting how she'd survive dawn without throwing up on the training field.

The moment her door shut behind her, she let herself sag back against it, the adrenaline bleeding away to leave a heavy throb in her ribs.

The bed was far too tempting. She didn't even bother to undress—just dropped onto the blankets and let the low hum of the Sanctuary wrap around her. She told herself it would be a short rest, just long enough to take the edge off.

When her eyes opened again, the light slanting in from the high window was thinner, tinted with the cool blue of late afternoon. Her stomach growled like an angry animal.

You're awake, Vaeronth said, his voice sliding into her mind like warm smoke.

"I'm starving," she muttered, pressing a hand to her stomach. "Where do you people even keep food in this place?"

You people? he echoed dryly. *There is a common hall three tiers down from your quarters. Follow the main corridor until you smell woodsmoke and roasted meat. If you get lost, I'll guide you.*

She pushed herself upright with a groan. "If I can survive three flights of stairs without tearing something open, I'll start asking for directions."

He made a sound somewhere between a sigh and a growl but didn't argue.

The directions proved easy enough, though the descent took her through parts of the Sanctuary she hadn't seen before—broader halls, open arches where the mountain wind rushed in, flickering light from sconces spilling over carved reliefs of dragons and Kin fighting side by side.

By the time she stepped into the dining hall, the air was thick with the scents Vaeronth had promised—roasting meat, fresh bread, fresh herbs. The space was enormous, long stone tables flanked by benches worn smooth with centuries of use. A broad hearth blazed at one end, the firelight gilding the wings and horns of the Kin seated throughout the room.

Conversation stopped.

Dozens of heads turned toward her. Massive, in-human faces—some carved with jagged ridges like mountains in miniature, others smoother but no less alien—stared in heavy, unblinking silence.

"Right," Eliryn muttered, low enough to herself. "This isn't awkward at all."

The Kin simply tracked her with those unearthly eyes as she strode toward the long serving table.

They were told you'd be resting until dawn, Vaeronth said in her mind.

"Guess I'm just full of surprises," she murmured, grabbing a heavy plate and piling it with bread, a thick slice of roast, and something that looked suspiciously like root stew.

The dining hall was warmer than the rest of the Sanctuary, lit by long stone braziers that filled the air with the scent of pine resin. She was almost to the end of the food line when the air shifted—not in temperature, but in weight.

A figure stepped from the far end of the hall, his presence parting the low conversation like wind through grass. Slate-dark stone traced with faint veins of gold, his form was all quiet strength—no wasted movement, no sharp edges of hostility, only the stillness of something carved to endure centuries.

The other Kin noticed him too. Conversations paused mid-word. Heads turned.

He crossed the space without hurry, the silence folding around him like a cloak. When he stopped before her, his voice was deep but not harsh—low enough she felt it more than heard it.

"Dragonrider."

She straightened instinctively, pulse quick. "That's... me."

His gaze held hers for a long moment, unblinking, and she had the strangest sensation that he wasn't looking *at* her so much as *into* her—not searching, not judging, simply... seeing.

"I am Druven," he said. "When the time comes, I will stand for the right to guard you."

Her lips parted, but for once, no quip came. There was no boast in his tone, no arrogance—only a certainty so steady it felt like the mountain itself had spoken through him.

"Guard me?" she asked finally.

"It is the way of the Kin. In the age of many riders, it is the way it was always done. Now..." His gaze drifted briefly to the others in the hall. "...you are the only dragonrider. And so we will prove ourselves worthy before you, your dragon, and the mountain."

Something about the way he said *worthy* made her throat tighten. Not because she doubted him—but because a part of her doubted herself.

"I didn't realize I would have the luxury of a personal stone wall," she managed, her voice a little unsteady.

A flicker of something warm touched his eyes. "Not a wall," he said softly. "A shield. For the one who carries the weight of the realm."

Before she could answer, he stepped back, inclining his head in a motion so precise it felt ceremonial. Then, without waiting for permission or acknowledgment, he turned and walked away—leaving the weight of his vow hanging in the space between them.

The hall began to breathe again, conversation returning in cautious ripples. Eliryn stood where he'd left her, the weight of his words pressing heavier than the plate in her hands.

By the time she reached her quarters, her pulse had settled into something hollow. She shut the door, leaned against it, and stared at the stone floor until her eyes blurred.

For all the oaths, all the prophecy, all the voices calling her chosen—she'd never felt more like someone trying to stand under something far too heavy.

She drew one long breath and let it out slow. The weight didn't lift—but it settled. Tomorrow, she'd learn how to carry it.

CHAPTER 5: THE FIRST STEP

"Even broken wings cast shade." —Proverb

The cold woke her first.

Not the sharp, metallic chill of winter air on skin, but the kind that seeped into muscle and bone, like the mountain itself had rolled over in the night and pressed its weight into her.

Up.

Vaeronth's voice slid into her thoughts, low and steady. Not unkind—but not offering room to argue.

"It's still dark," she muttered into her pillow.

So it is.

"So I don't need to be awake right now."

You do since you told Garrion you would train at this hour.

She cracked one eye open to the faint ember-glow from the hearth. "I said I'd *consider* training."

You did more than consider, Vaeronth said, the faint amusement in his tone infuriatingly warm. *And you are the one who wanted this.*

She shoved the blanket off and sat up, her ribs twinging in protest beneath the bandages. Eliryn couldn't believe this was her life right now. Her mother—gods, her mother—would just shake her head and say she was exactly where she was meant to be.

Her hand drifted to her collarbone—and stopped.

Empty.

The breath caught in her throat. The amulet was gone. The smooth obsidian pendant that had rested there for as long as she could remember—the only thing capable of housing Vaeronth's physical form—was gone.

"Vaeronth," she said quietly. "The amulet. It's missing."

I know.

Her pulse stumbled. "You knew?"

A pause, low and heavy. *I felt it break. Somewhere in the flight to the Sanctuary, the chain slipped free. It fell from you before we reached the peaks. There was no saving it.*

She stared at her hands, the hollowness in her chest spreading like cold water. For years, the amulet had been a constant—its weight against her skin a quiet reassurance that she was never truly alone. Without it, she felt... unmoored. Like part of her had been left in the sky to fall with it.

You feel its absence, Vaeronth said, his voice softer now, touched with something like sorrow. *But I no longer need a vessel to exist beside you. The time for being small has come and gone.*

She exhaled shakily. "It still feels wrong not having it."

I know. But you no longer need it, Little Flame.

Her boots waited by the bed. She pulled on the tunic and trousers the Kin had left her, cinching the belt tight before bending to lace the boots. Each tug of the leather straps felt like locking herself into a promise she wasn't sure she understood.

She finished lacing the boots and stood, running a hand through her hair. "Alright," she muttered to herself. "Let's get this over with."

The hall outside her room was still half-shadowed, the glow from the runes along the walls just enough to guide her steps. The air was cold this early, a thin mountain chill sliding down the back of her neck and under her collar.

She took the stairs slowly at first, and the steps seemed to go on forever, curling down along the inner wall of the Sanctuary. By the second flight her ribs were aching, breath coming sharper than she'd like to admit. By the third, she was seriously reconsidering whether Garrion had arranged this as some sort of pre-training endurance test. Funny how when she was hungry the pain hadn't seemed to bother her as much.

The stairs opened onto a wide stretch of grass cropped short and edged by low stone walls. Beyond that, the space widened again into the training courts—open to the sky, the wind threading sharp between the pillars.

Garrion was already there. Standing still as a cliff face, wings folded, eyes fixed on her like she was already a problem to solve.

And beyond him was Vaeronth. Massive. Watching. Waiting.

Her borrowed vision sharpened the sight into something almost too vivid to hold. The faint glimmer of frost along the black stone. The rippling shadow of Garrion's wings, stretched long in the early light. The silver-thread runes etched into the court floor, catching every flicker of dawn.

It wasn't her sight—she'd never pretend it was—but it was *clear*.

Clear in a way her own eyes hadn't managed since she was sixteen, when the world had begun to blur at the edges no matter how hard she squinted.

For years, she'd taught herself not to *want* this kind of vision—because wanting what you couldn't have was just another form of pain.

And yet, here it was.

Sharp. Whole.

A gift that didn't feel like hers to keep.

Her chest tightened. The court wavered slightly, her heart uncertain whether to race or slow.

"You're stalling," Vaeronth said aloud, his voice rolling across the court like distant thunder.

Her head lifted. "I'm thinking."

"Thinking," Garrion said, "will not build strength."

She met his gaze, something wry at the corner of her mouth. "Neither will freezing to death."

He didn't rise to it. "When the Riders of old trained," he said, "they began the day before sunrise. They ran the mountain passes until their breath became steady as wind. Then came blade practice and flight drills."

"That sounds like a good way for me to die a second time," she muttered.

"You will begin slower," Garrion said.

He started forward at an even jog. After a breath, she followed, boots striking the stone in uneven rhythm.

The silence stretched long enough for her thoughts to start wandering—and eventually, she broke it. "Yesterday, one of the Kin introduced himself to me. Druven. He said that when the time came, he would stand for the right to guard me."

Garrion's expression didn't change, but his wings shifted slightly, the sound like rock settling. "He spoke of the Rite."

"What Rite?"

"The Rite of Choosing," he said. "It is the oldest tradition the Kin still honor. In the age of riders, every dragonrider was bound to one of us—a guardian who protected them until death. When a new rider emerged, the Kin gathered to stand before the mountain. The Rite decided who would bear that duty."

She blinked. "How does it decide?"

"Through trial," Garrion said. "Of endurance, loyalty, and strength of spirit. The one who stands true is chosen by both the rider and the mountain. Once the vow is sealed, it binds them until death."

"So Druven meant it literally. He wants to compete—to become that guardian."

"Yes."

"Has he ever been chosen before?"

"No," Garrion said, his tone unreadable. "He has stood. None have called his name."

Her brows knit. "Why not?"

"That is his story," Garrion said. "If he means to stand again, he does so because he believes this time will be different."

Eliryn was quiet for a while. The rhythm of their footfalls filled the silence.

"So," she said finally, "I'm supposed to choose one of you. Someone who'd stand between me and everything that's coming."

"It is your right," Garrion said. "And your burden. The Kin have waited centuries for the chance to serve a rider again. Many will stand."

Her chest ached—not just from exertion. "And if I choose wrong?"

He didn't hesitate. "Then you learn. The gods do not weave without flaw. But the mountain remembers its own. You will know who stands true."

They slowed near the far edge of the court, where racks of stone-carved weapons and training dummies waited in orderly rows. Frost clung to everything.

"Your bond to Vaeronth will grow here," Garrion said. "Not only in sight and voice. There are other gifts yet to wake."

"Gifts?" she echoed warily.

"That depends on the rider," Garrion said. "And on what the gods took—and gave—when you died."

Her pace faltered. "That's... ominous."

"You will learn," he said simply.

She huffed out a quiet laugh, half breath, half disbelief. "You talk like someone who already knows exactly what I am."

"I know what the prophecy says," he replied. "The rest—you will show me."

For a few strides, silence stretched between them, broken only by the sound of boots on stone. Then Eliryn spoke again, voice low. "During the Trials of Sovereignty... there was a moment. I had to choose a weapon, and there was a sword that called to me. I thought it was a joke—gods, I could barely lift it. But when the fighting started..." She hesitated, brows pulling together. "It was like something else took hold. My body knew what to do before I did. Every strike, every turn—it felt like memory, not thought."

Garrion's head turned slightly, his gaze sharpening. "And you had never trained with a blade before?"

"Never."

"Then it was not memory," he said. "It was resonance."

She blinked. "Resonance?"

"The bond between rider and dragon is more than flesh and spirit. It is a current of power that threads through the soul. When you stood in those trials, you were already tied to Vaeronth, even if you did not yet understand the depth of it. His strength moves through you. Your instincts—your precision—are shaped by that bond."

Eliryn frowned slightly. "You're saying I wasn't in control."

"I'm saying," Garrion corrected, "that you and control have yet to agree on terms. What you touched in those moments was your own magic—untrained, but true."

Something about that settled in her chest, warm and heavy all at once.

He slowed to a stop, wings folding in with deliberate precision. "That's enough for this morning. The mountain is patient, even if I am not. Rest. Eat."

She nodded, stretching out the ache in her shoulders. "You know, for someone made of stone, you give decent advice."

"I have had time to practice," he said dryly, already turning toward the hall.

They made their way back through the carved corridors. The air grew warmer, the faint scent of bread and smoke guiding them toward the heart of the Sanctuary.

When they stepped into the dining hall, the space buzzed with quiet life. Dozens of Kin filled the long tables, wings catching firelight as they spoke in low tones. The scent of roasted roots and herbs curled thick in the air.

Eliryn hesitated, then joined the line, taking a bowl of porridge and a crust of bread still warm from the hearth.

When she turned, Garrion had already taken his seat near the great fire. She crossed the hall and sat opposite him without thinking.

He looked up, one brow lifting. "Dragonriders do not eat with the Kin."

Chapter 6: The Breaking Point

"No chain is stronger than its weakest link—so we carry the weight together." —Sanctuary Teaching

Eliryn stabbed her bread into the porridge, harder than necessary.

"What, we're good enough to protect but not good enough to share a meal with?"

Garrion's expression didn't shift. "No, Dragonrider. You misunderstand. Once, it was forbidden."

Her hand stilled halfway to her mouth. "Forbidden?"

"The old riders dined apart," he said evenly. "It was not arrogance—it was law. The Kin were sworn to serve, not to sit. The vow was bound into us when the first stone of the Sanctuary was laid. We could not lift a cup or touch food until dismissed."

Eliryn blinked, trying to make sense of the words.

"You mean... you couldn't eat because you weren't *allowed* to?"

"Yes." Garrion's gaze didn't waver. "It was said that to dine beside a rider was to presume equality. And there were few things the old orders feared more than that."

For a moment, she only heard the crackle of the hearth and the slow, rhythmic scrape of spoons against stone bowls. The words didn't just land—they hollowed something out inside her.

Something about the thought—the *smallness* of it, the cruelty wrapped in ceremony—hit her wrong. Deeply wrong.

She thought of the Kin she had met so far. Garrion, who had undoubtedly helped bring her back from death. Druven, who had all but vowed to protect her. The silent, watching faces in the halls—ancient beings carved from the mountain's bones, who still bowed to her name.

They had been made to serve at tables they had built. They had been asked to protect voices that once ordered them to silence.

The realization settled into her chest like a stone sinking into deep water—slow, heavy, inevitable.

Her throat tightened. "And it's still law?"

Garrion hesitated, and the pause said enough. "The vow has lost its binding, but not its shadow. Some traditions linger long after their meaning rots."

Her stomach twisted. "And none of you ever thought to put a stop to it?"

A flicker of something—sorrow, maybe—crossed the lines of his face. "We did not stop," he said quietly. "We endured. The Kin remember every command that chained us, even when the power behind it fades."

Eliryn's fingers clenched around the handle of her spoon. The thought of generations kneeling beneath the weight of obedience they no longer owed—it burned.

Not just anger, but shame. Old and borrowed and not entirely her own.

She looked around the hall at the faces that had gone still, the hands that hesitated over their plates, at the centuries of silence sitting beside them like another guest.

"That's not devotion," she said, her voice rough. "That's servitude."

The air shifted. A subtle pressure, like the mountain holding its breath.

Then—heat.

It began as a pulse deep within her chest, faint but sure, the rhythm of something ancient remembering itself. The warmth spread outward, coiling through her ribs and up her spine, filling the space behind her ribs with a light that wanted out.

The hum of conversation stilled.

Her dragonmarks ignited, thin veins of light threading down her arms, through her collar, across the faint shadow of the marks burned into her skin by the gods' choosing. It wasn't fire. It was something *older*.

The first breath caught in her throat—not pain, not fear, but release.

The light spilled from her sleeves, soft and molten at first, gilding the edge of the table. Then it grew.

It filled the cracks in the floor, brushed over the worn grain of the benches, climbed the walls like dawn over stone.

The nearest Kin drew in a sharp, startled breath. His arm, etched with old fissures from some ancient battle, began to glow faintly, the breaks sealing in slow, deliberate rhythm. The scars disappeared, leaving polished obsidian where ruin had been.

A sound rippled through the hall. The soft, sharp inhales of awe.

More followed. The fractures in the wings of another Kin knitted together, membranes turning smooth and whole. The ragged gouges along another's jaw softened and sealed.

Eliryn's pulse roared in her ears. She could *feel* them—all of them—like a thousand small threads tugging at her mind. Not as individuals, but as one vast, breathing whole. The mountain itself seemed to tremble under the weight of that connection.

The warmth swelled higher, cresting behind her ribs until it almost hurt.

It moved *through* her, immense and alive, brushing against the edges of something that felt like memory.

Eliryn. Vaeronth's voice struck her mind like iron through flame—low, warning, protective.

She didn't answer. Couldn't.

The heat reached its peak, spilling outward in one last wave before ebbing, leaving her trembling and hollowed, like the bell that's just finished ringing.

The light along her skin shifted—no longer gold, but blue and silver, the light of frost and flame twined together. It flickered softly across her hands, pulsing in rhythm with her heartbeat.

Dozens of Kin stood motionless, their eyes reflecting that light. Some touched their arms or faces in disbelief; stone once fractured now whole. Others bowed their heads, reverent, as if witnessing something they had not dared dream of seeing.

Garrion hadn't moved. His face remained carved from calm, but something behind his eyes had changed—recognition, awe, perhaps even the faintest trace of relief.

Eliryn's voice, when it came, wasn't raised. It didn't need to be. It carried through the hall with the quiet weight of truth.

"No more chains of service," she said. "No more walls between us. Kin, rider, dragon—we stand, we fight, we *live* as one."

The words sank into the stone, into the air itself. Not command. Not prophecy. Promise.

For a long moment, no one moved.

Then, one by one, the Kin rose. Not in defense or fear, but reverence. Fists pressed to their chests, heads bowed, wings folding close in perfect unison.

A silent vow rippled through the hall like the shift of the tide—ancient and wordless, yet louder than any oath ever spoken.

It was not the vow of servitude that had once bound them.

It was its undoing.

Even Garrion inclined his head, slow and deliberate. "As it should be."

Eliryn let out a shaky breath, the tension in her body releasing all at once. She sank back onto the bench, the bowl before her long gone cold, the room still trembling faintly with whatever power had passed through it.

The light on her skin dimmed to a faint shimmer. Silver to blue. Blue to ember. And when it finally settled, she could still feel it humming in her blood as a steady, unshakable rhythm that wasn't hers alone.

Vaeronth's voice curled into her thoughts, deep and rough with quiet pride.

Every Kin in this hall will remember the day you broke the old vows.

Her fingers brushed the faint shimmer tracing her forearm, the cool glow still pulsing faintly beneath the skin. "Good. Let them remember," she whispered.

The last of the light faded, leaving only the warmth of the hearth and the steady hum of the mountain beneath her feet.

For the first time since waking in the Sanctuary, she felt it—the weight of something shifting, the beginning of balance returning.

And somewhere deep in the stone around her, the mountain answered with a low, resonant hum.

CHAPTER 7: STONEWAKE

"The old magic sleeps in many forms. In some, it stirs slowly. In others it wakes all at once." —Keeper's Commentary on the Kin

The first thing Eliryn noticed was the quiet.

She opened her eyes to the dim blue of pre-dawn. The fire in the brazier had burned to ash, yet faint threads of silver-blue light still traced the lines of her dragonmarks, pulsing soft as breath. Her body felt whole, but different; balanced on the edge of something vast.

You did not rest long, Vaeronth murmured. His voice brushed against her mind like smoke, low and resonant.

"I wasn't sure I could," she whispered. "Last night... that wasn't normal."

No, he said. *It was not.* A pause, then—*But rare does not mean wrong.*

She sat up slowly, the blankets falling to her waist. "They all stood for me. Every single one. What was that?"

A vow, Vaeronth said. *One that has not been given in any age since the first. The Kin once swore oaths of obedience—chains of service bound in stone and blood. But this was not that. This was born of will. Of recognition.*

She frowned, studying the faint glow beneath her skin. "A vow to me?"

To you, and to what you are becoming. His tone deepened, the words vibrating through the air like thunder far beneath the mountain. *A vow that answers only to purity of heart and intention. To strength unbent by pride. You called it forth, and they answered.*

Her breath hitched, the weight of it pressing gently behind her ribs. "I didn't *mean* to call anything."

Power does not always wait for permission, he said. *It answers truth. And what you felt last night was its release.*

She looked down at her hands again, the light shifting through them like moonlit water. "It didn't feel like something I was controlling."

You weren't, he said. *Your body acted before your mind could. The bond between us opened fully for the first time, and your magic—* his pause was deliberate, heavy *—is greater now than it should be. Even for a rider.*

Her chest tightened. "Greater how?"

Vaster. Wilder. It will take your mind time to understand what it already carries. But it is there, beneath the surface, waiting. Do not fear it, Eliryn. What you hold was never meant to be small.

She sat in the stillness, her pulse syncing to the slow rhythm of his voice, and she felt the immensity of possibility.

She dressed quickly, tugging on the dark training leathers someone had left folded on her chair. The fabric was supple but reinforced at the joints, built to move without binding her in place. She laced her boots with brisk, efficient pulls, pausing only when she realized—

Her body felt... good. Not just "better than yesterday" good. *Strong.*

The ache in her ribs was gone. The stiffness in her side had vanished. Even her breathing was easier, deeper. She caught herself in the polished bronze plate by the hearth, tilting her head and trying to decide if her skin looked a little less like death warmed over.

You are preening, Vaeronth observed.

She scowled. "I'm assessing the damage."

There is no damage to assess.

"Yeah," she said quietly, "and that's the weird part."

The walk to the training courts was short, but the sharp air bit at her cheeks. Mist curled low over the stone pathways, veiling the open spaces between the sanctuary's towering walls. By the time she reached the broad grass-stretch where the pillars broke the skyline, she could see him.

Garrion stood at the far end of the court, still as if carved from the same stone as the Sanctuary itself. Wings folded in precise lines, eyes fixed on her.

When she stopped in front of him, he bowed.

The motion was not shallow, not perfunctory. It was deliberate.

"Eliryn, the Last Dragonrider," Garrion said, his voice carrying low across the court. "What you gave the Kin yesterday will be remembered for as long as the Sanctuary endures."

Heat crept up her neck. "I don't even know *what* I gave them," she admitted. "It felt like... losing control. Like something bigger decided to move through me and I just—let it."

The faintest curve touched his granite features, not quite a smile, but close. "That was no loss of control. It was awakening. Power unshaped, yes, but born of instinct. Few wield such grace the first time it answers them."

He stepped closer, shadow long and steady across the pale grass. "That is what your training will be, Dragonrider. Not to command such power, but to stand within it. To ground it before it consumes, to shape it without fear, and to learn how it strengthens the bond between you and Vaeronth."

Her gaze flicked toward the dragon's vast silhouette where he watched from the mountain's edge, wings half-furled, molten eyes fixed on her. "So I'm learning to master my magic."

Garrion inclined his head. "You are learning to master *yourself*."

He studied her for a moment longer, expression unreadable. "You look steadier today. The light sits differently on you. Let us see if your strength matches your recovery."

She exhaled slowly. "You're saying that like it didn't yesterday."

"I am saying only what I observe," he said, in a tone that somehow managed to imply everything else.

From above, Vaeronth's shadow rippled across the field. *Run, little flame. Let us see what your mortal legs can do now.*

Eliryn tilted her chin, half defiant, half amused. "If I collapse, I expect one of you to carry me back."

If you collapse, Vaeronth said, the air trembling with his amusement, *I will consider it part of the lesson.*

The first lap was easy enough; crisp air, steady rhythm, her lungs working in time with the heartbeat that thrummed faintly beneath her dragonmarks. The second began to bite. By the third, her breath came sharp and ragged, legs molten from effort.

When she slowed to a halt, bracing her hands on her knees, Garrion stood exactly where she'd left him, arms folded, impassive as the mountain itself.

He gave a single, thoughtful nod. "Endurance will come. Eventually."

From above, Vaeronth's low rumble of laughter filled her mind. *Still slower than a hatchling with one wing and three legs.*

Eliryn glared skyward. "You're both insufferable."

And yet, Vaeronth said, smug warmth curling through his tone, *we are not wrong.*

Garrion didn't waste the moment. "That, Dragonrider, is why we train. You have been given a body restored, but endurance is earned. And more than that—" His gaze sharpened. "—we must ground your power before it burns through you."

She tilted her head. "Grounding. What does that even mean?"

"It means teaching your magic to serve you instead of destroy you," he said simply. "The force inside you is not finite—it flows without end. Without discipline, it will spill over. It will break your body long before it reaches its true potential."

Her stomach knotted. "So... uncontrolled magic would kill me?"

"It would unmake you from the inside out," Garrion said, no trace of hesitation. "The gods have touched others, but never like this. Your power runs through you like blood, not in pockets like most riders. That makes you stronger. And far more dangerous to yourself and everyone else."

Vaeronth's mind brushed hers, warm but weighty. *And that is why you will master it. Quickly.*

She groaned. "Why do I feel like your definition of 'quickly' means no sleep and constant pain?"

Garrion's mouth almost—*almost*—quirked. "Because it does. Now—up again. We run."

Her groan deepened. "I am starting to think you *are* trying to kill me."

"If I were," Garrion said, already walking toward the track, "you would not be here to complain."

They jogged the length of the court again, Garrion's stride steady while hers... wasn't.

When she finally caught her breath, she said, "Alright, so humor me. From where I'm standing, I feel fine. Maybe healing is my gift?"

He didn't slow. "Riders are born with a single gift. One thread of power, woven into their bloodline. Some can see moments of the future. Others can call storms, sharpen their senses to a predator's edge, or call the earth to shield them. It is rare for a rider to have more than one."

She raised a brow. "And mine is healing... right?"

"That," Garrion said, "is what I am still deciding."

Garrion went on. "When your power manifested in the dining hall, the amount of energy you released should have drained you instantly. You should have collapsed, been unconscious for hours, perhaps days. And yet..." He glanced at her with something sharp in his gaze. "You remained standing."

"I was also moments away from falling if the table hadn't supported my weight."

"It is... unprecedented. The healing you did—" He gestured briefly with one clawed hand. "Restoring broken stone, knitting cracks in flesh that have lingered for decades—such things require not just skill, but vast reserves of power. Reserves you should not have."

"So... you're saying I cheated somehow?" she offered, lips quirking.

His mouth didn't twitch. "It means that, with training, your potential is limitless. That surge was only the beginning. If my guess is correct, your gift is healing—but healing on a scale that could reshape battlefields, cities... even the balance between life and death itself."

The air between them felt heavier somehow.

"Limitless sounds nice," she said, trying to keep her tone light. "But I'm guessing there's a catch."

"There is always a catch," Garrion said evenly. "Power without discipline burns. Even healing. Especially healing. Without grounding, it will take more from you each time until your body is hollowed out from the inside."

Vaeronth's mind brushed hers again, quieter now. *He's not wrong, Eliryn. What you did in the hall... it wasn't nothing. It was a promise of much more.*

She swallowed, the flush from their run suddenly not entirely from exertion.

Garrion stopped at the far edge of the court, wings folding close. "We'll begin simply. Sit."

Garrion crouched opposite her, talons curling against the floor. "Close your eyes. Breathe deep. Find the power inside you. Hold it. Then release it slowly into the stone beneath your palms."

"That's it? Sounds easy."

"Mm," Garrion said, which was apparently gargoyle for *you're about to regret saying that.*

She inhaled, trying to summon the heat she'd felt in the dining hall. The warmth rose in her chest, then into her arms, then—

Pop!

Craaaaaack.

She opened one eye. A hairline fracture split the flagstone beneath her. "Uh... was that supposed to happen?"

"No," Garrion said flatly.

Overhead, Vaeronth's laughter rolled down like a thunderclap. "Delicate control is *not* her strength."

"Oh, thank you for the vote of confidence," she snapped.

"This," Garrion said, ignoring the dragon entirely, "is why we ground your power. Without control, you will not heal—you will destroy."

"Noted," she muttered, cheeks warming. "So... round two?"

"Yes," he said, and somehow managed to make the word sound like a threat. "Palms down. Breathe. Find the warmth. Lower it into the stone."

From the terrace, Vaeronth rumbled—out loud, so it rolled the length of the court. "If she cracks the floor again, I am telling the masons you signed off on this."

"You broke three parapets in the Siege of Thornpass," Garrion replied without looking away from Eliryn. "Do not speak to me of repairs."

Eliryn's head tilted. "You two... know each other from before?"

Vaeronth's eyes cut toward Garrion, a flare of heat brightening the edge of his irises. "He taught me how to master battlefield maneuvers when I was young."

"And failed only once," Garrion said dryly.

"Twice," Vaeronth corrected, smug. "You forgot the river."

"The river wishes it could forget *you*," Garrion said, and then, as if the last few sentences weren't a window into centuries: "Focus, Dragonrider. Palms. Breathe."

Eliryn pressed her hands to the stone. The warmth was there on the first breath—quick and eager, like a hound catching a scent. She tried to pour it down through her hands in a thin stream.

Crrrk.

A hair-thin fissure traced under her right palm and stopped when she hissed and yanked back.

Garrion arched a brow. "We want it to *go into* the stone, not *argue* with it."

"Tell that to the magic." She shook out her hands. "It's like trying to carry soup in a sieve."

Vaeronth's tail thumped once. "The problem is not the soup."

"I hate you both," she muttered, setting her palms again.

"Good," Garrion said. "Emotion can be an anchor. Try again."

She breathed. Focused. Let the warmth slip through the heels of her hands instead of the center. The stone answered, faintly at first, then with a low hum she felt in her wrists. A small, neat glow bled into the etching between flags.

Garrion inclined his head. "Better."

She dared a smile—

—then the warmth jolted sideways like a spooked horse, and a training boulder three paces away coughed to dust along one edge.

Vaeronth exhaled a sound that was half-laugh, half-sigh. "She learned how to miss without aiming."

"You put these here to humiliate me," Eliryn said, pointing at the boulders.

"We put them here to survive you," Garrion said, already hauling over a round stone scored with faint practice runes. "This is meant to take excess magic. Hand here. Breathe deeply."

She planted her palm. Warmth rose, tested, pressed deeper.

The boulder pinged like a bell and hopped.

"Progress," she said.

"It moved," Garrion allowed.

"I moved it."

"Unintentionally." He set a second boulder beside the first. "Again. Do not snatch from the magic. Invite it."

She tried. The rune-lines flushed like banked coals. She held steady, teeth set—

—and a *snap* licked from the second boulder, a clean split right along a faded sigil.

Eliryn closed her eyes. "I am a menace."

"Accurate," Vaeronth said, pleased.

"Again," Garrion demanded without further comment.

They worked until her hands felt like they were full of bees. The warm-fast spike, the hot-lurch sideways, the nearly—*nearly*—there drip of controlled magic that lasted precisely two heartbeats before it flared like lightning. On the fifteenth attempt, the first boulder warmed evenly, then cooled without drama.

Eliryn stared at her hand like it didn't belong to her. "I didn't break it."

"Not breaking is a start," Garrion said. "Stand."

She stood. He put her through joint-and-sinew stretches until her muscles softened and lengthened, breath settling into something like rhythm. Then he pointed to the track that circled the court. "Run."

"Ha," she said. "You're very funny."

"Run," he repeated.

She ran. Two laps in, her lungs were on fire. By four, her legs negotiated a peace treaty with gravity. By six, she tripped, swore, and did not, by some miracle, faceplant.

"You run like a sack of wet grain," Garrion observed.

"Did you rehearse that?" she wheezed.

"He has said it to me as well," Vaeronth offered helpfully.

"You do not run," Garrion said.

"I did when I was young," Vaeronth said. "It was alarming."

"Lets go back to the magic," Garrion told Eliryn. "Breathwork, then bowls."

He led her to a circle of shallow stone bowls etched with thin script and filled to the lip with water. "Ripple the nearest bowl," he said. "Only the nearest. Nothing else."

"Fine. Focus. Ripple. Got it."

She breathed, coaxed the warmth, and *suggested* to the nearest surface that it might want to move.

Three bowls away, water hissed, flashed to steam, and left a scorching ring.

Eliryn didn't look up. "We are not speaking about it."

"We are learning." Garrion said. "Again."

She adjusted. Slower. Quieter. A neat ring lapped once, twice, and stilled in the closest bowl.

She beamed.

A bowl behind her geysered an accusatory arc that splashed her boots.

Vaeronth lowered his head, golden eye amused. "If you wish to bathe, there are better options."

Garrion's mouth didn't change, but his tone did, the faintest edge of approval. "Again."

They went until she could call a ripple without incident more often than not. Until the court smelled like wet stone and the bowls wore little crescents of spilled water along their outer rims. Until her breath and the warmth tracked together like two lines of a braid.

"Pole," Garrion said, and handed her a weighted staff. "Not for striking. For stillness."

She took it. The balance was clean and honest, the sort of weight that pressured her wrists and shoulders. He set her in stance, feet under hips, knees soft, spine long, pole across her open palms, and said, "One hundred heartbeats."

"That's a lot of heartbeats."

"You have them to spend. Spend them wisely."

She held. Ten beats: fine. Forty: wrists ached. Sixty: warmth snuck up her arms to her throat; she told it later, and it tested her anyway. Eighty: a gnat investigated her eyelid, and she considered murder. Ninety-nine: her calves trembled. One hundred: the pole slipped a fraction, and she caught it, heart banging victory against her ribs.

"Again," Garrion said.

"I could perish."

"You could," he agreed.

"Garrion," Vaeronth said, dry. "Remember when you made me hold a boulder on my back for an entire afternoon?"

"You complained less," Garrion said.

"I was younger then. And more concerned about appearances."

Eliryn snorted, which almost cost her the pole. "Do you two take this act on the road?"

"We took it to Thornpass," Garrion said. "And Grey Fell. And once—regrettably—to Riverford."

"That was the one with the river?" Eliryn asked.

"The river dragged him half a mile," Garrion said. "He refused to drop the enemy's banner."

"It was a good banner," Vaeronth said, as if this explained everything.

"You won the fight," Garrion allowed. "And destroyed both banks, flooded three farms, and nearly drowned yourself in the process."

"The current was unnecessarily hostile," Vaeronth said.

"You were nearly offed by water," Garrion deadpanned.

The pole wobbled because she was laughing, and because some part of her, the part that had woken in the dark not knowing if she was alive, was relieved by the shape of their old argument. It made the world bigger than her mistakes. It said: *you are not the first disaster we have shepherded toward usefulness.*

They broke for water at a small alcove where a basin fed from the mountain and a shelf held wrapped oatcakes that tasted like virtue and grit. Vaeronth drank from the basin, drops beading along the edges of his fangs.

"Question," Eliryn said between bites. "Something's not adding up. Why does everything I do feel like—" she searched for the word "—*more* than just myself? The Flame left me, so why do I feel more power now than I ever have before?"

Garrion's gaze sharpened. Vaeronth went very still.

"The gods," Garrion said, careful, "give dragonriders their gifts. It is also the will of the gods that made the Flame, meant to aid the realm's ruler. Riders have always had gifts from their bloodlines. Sight.

Storm-calling. The knack of steel or root or beast. The Flame is... governance, not lineage."

"The crown's cheat code," Eliryn said, grim. "So when I was chosen—"

"The Flame rested in you because you were Sovereign," Garrion said. "When your heart stopped, it left. That is the law of it."

"Then what is *this*?" She gestured to the court, to the bowls, to the ache in her hands. "Because that wave in the dining hall, whatever it was, that wasn't some tiny flicker of a magical gift. And I felt... different after. Stronger. Healthy. Not—" she grimaced "—not *powerful*, but... rebuilt."

Vaeronth's voice dropped, all the humor washed from it. "Because you were."

Garrion set a hand on the stone shelf, talons tapping once, twice. "When Vaeronth brought you to us, you were already beyond the Veil's threshold. The Flame was gone. Your body failing. He asked us to perform Stonewake."

Eliryn's mouth went dry. "Stonewake."

"An old ritual," Garrion said. "Older than the city of Vireth, older than thrones. We call the spirit back to flesh with blood, magic, and stone. It is not resurrection. It is recall. It leaves marks."

"What kind of marks?" she asked, quiet.

"You will feel the halls wake when you pass," he said. "You will hear voices through stone. Your warmth runs constantly. That is Stonewake's bind—you are tied to the Kin, to the Sanctuary, and to the one who called us to you." He nodded toward Vaeronth. "And your dragonrider blood, the line that gave your mother visions without ever touching a dragon, wove with that bind and your bond."

"A braid," Vaeronth said softly. "Dragon. Kin. Blood."

"And the Flame is not one of the strands," Eliryn said.

"No," Garrion said. "It is not."

"So the healing in the dining hall—"

"—was three magics pulling in the same direction," Vaeronth finished. "Our bond fed your magic, the Kin steadied you, and your lineage *remembered* how to mend. You pushed, and the realm answered."

"And without grounding?" she asked.

Garrion's answer was blunt. "Without grounding, the braid frays you. Not in a blaze. In a grind. Your mind would go first because it is the hardest to still. Then the body. Then your bonds."

Eliryn swallowed. "So this isn't just about not breaking floors."

"No," Garrion said. "It is about keeping you alive."

Vaeronth leaned closer, the terrace railing creaking softly beneath his weight. "And about making you something the realm will have to reckon with."

She looked up at him. "Is this where you both assure me I'm special?"

"No," Garrion said.

"Yes," Vaeronth said at the same time.

They glared at each other like the old men they were.

Eliryn snorted then raised her chin. "Fine. Back to work before I start thinking too much."

"Good," Garrion said, as if she'd finally said something sensible. "Ground-steps."

He took her to the long strip of sand and scratched a thin line down its center. "Heel, ball, toe," he said. "Hips steady. Spine tall. Breath in for four, out for six. Do not step off the line."

"I can walk," she said.

"You can *move*," he corrected. "Walk."

She did. The first ten steps were insultingly easy. The next ten required attention. By twenty-five, the line was a thread drawn tight through her skull. The breath count skimmed her ribs, the warmth hummed low, and she felt everything inside her agree.

She reached the end without stepping wide.

Garrion made a pleased sound so small she might have imagined it. "Again."

She did it again. The wind pushed; she adjusted. A shout echoed from a far court; she let it slide by. The warmth pawed at her palms; she told it *later*, and it waited.

She finished, grin tugging despite herself.

"Now make it boring," Garrion said.

"What?"

"Do it until it bores you," he said. "Mastery is not made of triumph. It is made of repetition."

They finished with what Garrion refused to call meditation. "Sit," he said. "Spine tall. Hands easy. The warmth is a hearth, not a forge. Keep it banked."

She sat. The mountain breathed. The court murmured. The braid of power inside her prowled the edges of her attention like something half-wild, curious but contained. When it pushed, she didn't push back; she set a palm on the metaphorical muzzle and said, *later*. It snorted and settled, and some small, ridiculous part of her felt proud.

"Enough," Garrion said at last.

Her eyes opened. The light had shifted. The court's shadows had moved. Her muscles trembled in that clean, used way that promised stronger tomorrow. Not powerful. Not yet. But... *possible*.

Garrion offered a hand up. "You did not die," he said, as if noting the weather.

"High praise," she said, taking it.

Vaeronth lowered his head until one molten eye was level with hers. "She did more than not-die," he said, and there was an old, quiet pride in it. "She did not quit."

Eliryn watched them, warmth pricking her throat for a reason that had nothing to do with magic. "What now?"

"Now," Garrion said, "you eat."

"And at dusk," Vaeronth added, satisfied, "you do it again."

She groaned, but it didn't have much heart. As they turned toward the alcove, she glanced back at the circle of bowls, the thin line stitched into the sand, the boulder that had *not* shattered.

Healthy? Yes. Powerful? Not quite.

But now she understood what the difference might cost, and why it might be worth paying.

Chapter 8: The Well Within

"Stone holds memory. Blood carries fire. But only in the joining of both can truth be seen." —Saying of the First Kin

The food hall had been nearly empty when they arrived—just a few warriors finishing late meals, their voices low and steady. Garrion had left after eating, mumbling something about "letting the joints cool" before the evening session, and Vaeronth had stayed outside, wings snapping wide before he launched into the skies in search of his own meal.

That left Eliryn with a half-full belly, a restless mind, and an entire sanctuary she'd barely seen.

She started walking.

The stone corridors were cool under her palms, worn smooth by centuries of hands, claws, and wings brushing past. Light spilled in patches from high, narrow windows; her steps echoed alongside the faint rumble of voices and the clang of distant steel.

She wasn't far along before she passed two gargoyles in conversation near an archway. Their eyes tracked her first and then, inevitably, dropped to the faint gleam of her dragonmarks where her sleeve had shifted. One inclined his head in a bow, his granite-cut features unchanging, yet weighted with something that felt... like awe. The other mirrored him before returning to their talk, but she felt the press of their attention long after she'd moved on.

It kept happening. In twos or threes, in passing doorways or along walkways above; gargoyles whose eyes flickered to the marks, whose stares held for just long enough to make her skin prickle. She tried to smile, sometimes. Other times she just nodded, feeling awkward and unsure whether she was supposed to be bowing back.

Rounding a turn, the air changed into something warmer, heavier with the metallic tang of sweat and steel.

It was almost a relief to hear the clash of stone on stone. The sound drew her toward an open courtyard, half-hidden behind a colonnade. She stepped into its shadow and froze.

The sparring ring lay in a half-shadowed courtyard, the air ringing with the clash of weapons and the deep, resonant thud of stone against stone. One gargoyle dominated the center of the fight—deep green granite streaked with gold veins, thick black braids swinging behind like whips. Their opponent was bigger but slower, and the one with braids moved with a predator's ease, talons flashing, wings catching the light like shards of glass.

Eliryn lingered at the edge, watching as the gargoyle whispered something sharp and fast. The air warped, golden light flickering around their fingertips, and their opponent's weapon cracked neatly in half. The crowd roared, the victor dipped their head, and then—unexpectedly—those amber eyes found Eliryn.

Eliryn blinked. So—*not all Kin were male.*

The gargoyle crossed the ring toward her, every step deliberate. Up close, her presence was like standing too near the edge of a storm, beautiful in its danger, carved strength wrapped in poise. The air around her felt charged, alive.

"You wish to join?" the gargoyle asked. Her voice was low, smooth as polished obsidian, carrying no challenge, only curiosity.

Eliryn met her gaze, steadying herself beneath its weight. "I think I'll spare everyone the spectacle," she said, a faint smile tugging at her lips. "I'd probably embarrass myself."

A flicker, something like amusement, or perhaps approval, moved through the gargoyle's eyes. "Caution," she said. "Rare, for one who carries such power."

Eliryn tilted her head. "Power's easier to handle when you know more about its source. I'm still learning."

For a heartbeat, the gargoyle studied her in silence. Then she said, "I saw you. In the hall. After the feast. The magic that answered you..." She hesitated, as if searching for the right word. "It should not have been possible."

Eliryn's pulse jumped. "I didn't mean for it to happen," she admitted quietly. "I just—reacted."

"Then the Kin reacted with you." The gargoyle's tone held no accusation, only fact. "We have all been waiting a very long time."

Before Eliryn could respond, the warrior turned and walked back toward the ring, braids catching the sun as she moved.

Eliryn watched her go, the echo of her words lingering long after she'd vanished into the sparring crowd. Something about the steadiness in her movements and the quiet gravity of her presence pulled at Eliryn in a way she couldn't name.

She stayed to watch the fights.

The sparring ring beat with rhythm and light; stone striking stone, wings cutting air, power threading through every motion. None of the Kin tired. Their precision was absolute, their strength relentless.

Eliryn leaned against the railing, chin resting in her hands, watching them move like water shaped into war. *And I can barely run a few laps without collapsing,* she thought wryly.

When the green-and-gold warrior stepped from the ring again, talons flexing as if to shake off the ghost of battle, Eliryn pushed off the wall and crossed to meet her.

"Meyra," the gargoyle said before Eliryn could speak, her tone unreadable, as though she'd already decided to meet her halfway.

"Eliryn," she replied, nodding in return.

Meyra's gaze traveled over her once, assessing but not unkind. "The power that answered you, it does not come often. Not in any age I remember."

Eliryn held her eyes. "Then let's hope I learn to wield it before it decides to wield me."

Something flickered in Meyra's expression, a subtle shift, sharp and fleeting. Respect, maybe. Or warning. She inclined her head, a gesture that felt old, almost ceremonial. "We will see," she said.

And then she was gone, disappearing into the barracks' shadowed archway, leaving Eliryn with the faint hum of her own pulse and a new, restless certainty coiling low in her chest.

For a long moment, Eliryn stayed where she was, the sounds of the sparring ring fading into the steady rhythm of her breathing. The sun had begun its descent behind the peaks, painting the courtyard in gold and violet. Every stone seemed to hold memory here—oaths made, battles fought, lives carved into the mountain's marrow.

She glanced once toward the horizon, where the light fractured against the spires, and wondered if this place remembered the last rider who had stood where she did now.

Whatever it remembered, it was watching her.

Eliryn turned toward the main walk, her boots whispering over stone, the echo of Meyra's words still tugging at her mind: *It should not have been possible.*

She didn't know whether to feel impressive or terrified by that truth.

———◆———

The Sanctuary breathed differently at dusk.

Torches hissed to life along the walls, their flames bending in the canyon wind. Shadows stretched across the training courts, long and sharp, making the carved pillars look like silent sentinels. The stone beneath Eliryn's boots still held the day's warmth, but a cool draft tugged at her sleeves, carrying with it the faint scents of resin smoke, sweat, and mountain air so crisp it stung her nose.

Her thoughts circled stubbornly back to the gargoyles she had saw training.

Eliryn hadn't seen any other women among the Kin—not yet. Maybe Meyra was an outlier, the way Eliryn herself always seemed to be.

But gods, she'd looked nothing like an outlier in the ring. She'd been sure. Grounded. A warrior from soul to stone. Eliryn couldn't help comparing herself—stumbling through stretches, tripping over her own feet, nowhere close to being a warrior. She had a long way to go before she was even half the fighter Meyra already was.

By the time she reached the training courts, her stomach was knotted tight with restless energy. The wide expanse lay open to the night sky, ringed by high arches that cut jagged shadows across the sand. Garrion stood at the center, arms folded, wings casting long silhouettes behind him. Vaeronth crouched nearby, molten eyes gleaming in the torchlight like banked fire.

"You're late," Garrion rumbled.

"I was... sightseeing," Eliryn said, brushing a lock of hair from her face. "Wasn't too long ago I couldn't see much of anything at all, so you'll have to forgive me if I get distracted."

The silence stretched. Garrion and Vaeronth exchanged a glance—quick, unreadable. It made something twist low in her stomach.

Garrion only said, "Stretch."

She sighed but obeyed, dragging through the motions until her muscles loosened and the air burned in her lungs. The sand was cool beneath her boots, the night wind tugging at her hair.

When she straightened, Garrion stood at the center of the court, wings half-furled. "Tonight," he said, "we do not test your strength or your endurance. We measure something far more dangerous."

Eliryn tilted her head. "Which is?"

"The depth of what lives within you." His gaze caught the faint shimmer of her dragonmarks. "Yesterday proved your power has no leash. Tonight, we see if your Well has a bottom."

Vaeronth's growl rolled low and approving through the dark. *A wise place to begin.*

Eliryn's pulse kicked. "And if it doesn't?"

"Then we will learn how to stand at its edge without falling." Garrion stepped back, motioning her forward. "Breathe. Quiet your thoughts. Do not reach for the surface of your magic—sink beneath it. Follow it as far as it allows."

"That sounds," she said carefully, "like the exact opposite of safe."

"Safety is a lesson for later," Garrion said, utterly calm. "Tonight is for truth."

The words sent a chill down her spine. But she nodded, grounding herself in the rhythm of her breathing, the scrape of her boots in the sand, the steady heat of Vaeronth's presence behind her.

The realm narrowed. The whisper of wind between the arches. The scent of stone and torch smoke. Her own heartbeat. She turned her senses inward, past the ache of muscle, past the hum of thought, searching for that strange current she had felt in the hall.

At first, nothing.

Then—pressure. Slow. Relentless. Vast.

It wasn't like touching flame or storm; it was like standing at the edge of an ocean at night, the tide rising soundlessly at her feet. The depth of it made her chest tighten. The dark below wasn't empty—it was full. Waiting.

Her hands trembled. The air thickened.

"Do not fight it," Garrion said, voice rough as stone and steady as the mountain. "Do not fear the drop. The Well is not meant to be conquered. Only known."

Easy for him to say.

Eliryn drew one more breath. Then she let go—and began to fall.

At first, nothing. Just the usual hum under her skin, the warmth of her dragonmarks. Then—

A pull.

Not gentle. Not welcoming.

It seized her chest, yanking her downward into something endless and black. Her lungs seized. The air thickened. For a wild moment she thought she was drowning, sucked into a river with no surface. Voices—no, echoes—slid along the edges of her mind. Too many to count. They whispered in tongues she didn't know, their syllables heavy as stone, bright as fire.

Her heartbeat stuttered. The marks on her arms flared, molten gold flooding her veins. Pressure built in her bones, in her teeth, behind her eyes. Like the whole mountain was leaning its weight against her body.

"Eliryn!" Vaeronth's voice was louder than thunder. Sharper than the first crack of lightning.

But she couldn't stop. Couldn't let go. The Well had her.

Then—

It broke.

The ground cracked beneath her knees, runes on the walls igniting in a furious cascade of gold. Light exploded from her chest, a column that shot upward like a spear. The shockwave slammed outward, rattling the very foundations of the Sanctuary.

Stone shuddered. Dust rained from the ceiling. Somewhere distant, wings unfurled in alarm.

And then they came.

One by one at first, then in a flood—gargoyles drawn to the call like moths to a flame. Their claws scraped the stone as they landed, wings snapping closed, eyes locked on her blazing form. Some stumbled, forced to one knee as the raw pulse of her power pressed against them. Others froze where they stood, staring with something between awe and terror.

A cry rippled through the chamber in their tongue, low and reverent. Fists pressed to hearts. Bows of instinct, not choice.

But Eliryn didn't see it. Her vision had gone white. The Well was swallowing her whole.

Her body arched, spine bowing under the pressure. The energy was too much, too vast, tearing at the edges of her skin like it wanted out. Every beat of her heart felt like it might be her last.

Let go, the Well seemed to whisper. *Fall, and be unmade.*

Something slammed into her awareness, fierce and furious. Not the Well this time, but Vaeronth.

His presence lashed through her like molten iron. *No. You will not fall, Little Flame. Not again.*

The words anchored her just long enough for the power to crest, then collapse inward.

The world went black.

Chapter 9: A Vessel Strained

"The brightest fire does not need an enemy to burn. It will consume itself, if left untended." —Fragment of forgotten lore

When awareness returned, it didn't come gently.

Her first breath tore through her chest like fire, dragging air into lungs that felt too small, too raw. The stone beneath her back was cold, damp with grit, and for a disorienting moment she thought she was buried alive—swallowed by the mountain, pinned beneath its weight.

Her fingers scrabbled against the stone floor. Her tongue tasted of iron. Her ears rang like struck metal, drowning out everything except the dull roar of her own pulse.

She forced her eyes open. The realm was blurred at first, shapes smeared together—light and shadow bleeding in wrong directions. Then the blur shifted, sharpened, and she realized the heat above her wasn't the stone collapsing.

It was Vaeronth.

His body loomed, wings arched wide enough to blot out the runes glowing along the walls. Smoke curled from his open maw, each exhale a furnace blast across her face. His tail lashed in restless arcs, gouging trenches into the floor.

And his snarl—deep, guttural, vibrating through the stone itself—wasn't for her.

It was for *them*.

The chamber was full. Every archway. Every ledge. Dozens—no, more than dozens—of gargoyles crowded the space, their granite faces lit by the dying glow of her runes.

Not moving. Not speaking. Just watching.

And every single one of them was staring at her.

One gargoyle near the front had dropped to one knee, his hand pressed over his chest like a knight swearing fealty. Another—an older male with horn ridges worn smooth by time—looked as though tears might crack through the stone of his face. Further back, a younger gargoyle whispered something sharp and urgent to the one beside him, their eyes wide as if they had witnessed something unspeakable.

Her stomach lurched. The last thing she remembered was falling—being dragged down into that impossible Well inside her, voices clawing at her bones. A chorus of whispers, old as the stone itself, pressing against her ribs as the realm had ripped apart in light. And now? Now every protector in the Sanctuary was here, as though her heartbeat had torn them from their barracks and bound them to this chamber.

And there—front and center, storm-gray and severe—was Druven.

The one who had promised he would compete for the right to guard her. His arms were folded now, his expression carved from stone, unreadable. But his eyes—dark, steady, and fixed on her—held something she couldn't name. Not reverence. Not doubt. Something heavier.

Her chest tightened. After this, after nearly exploding apart on the training floor, did he regret saying he'd stake his claim? Or worse, was he silently deciding that something this unstable wasn't worth guarding at all?

"Enough," Garrion's voice cut through the suffocating silence, rough as grinding stone. "Stand down."

The command rippled outward. Slowly, the gargoyles shifted. Lowering. Knees bent. Heads bowed. Claws pressed to hearts.

Eliryn swallowed hard and tried to sit. Her ribs flared in protest, the whole realm tilting sideways.

Vaeronth's wing snapped down across her body, blocking her from view. His growl deepened, rolling like thunder through the cavern, a sound that vibrated against her ribs and into her bones.

"They wouldn't harm her," Garrion said, stepping forward into the circle Vaeronth had claimed. His eyes swept from Eliryn's pale face to the dragon's bared teeth. "You know this."

Vaeronth's molten gaze didn't waver. Smoke hissed between his teeth, heat building in his throat. "She will not die again."

The words shattered what little air remained.

The hall went utterly still. The gargoyles froze mid-breath, their reverence deepening into something sharper.

Eliryn blinked up at Vaeronth, throat thick. He wasn't posturing. He wasn't simply being protective. He was *afraid*. Truly, viscerally afraid. The kind of fear born only from loss already endured.

Her fingers curled weakly against the stone. She wanted to speak, to ease the fury in her dragon's stance, to explain the storm that had ripped through her body—but nothing came.

Because she didn't understand it either.

Her lashes fluttered, her vision swimming as she forced her eyes to focus. Cool stone beneath her palms. Smoke in the air. A wall of tense silence pressing in from every side.

"What... happened?" Her voice cracked.

Garrion's granite face leaned into view, the carved lines of his features grave. "Your Well is vast, Dragonrider. Too vast. You reached into it, and it answered." His tone had the weight of warning—but when his gaze flicked briefly toward the other Kin, there was something else there too. Something unspoken, as if he knew more than he was willing to lay bare in front of so many witnesses.

Her breath caught. The memory of it crashed back—light and pressure, drowning heat, voices like echoes from a place older than the mountains.

She turned her head again, seeking an anchor—and found Druven's eyes still locked on hers. A shiver ran down her spine. Was that loyalty in his gaze... or warning?

Eliryn looked away fast, pressing her palm harder to Vaeronth's scales, grounding herself in the heat beneath her hand. "I'm here," she whispered. "I'm not dying."

The words trembled out of her before she could stop them—and for a heartbeat, she wasn't sure who she was trying to convince more: herself, or the dragon above her.

Garrion crouched closer, his wings folding in tight. His gaze pinned her. "This is what I warned you of. Unchecked, your Well will spill over. And when it does, it will not only burn you out from the inside—it will call every Kin within reach. You felt it, didn't you? The power trying to claim you."

Eliryn swallowed hard, throat dry. "It was like... drowning. Like being pulled under by something too big to fight."

"That," Garrion said, voice low, "is what happens when a vessel is not yet strong enough for what it carries. Yours is already straining its bounds."

Her mouth went dry. "So what—you're saying if I don't learn control, I'll just..." she gestured weakly, "...explode?"

The faintest flicker of grim humor crossed Garrion's stone features. "If you're fortunate. If not, the power will hollow you out piece by piece until nothing remains."

Her hand curled tighter against Vaeronth's scales, heat prickling behind her eyes. She had no quip. No shield of humor to hide behind. Just the cold, raw knowledge that what she carried inside her wasn't a gift at all—it was a storm waiting to break.

Vaeronth's growl still rattled the stone, though it had dimmed to something low and seething. His wings twitched above her, unwilling to fold, every line of his body locked in the language of defense.

"There are no threats here," Garrion said again, firmer now, the words like granite blocks laid one atop the other. His gaze swept the gathered Kin, then returned to Vaeronth. "They are protectors. They answered the call of a dragonrider—that is their most sacred purpose. You know this."

Vaeronth's molten stare shifted from the ring of gargoyles to Garrion. Smoke hissed once more between his teeth. Then, with visible reluctance, his wings folded tight to his sides. His body curved still around Eliryn like a wall, but the promise of violence in him eased a fraction.

Garrion crouched, extending a hand to her. The stone of his palm was cool, grounding as it closed around her unsteady grip and helped her rise. Her legs trembled, not entirely from weakness.

"I feel like I could be knocked over by a stiff breeze," she muttered, trying for humor.

But Garrion's expression didn't shift. "No. You are stronger than all of us. That is why your training must be taken more seriously than any before you. What you carry will not forgive hesitation."

The words sank into her chest like iron. Around them, the gargoyles had not scattered. They lingered in alcoves, on ledges, along the walls, just watching.

Druven stood closer than the rest, nearer than caution should have allowed. His dark eyes hadn't left her since she'd woken. And it struck her then—he must have pushed forward, through whatever storm of light and power she'd unleashed, because he was here now. Not cowed. Not shaken back. He had moved toward her, as though it was unthinkable to do anything else.

He would have walked into her collapse—into that raging magic—for no reason other than the sense of duty woven into his marrow. Protector, through and through. For a stranger. For her.

And what had she been doing all those years while her mother whispered prophecy in half-shaken tones? Taking each day as it came. Sulking at her fading sight. Pretending her bloodline was just another curse to bear. She should have been preparing. Training.

Instead, she'd wasted time.

Never again.

She straightened as best she could, though her knees wobbled, one palm still pressed firm to Vaeronth's scales. *This is real. Serious. Every moment matters.*

Garrion's gaze lingered on her for a heartbeat, then shifted toward the shadowed edge of the courts where a stone archway waited, half-swallowed by torchlight and mist. "Come," he said quietly. "There is more you need to understand. The knowledge of the Kin is old—and it is time you saw it for yourself."

The training grounds had fallen silent. The sand was scored with claw marks, faintly glowing runes still pulsing beneath the surface where her power had cracked the earth. Around them, the gathered gargoyles began to withdraw. Wings folding, heads bowing; the weight of their gazes followed her as she moved.

Vaeronth lowered his head as she passed, his breath a hot rush against her shoulder. *I will follow.*

She fell into step behind Garrion, her boots whispering over the sand. The archway loomed ahead, one of the many carved passages that honeycombed the mountainside, and for a moment, she hesitated. The space beyond it was darker, the light of the courts fading into an ancient hush.

She cast one last glance over her shoulder. The gargoyles still lingered along the colonnades, silent and unmoving.

Then she followed Garrion beneath the arch.

The noise of the courts fell away at once. The air turned dense and still, carrying the scent of old stone and the faint hum of something alive just beneath the surface. The tunnel sloped downward, the walls close and veined with faint light that flickered in rhythm with her dragonmarks.

Each step carried her deeper, until the hum grew louder—not in her ears, but under her skin. The tunnel opened, the air shifting again, and suddenly the floor dropped away into a cavern so vast Eliryn forgot to breathe.

Pillars rose in solemn lines, carved with ancient runes that glowed like veins of light. Alcoves lined the walls, some cradling relics wrapped in dust and shadow, others empty but thrumming faintly with presence. High above, the ceiling disappeared into darkness broken only by faint threads of gold, like constellations etched into the stone.

"This is the Sepulcher of Oaths," Garrion said. His deep voice carried easily in the hush. "Here, every protector has sworn their vow. It is where ceremonies are held. Where promises are bound."

Eliryn's gaze swept the vast chamber, her chest tight. The air itself felt alive, pressing close, carrying whispers she could almost hear.

Her dragonmarks prickled faintly.

She stepped closer to one of the pillars, tracing the carved runes with her gaze. The symbols pulsed at her nearness, slow and steady, like a heartbeat.

"What are they?" she whispered.

"Names," Garrion replied. "Vows. Declarations of service, carved into eternity. Every protector swears here, and every dragonrider with great power stood where you do now."

Eliryn's throat went dry. She could almost picture it—rows of warriors on bended knee, stone voices ringing out their oaths while dragons watched from above. She wasn't sure if she felt awe, or smallness, or some muddled knot of both.

Too much. Too vast. The weight of all of it pressed on her shoulders until her breath felt shallow. She had thought she was beginning to grasp her place here—but this place reminded her she was a speck standing inside centuries of legacy.

She lingered as Garrion's explanation rolled on—about ceremonies, about the permanence of stone, about the bond between dragonrider and protector—but her mind was already blurring, too full to take more in.

By the time they turned back toward the tunnel, her legs felt unsteady. She didn't remember walking the length of the cavern, only the echo of her footsteps, and the way the runes pulsed faintly as she passed—as if acknowledging her, or warning her.

When they emerged into cooler air, Vaeronth peeled away, wings unfurling as he leapt into the night sky. His departure shook dust from the high stone arches.

By the time she stumbled back to her chamber, she was wrung hollow—her head buzzing, her limbs heavy. She fell onto her bed without undressing, without thought.

Sleep claimed her fast, before she could even wonder if any of it had been real.

Chapter 10: Eyes Beyond Stone

"The realm does not hand you power. It hands you weight, and waits to see if you will carry it." —Attributed to Garrion of the Kin

Eliryn woke with sight that still shocked her.

The ceiling above her was sharp, every crack in the stone etched with perfect clarity. Light filtered in from a narrow slit of a window, dust motes spinning lazy circles in the beam. She could see it all—details so crisp her chest ached.

For so many years, her vision had slipped further and further into shadow, until the realm had narrowed to blurred outlines and soft shades.

Even after bonding with Vaeronth, she had only glimpsed the world again in fleeting moments, borrowing his sight through sheer concentration. Each time it had felt like fighting to hold water in her cupped hands—beautiful, impossible, and temporary. And then, in the citadel, it had gone completely dark. One blink and everything had been stolen.

But now, there was no effort. No reaching. No strain. The bond was seamless.

She didn't have to *ask* to see anymore.

She simply opened her eyes, and their bond magic was there—vast, sharp, edged in the impossible colors of a dragon's world.

It still rattled her. This wasn't her sight. It never would be again. She was blind. That truth hadn't changed. And yet, with Vaeronth, she walked and breathed and lived as if the darkness had never claimed her.

It was a gift. A miracle.

And a reminder that every part of her life now rested on borrowed clarity.

Her thoughts tangled, chasing themselves in circles—how sight could return to someone who no longer had eyes to claim it, how a bond could blur the line between two souls so completely that she wasn't sure where she ended and Vaeronth began.

Your thoughts are loud this morning.

The voice cut clean through her reverie, low and dry and unreasonably calm.

Eliryn startled, the blanket slipping from her fingers. *You were listening again,* she accused, half-hearted.

I do not listen, Vaeronth said. *I simply cannot escape the noise you make when you think too hard.*

Despite herself, she smiled. "It's not my fault the universe dropped me into a realm where magic keeps rewriting the rules every day." She shifted onto her side, the light from the narrow window tracing gold across the sheets. "A few weeks ago, I thought I had only days left to see shadows. Now I wake up and everything's... sharp. Effortless. Like it's mine."

It is.

The certainty in his tone stilled her.

She hesitated. "You're not near me, are you?"

No. His voice rumbled faintly, carried on a wind that wasn't in her room. *I am above the canyon. The cliffs are bright today.*

Even as he spoke, her vision tilted—lifting into sky and sunlight, cliffs sweeping beneath her as if her body had taken flight. She gasped softly, pressing a hand to her chest. "I can see it. Through you. Without even trying."

Vaeronth's presence shifted, quieter now, the heat of his mind brushing hers. *Our tether deepens. You no longer reach for sight—it reaches for you. The Kin's magic woke something in us when they performed Stonewake.*

Her brows furrowed. "Stonewake is what they called the ritual that brought me back to life, right?"

A hum rolled through their bond, ancient and solemn. *It is the oldest rite of the Kin,* he said. *A call to rouse what has fallen beyond life's reach. When a soul teeters between breath and oblivion, their Stonecallers sing to the mountain itself. It lends its strength to restore what is not yet ready to fade.*

Eliryn went still. "So when they pulled me back—"

They did more than heal your body, Vaeronth finished. *They wove the mountain's essence into ours. The magic of Stonewake is patient and deep, meant to wake slowly over years. But in you, it surged all at once. You are past what you should be, faster than what should be possible.*

Her breath hitched. "Because I died."

Because you live again, Vaeronth corrected, his tone softer now, the words rumbling like distant thunder. *Stonewake does not return what was lost—it remakes it.*

She sank back against the mattress, fingers brushing her temple. "So this—my sight, the bond—it's all because of that?"

It is part of it, he said. *But what has begun will not stop now. The line between us will keep thinning until much more than your sight changes.*

Eliryn exhaled, slow and careful. "That's... a lot."

It is only the beginning.

Silence stretched between them for a beat, her heart syncing faintly to the pulse of his wings high above. Then Vaeronth's tone shifted—lower, steadier, threaded with something heavier.

There will be no training today.

She frowned. "What do you mean?"

The Kin gather, he said. *They will fight for the right to guard you. The Rite of Choosing begins soon.*

Eliryn sat up, the blanket tumbling into her lap. "Already?"

Stone does not wait, Little Flame, Vaeronth said, the faintest edge of pride threading his voice. *Your call reached them all last night. Now they will answer it.*

Eliryn's throat tightened. Memories flickered—Druven's storm-gray stare, Garrion's solemn presence, the way dozens of protectors had filled the chamber like her heartbeat had summoned them. Now they would fight because of her—because of what she was becoming.

She pressed her palms to the mattress, steadying her breath. "Then I won't let doubt ruin this," she murmured. "If they're willing to fight for me, the least I can do is be the rider worthy of it."

Vaeronth's rumble threaded through her chest, warm and low. *That is all the Kin ask. Not perfection. Only purpose.*

A small, quiet smile tugged at her mouth. "Then purpose is what they'll get."

She rose—legs still heavy, but her spine straight—each movement a promise she hadn't quite spoken aloud.

A basin sat against the far wall, carved into the stone floor. The water shimmered faintly with light from the slit of a window above. She crouched, dipped her hand in and hissed. Cold. Not the enchanted warmth of the citadel's chambers in Vireth, where everything had been gilded in magic's luxury. This was mountain water, biting and raw.

Still, she stripped and sank into it with a sharp inhale, submerging herself until her scalp prickled. It wasn't comfort she sought, but clarity. She scrubbed until her skin flushed pink, dragging away dust and sweat, until it felt like she was scraping off doubt itself.

When she emerged, the cold clung to her like armor. She twisted her hair into tight braids while it was still wet, fingers fumbling only twice before finding rhythm.

Clothes awaited her on a bench near the wall. Simple: a dark tunic, sturdy trousers, boots with steel at the toe. Practical. No embroidery, no gilding, no softness. She ran her fingers along the stitching, frowning.

"Where did these even come from?" she asked aloud as she dressed, fastening the belt with deliberate precision.

From the Kin, Vaeronth's voice rolled through her mind like distant thunder. *The Sanctuary provides for its own. One among them tends to your chamber—leaves what you need, repairs what's worn. It is an old custom, one of quiet service.*

Eliryn paused, the tunic half fastened. "Someone's been doing this for me? Every day?"

Yes. A faint warmth rippled through the bond, like the brush of wind over embers. *The Kin honor those who train beneath these mountains. You are watched over, even when you do not see it.*

Her throat tightened around something she couldn't name. She glanced toward the door, voice softer now. "Then I'll have to find them someday. Thank them properly."

They will not expect thanks, Vaeronth murmured. *But they will appreciate it.*

She nodded, a quiet promise to herself, and finished dressing. No vanity. No hesitation. This was just another kind of armor.

She made her way from her room with haste born of anticipation and nerves.

The sound of the Sanctuary carried differently that morning—low voices echoing through the halls, heavy footsteps that felt measured, purposeful. It wasn't the usual rhythm of training. It was the hum of anticipation.

Eliryn stepped into the corridor, braids damp against her shoulders, her new tunic snug across her frame. Every gargoyle she passed gave the same quiet acknowledgment—some with a dip of the head, some with a claw pressed briefly to their chest. None spoke. The silence was almost ceremonial.

Already, they gather, Vaeronth murmured in her thoughts, the beat of his wings punctuating the words.

"Dozens of them?" she asked, voice low as she walked.

More. Not every Kin will fight, but many will watch.

Her pulse stuttered. Fighting was one thing—she wasn't the one swinging blades today. But the thought of being watched, measured, weighed by those stone-carved eyes made her stomach knot.

The corridor widened into daylight, and the air shifted—open, vast, touched by the sharp tang of dust and stone warmed by sun. The arena spread out before her, carved directly into the mountainside. Rows upon rows of seating rose in an arc, packed with gargoyles who had already taken their places. The sheer number of them stole her breath.

At the far end, banners rippled in the canyon wind—black cloth emblazoned with the Kin's crest: a horned face set within a shield. The same sigil gleamed from silver clasps at the warriors' shoulders below, each one dressed in ceremonial garb as they assembled in formation.

Her steps faltered. Standing there in the sand, lined shoulder to shoulder, they looked almost... human. Broader, harder, their skin veined with stone, their talons gleaming like onyx—but the shape was familiar. The slope of shoulders, the bend of knees, the rhythm of breath in broad chests. They were men and women who had been reforged, not something wholly other.

Garrion's presence appeared at her side, grounding and immovable. His wings flexed slightly as he spoke, voice low but edged with gravity. "This is the Rite of Choosing, Dragonrider. It has been performed since the First Bond. The Kin do not give their service lightly—they earn the right through combat, through magic, and through spiritual bond. To guard a dragonrider is the highest honor they can fulfill."

He tipped his chin toward the waiting ranks. "There will be three rounds. The first—flesh against flesh, strength alone. The second, magic. And the third is a bonding test. Only those who prove themselves in all may stand before you at the end."

Eliryn swallowed, throat dry. "I understand."

Garrion's gaze sharpened, the lines of his granite face cut deep. "Do not mistake this for spectacle. You must not interfere. Not with word or will. Their fight must be theirs alone."

Vaeronth's shadow swept overhead, circling once before folding into place beside the dais carved for them at the arena's heart. The platform overlooked the ring, etched with faintly glowing runes, a place of honor—and of judgment.

Eliryn climbed the steps, heart hammering as she sat at the edge, her dragon's warmth radiating against her back.

Dozens of contenders shifted below. Dozens more watched from the stands.

The air itself seemed to pause, waiting.

The horn sounded, deep and resonant, reverberating through the mountain like a heartbeat.

The first round would soon begin.

Chapter 11: The Sightless Measure

"Strength can be measured in stone, but loyalty must be weighed in silence." —Kin proverb

The horn thundered again, and the mountain answered.

Sound rolled down the terraces like a physical thing—shaking grit from the colonnades, waking a thousand faint carvings along the walls until old runes seemed to catch and hold the vibration. Eliryn felt it in the bones of the dais, in the soles of her boots, in the soft place beneath her sternum where fear and awe liked to curl together and pretend they were one feeling.

The arena had been cut straight from the cliff face in a great crescent. No mortar. No added stone. Just mountain, persuaded. What must it have taken to carve this? Entire slopes were scalloped into tier upon tier of seating, each bench worn smooth where generations of Kin had braced their weight. Claw-scratches scored the edges like tally marks. At the very top, the wind hunted through narrow archways and brought with it a cold, clean bite—melted snow and sky.

Below, the fighting floor gleamed pale against the dark rock, a circle of stone so tightly polished it reflected the banners above like a shallow pool. Runes were etched there—faintly luminous veins spiraling out from the center. They didn't blaze the way the Sepulcher's did; these only pulsed when the horn called, as if the arena itself were breathing.

Vaeronths' wings cast the kind of shade that made the air itself shift temperature. *Do not fidget.*

"I'm not fidgeting," she whispered, and immediately realized she was.

You are vibrating with nervous energy, Little Flame, he said, dry as heat on stone.

Her mouth twitched. "And whose fault is that? They just called an entire species to spar for my attention."

This is not for you, he corrected, and that thread of old pride wound through the bond, iron and ember. *It is for the sake of the prophecy. For what you carry. For what must be guarded.*

Eliryn forced her shoulders to lower. Forced air into lungs that wanted to only sip, not swallow. From the dais—raised a few steps above the ring and ringed in sigils of its own—she could see the whole of it: the long entry tunnels yawning like throats at cardinal points; the tiered benches already knit with bodies; the black banners snapping from high spars.

The crest of the Kin was everywhere. On cloth. On armor clasps. Carved into the faces of the great pillars that supported the upper tiers: a horned guardian's visage set within a shield, with vinework curling from the rim like captured roots or tongues of ivy-flame. Seen up close, the vines weren't abstract at all—they braided into smaller figures: a rider with a spear; a dragon coiled around a mountain; a line of Kin standing shoulder to shoulder, wings mantled over all. The sigil wasn't just decoration. It was history rewritten small enough to wear.

She dragged her gaze from it and tried not to count. Rows upon rows of bodies. Hundreds. Maybe more. Most had come only to watch—stone-still, arms folded, eyes like banked coals. Some leaned forward on their knees, intent; others reclined with the casual arrogance of veterans who had seen a dozen such rites and knew the rhythms by instinct. A few shared quiet words, lips hardly moving; the sound of them was a low river through the whole space, steady and inevitable.

Eliryn was again struck by how humanoid the gargoyles were. These were not statues pretending to breathe. These were people. Harder than she was. Older than her line. But still people.

Garrion quietly cleared his throat, drawing her attention back to him. "You will learn the measure of those who would stand between your body and a blade. When the rounds are done, you will formally choose."

A cold prickle slid along her arms. "And if I choose wrong?"

Garrion's profile did not change. "Stone endures poor choices. Flesh does not. Choose well."

Right. Comforting.

Vaeronth's large frame lifted to the sky, raising above the dais and settling into an outcropping that jutted like a knuckle of rock above them. He did not fold himself down into idle elegance the way he sometimes did. He was alert, the cords of his long body tight.

The horn sounded a third time.

The runes along the circumference of the ring brightened by a shade.

The far gates groaned.

A procession emerged.

They came two by two, then three by three as the tunnel's width allowed, wings folded close or half-mantled like stormclouds about to part. They wore their ceremonial harnesses over training leathers—black sashes crisscrossing broad chests, silver clasps bearing the crest at each shoulder. No helms. No masks.

Eliryn's eyes dragged over every detail. A marble giant with a ridge of broken horn and a smile like a crack splitting ice. A lithe obsidian female whose wings were webbed with thin, pale scars like frost tracing glass. A weathered elder in basalt whose right forearm had been rebuilt at some point—the seam a faint lightning-bolt of lighter stone that ran wrist to elbow. A young onyx warrior whose talons were notched from obsessive sharpening. A broad-shouldered figure the color of wet slate with gold veining like river-maps winding up his throat.

Eliryn found herself leaning forward despite herself, palms braced on her knees as the line curved and curved again, spilling into the ring until there were dozens standing shoulder to shoulder, wing-shadow crowding wing-shadow. The air was different down there—she could see the way dust lifted around their ankles with each breath. The ring smelled like iron and cedar resin and the warm mineral tang of stone in sun.

Breathe, Vaeronth murmured in her mind.

"I am," she lied.

You are tasting air and calling it breath.

She exhaled through her nose, slow, and tried to find a shape inside herself big enough to hold this moment. Her mother and grandmother would have stood, chin up, eyes steady, as if they had been born to be weighed by a world and not found wanting. Eliryn had never felt particularly born to anything. Yet here she was, the focus point where a thousand histories crossed.

"This place was made for proving worth," Garrion said without looking at her, as if he could hear the way her thoughts ran in circles. "Today will mark an important moment in our history."

The herald lifted a hand; the crowd's low hum thinned. A last file of Kin emerged from the shadowed gate, then the bronze gates swung shut with a rumble that rolled through the bones of the cliff.

Eliryn let her gaze stray across the tiers one more time.

Vaeronth's tail tapped rock above her once. *Ready?*

"As I'll ever be," she murmured. "Which is to say: not at all."

Honesty looks good on you.

"Shut up."

The corner of Garrion's mouth might have moved, just a fraction, as if guessing at their conversation.

The herald's staff struck stone three times. Runes along the ring brightened by another shade.

The contenders moved into formation, shoulder to shoulder across the sand. For a breath, no one moved, and then hundreds of eyes shifted to the dais where Eliryn sat.

Then the first name rolled like thunder across the amphitheater.

"Kareth, son of Orun, breaker of the southern siege, shield who did not fall."

The marble giant stepped forward. Pale stone gleamed in the sun, veins of silver light rippling faintly as if his skin held molten ore beneath. Horn ridges crowned his skull, one broken at the tip. His eyes—pale as moonlight—didn't waver. When he moved, it was deliberate, every step the stride of someone who had never been turned aside.

Murmurs rose along the benches, ripples of respect.

Even standing still, Kareth looked like a fortress given flesh.

The herald's voice cut again.

"Veyra and Veyrik, twins of the Shadow Cornice; two against ten at Dawnfell, mirrors who did not falter."

Two basalt figures stepped forward in perfect unison. They were nearly identical—the same sharp jawlines, the same heavy-set shoulders, the same eyes of volcanic glass. When they flexed their talons, they did so in mirrored rhythm, as though a single thought coursed through both bodies. The crowd's hum thickened into something darker: admiration tinged with unease.

"Do they always move like that?" Eliryn whispered, leaning toward Garrion.

The gargoyle's wings twitched faintly. "Always."

She shivered, unsure if she found it beautiful or terrifying.

The names rolled on.

A lean figure with ash-gray wings etched in faint scars: Serrik of the Hollow March, who carried three Riders from the fire-fields when his own wings burned.

A lithe obsidian female whose movements held the grace of a dancer: Nyssa, the Emberthread, whose speed turned the tide at Blackspire.

Each name bore a deed, and each deed was a weight Eliryn felt pressing against her ribs. These weren't just warriors, they were legends.

And then—

"Meyra of the Goldvein, first through the breach at Frostgate, magic that does not waver."

Eliryn's heart caught. Meyra stepped forward, gold-green skin catching the sunlight, braids swinging against her shoulders. She moved with a calm certainty that made others seem louder by comparison. No wasted movement. No flaring of wings. Just presence—solid as a pillar, sharp as a drawn blade.

Eliryn couldn't help herself. She leaned forward, hands gripping her knees. *She makes it look so easy.*

A low ripple of amusement slid through their dragonbond. *Admire her,* Vaeronth said, his voice a purr of stone on stone. *But remember—your guardian must be more than just someone you want to be friends with.*

She bit the inside of her cheek. "I know," she murmured out loud.

More names followed. A veteran with one eye clouded in white. A young warrior whose muscles twitched ever so slightly, betraying his nerves. A slate-skinned gargoyle whose veins glowed faintly gold, like a river-map drawn across his body.

Dozens filled the arena floor, the sand darkened by their weight, their wings like a storm waiting to break.

The horn bellowed once more.

Pairs split from the line and stalked into the center.

No weapons. Only stone.

The first clash rang like boulders colliding. Talons locked. Wings flared. Dust leapt as one slammed the other to the ground, only for him to rise again as though pain were no more than an afterthought. Blows that would have shattered mortal ribs barely staggered the Kin.

Eliryn's heart thudded in her throat as the fights unfolded in brutal rhythm. Each was a display of endurance, of precision. Of what it meant to be forged for this.

The twins circled an opponent, their mirrored strikes so fluid they seemed choreographed by something better than practice. Their foe held as long as he could—longer than Eliryn would have believed possible—before one blow cracked him to his knees and the other sent him sprawling.

The crowd did not cheer. They marked it with a low rumble of acknowledgment, heads dipping, wings twitching in subtle tells Eliryn couldn't yet read.

Her gaze found Meyra. Her opponent was larger, broader, but Meyra moved like water, slipping beneath a swing, talons hooking, turning the force against him. With a twist that looked almost effortless, she sent him sprawling in the dust.

No flourish. No smile. Just a dip of her head as she acknowledged her victory before stepping back.

Eliryn's pulse quickened. She couldn't look away.

"They're..." She searched for the right word, breathless. "...incredible."

They are protectors, Vaeronth rumbled. *Their bodies are honed for this purpose. Do not gape so.*

"I wouldn't last a minute down there," she muttered.

No comment. His amusement whispered around their bond like smoke.

The bouts kept coming. Stone cracked. Dust rose. Sweat and iron filled the air until Eliryn swore she could taste it. The floor became a map of gouges and scuffs, each one a signature of violence endured.

And then the names were called for the second wave of fighting. Eliryn was too busy looking at all the contenders to pay attention to all the names being called, but then there was a subtle but undeniable shift that swept through the arena.

A a ripple of unease that stiffened shoulders, furrowed brows, sent whispers threading like cracks through the stone silence.

Eliryn's gaze sharpened on the final figure.

Druven.

Storm-gray skin darker than basalt. A frame less polished, less honed, as though the mountain itself had tried and failed to break him clean. Wings ridged and sharp as broken rock. His presence was not like the others—it was heavier, rougher, a silent defiance that drew every eye whether he wanted it or not.

The hush that fell was not reverence.

It was darker than that.

A name should have come next—another recitation of deeds and lineage, the final thread in the tapestry of the chosen. But instead, the silence stretched. Long enough for the sound of wings above to shift. Long enough for the crowd to realize what wasn't being said.

No name. No title. No proclamation.

The crowd shifted, unease sparking like a storm on the horizon. Low growls rose, sharp whispers cutting the air until one voice broke through, jagged as shattered glass:

"He should not be here!"

The words cracked across the arena like a whip. Another voice joined, then another, until the tiers hummed with discord. Some glared openly at Druven, others turned their faces as though his very presence tainted the Rite.

Eliryn leaned forward, eyes fixed on the storm-gray figure. Druven didn't bare his fangs. Didn't flare his wings. He just stood, talons flexing once, gaze steady as though the weight of a hundred stares meant nothing.

The sound pressed against her skin until it itched, until her ribs felt too small. "Why are they—"

Garrion's shadow loomed, his presence suddenly closer, his granite voice steady. "Stay calm, Dragonrider."

Her heart hammered. "They're singling him out. Why?"

Vaeronth's growl coiled through the bond, low and molten, like stone grinding beneath the earth. *Because they remember.*

Eliryn's gaze flicked between her dragon in the heights, Garrion at her side, and Druven silent in the dust below. Something cold coiled in her gut.

"Remember what?" she whispered.

Garrion's eyes finally met hers, heavy as the weight of the mountain itself. His words fell like stone dropped into still water.

"He is not just a warrior, Eliryn. Druven is a killer."

Chapter 12: The Weight of Fear

"Power does not make monsters. Fear does." —Fragment of the Lost Oath

"Druven is a killer."

The words rippled through the arena like a stone hurled into still water—concentric silence, then noise, then something uglier. A dozen voices surged at once; talons rasped along stone benches; dust sifted down from the colonnades in shivers.

Eliryn's mouth went dry. "A—what do you mean?" The question scraped raw. "In battle? Or... murder?"

Vaeronth's shadow swept over her as he landed with thunderous force on the dais. Heat rolled off his body in waves, wings mantling wide as runes glared bright beneath his weight. "Tell her all of it," he commanded, voice cracking through the tiers. "She chooses with truth, or not at all."

Garrion's granite face shifted toward her, eyes heavy as iron filings. "The brief version, then." His voice carried only for her. "In the last Rite of Choosing, Druven killed another protector in the ring. Not by malice. Death was not his intent."

The crowd seethed, the word *killer* hissing from stone throats.

Eliryn's pulse stuttered. "Rites can end in death?"

"Rarely," Garrion said, his voice like slate splitting. "The Rite is meant to test, not to break. But Druven's body is a weapon few can match. His strike landed too deep, too hard. It shattered what should not have broken."

Her breath caught. "And he just—"

"He tried to save him," Garrion cut in, jaw tight. "Poured magic into the wound until the ring reeked of it. But some damage cannot be undone. The Kin carried out judgment. It was ruled an accident. Lawful, even." Garrion's mouth hardened into a grim line. "But it was not forgotten."

Eliryn's gaze dragged back to Druven. Storm-gray and silent, wings ridged like blades, he stood unbowed in the ring, simply waiting. He hadn't flinched when they shouted, hadn't risen when they spat his name. His talons only flexed once before stilling again.

"So he's dangerous?" she whispered.

"To anyone who underestimates him," Garrion said evenly. "To you? No. His strength does not bend toward betrayal. Only protection."

Vaeronth's eyes glowed like banked coals. *Good,* he rumbled, satisfaction rolling through their bond. *We do not need docility guarding our backs. A guardian must be capable of killing—swiftly, without hesitation. Mercy belongs to you, Little Flame. Not to the ones who will stand between you and death.*

Eliryn considered his words as the arena seethed. Entire rows of gargoyles leaned away without meaning to, their bodies betraying the instinct their pride refused to voice: distance.

Eliryn's stomach knotted. They weren't just watching him. They were bracing.

And still Druven didn't move. He stood with storm-gray wings half-fanned, his bulk as unyielding as the cliff walls themselves. If the crowd's mutters pierced him, if centuries of being feared pressed heavy against his skin, he gave no sign. He was stone, he was shadow, and he was utterly still.

The sharp crack of staff against stone split the unrest like a blade.

The murmurs died at once.

"Kin." The herald's voice boomed, vast and cold as the cliffs themselves. "You forget yourselves."

The sound rolled through the tiers, not shouted, but weighted—every word a hammer. "This is sacred ground. Judgment is not yours to give, nor your scorn to hurl. The Rite sees all, and it will decide what stands... and what falls."

The crowd stilled, but the silence that followed was brittle, tight as stretched wire. Dozens of eyes still flicked toward Druven as if even the herald's authority couldn't scrape away the stain of what he'd done.

The old gargoyle lowered the staff, its end ringing faintly against the stone. "Restrain your tongues," he said, voice like cracking granite. "The stone will remember who cannot hold theirs."

The runes flared brighter, one after another, igniting around the arena in a circle that pulsed like a heartbeat.

The crowd bowed their heads. Some reverently. Others reluctantly.

Eliryn drew a breath that scraped her throat raw. Garrion's words rang still in her ears—*he has never been chosen.*

And beneath that, the unspoken truth: because they fear him.

Because to them, Druven was a reminder of how thin the line between protector and destroyer could truly be.

The herald's staff lowered, the last flare of the runes crackling like lightning across the arena floor. For a moment, there was only silence—the collective breath of the Kin held tight in their stone-carved chests.

Then the horn thundered again.

Warriors surged forward.

The ring dissolved into a storm of bodies and wings, talons striking sparks against stone, the thunder of impacts shaking dust from the colonnades above. Gargoyles collided with a violence that bordered on primal, each one desperate to prove strength enough to carry a protectors' oath.

Eliryn's breath caught as she tried to follow it all. Everywhere she looked, pain blossomed. A wing slammed into a chest, a talon carved trenches into the sand, two warriors locked in a grapple so brutal the earth itself seemed to wince.

They fight like it is their sole purpose, she thought, awed and horrified at once. *Like nothing else matters.*

At first, the chaos was strangely balanced. Fights broke apart and reformed, opponents clashing in sudden bursts before peeling away again. But then—like gravity bending around a star—the current shifted.

Toward Druven.

Warriors veered to him as though drawn by some invisible pull. Not one challenger. Not two. Four. Five. They converged at once, wings flaring, talons gleaming, faces hard with the kind of resolve that came from fear.

Eliryn's stomach lurched. "That isn't fair—"

Watch, Vaeronth growled through the bond, heat rippling in her bones.

The first attacker lunged. Druven caught him mid-strike, talons snapping around the gargoyle's wrist with enough force that Eliryn winced. He pivoted, used the momentum, and hurled the male across the ring.

The second and third slammed into him together. Dust exploded. For a heartbeat Eliryn couldn't see—then Druven's wings tore free of the haze, beating once, twice, a gale that sent both opponents staggering back. His talons carved the air in brutal arcs, striking with such precision it looked less like rage and more like inevitability.

The crowd hissed. Some shouted. But beneath it all ran that same undercurrent of unease, louder now, sharper—because for all their numbers, Druven didn't falter. He *thrived*.

Eliryn leaned forward on the dais, heart in her throat. He wasn't elegant like Meyra, or seamless like the basalt twins. He was raw force, brutal and unrelenting, every motion meant to end a fight before it began. There was no flourish. No showmanship. Just purpose.

And the purpose was terrifying.

Her nails bit into her palms. *He's not fighting like the others.*

Below, two more gargoyles tried to flank him, talons raised for his unguarded back. Druven turned before they'd closed half the distance. One vicious sweep of his wing sent the first crashing into the sand, and his other hand shot out, catching the second by the throat. For a sick heartbeat, Eliryn thought he'd crush it—thought she'd see a gargoyles' body crumple under that impossible strength.

But Druven's grip shifted. He threw the warrior aside instead, sending him skidding across the runes. The crowd gasped, half in outrage, half in disbelief.

"Why are they all going for him?" Eliryn whispered.

Garrion's face was stone. "Because they've been waiting for the opportunity to avenge their fallen brethren."

Eliryn's chest tightened, her gaze locked on Druven as the dust rose around him again, as the free-for-all bent into a war with one center, one storm.

One by one, fighters began to fall—some crumpling to the sand in exhaustion, others carried off with their wings bent or shoulders split. The runes caught each collapse, flaring once in judgment before dimming again, marking the defeated.

The numbers dwindled.

Eliryn gripped the edge of the dais so tightly her knuckles ached. Every bout was fiercer than the last—stone crashing against stone, dust clouds rising like storms, roars splitting the air. The arena smelled of iron and earth, the heat of bodies straining against limits.

But through it all, Druven never faltered.

Where others tired, he endured. Where others re-lied on paired moves or quick flourishes, his every strike landed with inevitability. He didn't waste motion. He didn't toy with opponents. He finished them—fast, decisive, without flair.

It wasn't wild. It wasn't uncontrolled.

Eliryn saw it, even when the crowd refused to. Every choice he made was measured. He did not fight to maim, though his blows could have split stone in two. He pulled just short of killing force, ending fights without leaving ruin. But his sheer power was so great, so overwhelming, that no amount of restraint could make it *look* merciful.

Her chest tightened. *How must it feel—to be so strong that even pulling your punches still terrifies your people?*

Twenty remained. The horn thundered its judgment, shaking the dust loose in rivulets down the carved walls. The victors stood in a loose circle, chests heaving, wings half-spread. Among them: the marble giant Kareth, the basalt twins, Meyra with her amber eyes steady, a dozen others whose names Eliryn only half-remembered—each marked by sweat, grit, and pride.

And Druven.

He stood a little apart, dust streaking his storm-gray skin, shoulders squared, eyes fixed not on the crowd, not even on her—but straight ahead, unyielding. As if daring anyone to say he hadn't earned his place.

The crowd erupted in fractured noise. Some clapped claws to chests, giving reluctant acknowledgment. Others muttered. A few hissed outright. And one, a stocky gargoyle with jagged horns, spat into the sand at Druven's feet.

Druven didn't react. Not a twitch, not a flicker of his eyes. The spit sizzled against the rune-lit ground, and he simply stood, as immovable as the mountain itself.

Eliryn's throat worked. A flare of anger rose sharp and hot in her chest. *They fear him because of what he is capable of. Because his strength cost more than it should have. But is that so different from me?*

Her hand curled against her thigh. *My magic almost destroyed me. Without control, I could hollow out the realm around me just as easily. If they despise him for what he can't help... then what will they do when they see me lose control again?*

She looked down at Druven, at the unshakable way he held himself against a crowd that hated him.

Something in her chest shifted.

The herald's staff struck the stone, silencing the stands once more. His voice boomed across the ring: "Twenty stand. Twenty endure. Flesh has proven its worth—now let power take its turn. Strength has spoken. Let magic answer."

The runes flared brighter, casting the victors in a wash of fire-light. Eliryn's gaze lingered on Druven until the glow swallowed the sand and the crowd began to roar again.

Eliryn wondered—*If I must choose, why not the one who already knows what it means to carry a burden too heavy to bear?*

CHAPTER 13: THE HOLLOW GAZE

"Sightless shall one rise, bearing truths the world cannot endure." —From the Prophecies of Ashenstone

The horn's echoes still trembled in the stone when silence fell again. Eliryn's heart thudded against her ribs, too fast, too uneven. She forced her hands to still against her knees, though her fingers itched to move, to do something.

She had thought the Rite would stretch across days—rituals divided by dawns and dusks, time enough for breath, for rest.

But the Kin pushed themselves harder, faster, because of her—because everything was now bent toward her survival.

Her gaze drifted over the stands, over the countless granite faces lit by sun and rune-light. Not just spectators. Witnesses. Hundreds of protectors who had gathered for *her*.

A memory pressed through, sharp and unbidden: her mother's voice, low and trembling, discussing the prophecy. *You will be sightless, but not blind. You will be last, but not alone.* As a girl, Eliryn had thought those words cruel riddles, half-curses from a mother already fading into visions that left her shaking in bed. She had hated them, hated the way they painted her life as something already decided.

But now—now she sat in a mountain carved to hold oaths older than her bloodline, hundreds of stone warriors watching her like the tilt of her chin might shift the balance of the realm. Her mother hadn't seen *this*, had she? Hadn't seen the endless tiers of gargoyles pressing in, the weight of dragon fire burning steady at her back, the ache of destiny tightening its hold like a collar around her throat.

Her fingers curled against her knees, breath sharp. If her mother had seen this, if she had known what was coming, why hadn't she prepared Eliryn better?

Why had she left her to stumble half-blind through the years, clinging to fragments, wasting time pretending she could live as anything other than what prophecy demanded?

You are the last, Eliryn, the memory whispered, cruel and inevitable. *The last, and the realm will bend around that truth.*

At her back, Vaeronth's shadow shifted with the slow sweep of his wings. He said nothing, but she felt the steady pulse of him through the bond, anchoring her as her mind twisted.

The herald's staff struck the arena floor once, sharp as a crack of thunder. Runes stitched along his staff flared to life, circling the rim of the arena in a steady glow.

"Kin!" His voice carried, vast and resonant, filling every hollow of the canyon. "Step forth, those who remain."

One by one, the contenders advanced from the shadows of the gate, called by name in tones that shook the mountain. Kareth, son of Orun, announced like a fortress incarnate. The basalt twins, Veyra and Veyrik, their names spoken as one, drawing cheers from the stands. Meyra, whose golden braids caught the light as though flame itself crowned her, her name carrying a weight of expectation that pressed as sharp as a blade.

Others followed—onyx warriors, green-veined veterans, obsidian figures with talons that glinted like polished steel. The herald's cadence rolled steady, each name an affirmation, each warrior met with a wave of approval from the tiers above.

And then—

"Druven." The name cracked like slate. But the herald did not stop there. His tone shifted, cutting colder, crueler. "Druven, the Oathbreaker."

The title landed like a blade across the arena floor. Eliryn's head snapped up, breath catching.

The word slithered into every corner of the stands. *Oathbreaker.*

Unease rippled through the Kin like a living thing. Some hissed through their teeth. Others spat into the sand at his feet. A handful bowed their heads—not in respect, but to avoid looking at him at all. The air itself soured, thick with the taste of old judgment.

Druven strode forward. He did not flinch. Did not lower his gaze. Storm-gray skin caught the sun, wings half-spread, his stride measured as though the venom in the air could not touch him. Yet Eliryn's throat tightened as she studied his face. Not blank. Not detached. He carried the weight of his title like a stone long since fused to him—part burden, part armor.

Vaeronth's voice slid through her thoughts, low and edged with smoke. *They spit at what mirrors them too closely.*

Eliryn frowned. "They're all soldiers. Why turn on one of their own?"

Because he crossed the line they all walk, Vaeronth said. *Every warrior knows the edge between control and ruin. Druven stepped over it—and lived. They see him and remember how thin that line truly is.*

Her gaze dropped back to the ring. "So they hate him for surviving?"

Mhmm. A pulse of heat moved through their bond, like a dragon's sigh. *And for what it means. They fight with rules. He fights to end the fight. That kind of will unsettles even the hardened.*

She hesitated. "You approve."

Vaeronth's answer was a low growl of satisfaction. *We do not need softness at our side, Eliryn—we need certainty of strength.*

Her heart kicked once, hard. There was no cruelty in his tone—only truth. The kind that didn't bend to comfort.

The herald's staff struck stone again, shattering the silence before she could speak.

The second trial began.

The first contender stepped into the circle—a young male with skin veined in copper. He raised his clawed hands, and fire leapt to life. Not simple flame, but a whirling vortex of molten sparks, weaving around his body in a spiral dance. The heat rolled across the arena, crackling so sharp Eliryn swore she could hear it. With a sudden thrust of his palms, the fire coiled upward and split, forming twin serpents of flame that snapped their jaws before dissolving into ash.

The crowd roared approval.

Another followed—a female with obsidian wings etched in pale scars. She crouched low, palms pressed to the ground, and the very stone of the arena rippled. Spires of crystal surged upward, refracting light into a dozen colors, a forest of jagged glass rising where the floor had been smooth. She exhaled once, and the crystals shattered in a rain of diamond dust that glittered like stars before it vanished.

Eliryn's mouth parted. Magic here wasn't gentle. It wasn't ornamental. It was raw, carved into the very fabric of the realm.

Then Meyra stepped forward.

The crowd hushed in instinctive reverence. She closed her eyes, braids swinging as she lifted her chin. The air shifted. Thickened. A hum built—low at first, then climbing, until the runes around the arena flared like sunlight on water.

Eliryn gasped. Light itself bent around Meyra's hands, pulled like threads from the air. She wove it as if it were silk, spinning radiance into a spear so sharp it made the air quake. When she drove it into the earth, the arena shook, runes flaring even brighter than before.

For a long breath, silence reigned. Then the stands erupted, cheers breaking like surf on stone.

Vaeronth's voice brushed her mind. *That one is gifted.*

"No kidding," Eliryn whispered, pulse hammering. Her gaze remained fixed on Meyra, her silhouette radiant in the dust. "She didn't just summon light. She commanded it."

And it obeyed. Vaeronth's tone was taut, unreadable. *Not many can make light kneel.*

Eliryn swallowed, throat dry.

Another stepped forward—a hulking gargoyle with skin marbled in dark blue and white, like veins of ice running through stone. He raised one hand, talons curling, and the temperature plummeted. Frost blossomed across the arena floor in jagged streaks, ice climbing up his arms until he looked carved entirely from frozen granite. With a guttural roar, he slammed both fists down—and a glacier erupted from the ground, shards of ice exploding outward in a deadly halo before it shattered into glittering dust.

Gasps rippled through the crowd. Eliryn's breath clouded in the sudden chill.

Then came a lithe female with onyx wings. Instead of raising her hands, she closed her eyes and let the silence deepen. The dust at her feet began to swirl. Faster. Faster. Until wind wrapped around her in a column that screamed like a banshee. She leapt into the air, suspended by the cyclone, wings spread wide as lightning arced across her talons. With a sharp twist, she flung the storm outward, and the arena floor bore the scars of wind and crackling sparks long after the magic faded.

"She commands the air," Eliryn whispered, awe dripping from every word.

And the storm answers, Vaeronth said, his tone edged with a grudging respect. *That one could shear battalions if she wished.*

Next, the basalt twins Veyra and Veyrik stepped together into the circle. The crowd roared before they'd even lifted a claw. In perfect synchronicity, they pressed palms together, then apart. A ribbon of molten stone stretched between them, flexing like a living thing. With each motion, they twisted the lava into shapes—blades, shields, serpents of fire—passing control back and forth as though their bodies shared one mind. When they finally slammed their palms to the ground, the molten ribbon surged forward and solidified in a wall of black obsidian that gleamed in the sunlight.

Eliryn's mouth went dry. "They're not just fighters—they're creators."

Creation and destruction are one with them, Vaeronth murmured.

One after another, the displays came:

A copper-skinned gargoyle who called roots from the cracks in the arena floor, thorned vines writhing like snakes before he snapped them into ash with a gesture.

A pale, silver-eyed female who wove illusions so real Eliryn swore she could smell saltwater when a phantom sea crashed into the ring.

A scarred veteran who bent shadows into blades, each strike slicing through stone as if it were silk.

The arena roared for each, voices echoing against the mountain walls. And through it all, Eliryn sat frozen, her chest tight with awe and something colder. The Kin were weapons, each honed differently, each deadly in their own right, their powers perfect for war.

And then—

The herald's staff struck again. Dust leapt from the floor at the sound.

"Druven," the voice boomed, low and merciless. "The Oathbreaker."

The arena shifted like a living thing. Cheers dulled into a hiss of unease. The air itself seemed to thrum with judgment.

Druven strode into the circle, unhurried. Storm-gray wings trailed dust with every step, his talons curling and flexing once before stilling. He didn't bow to the crowd, didn't acknowledge their hatred. His eyes remained fixed on the ring's center, as if nothing beyond it mattered.

Eliryn's pulse hammered. She leaned forward, nails biting into her palms. For all their venom, the others had fought with flourish, with spectacle. But

Druven carried no theater with him. Just silence. Just inevitability.

"Vaeronth," she whispered. "Are they waiting for him to fail?"

No, Vaeronth rumbled, wings shifting against the mountain's wind. *They're waiting for him to prove their fear right.*

Eliryn's breath stuttered. Every other contender had begun their display with some flourish: a lifted hand, a bowed head, a deliberate stance. Druven did none of that. He only stood there, broad chest rising once, wings shifting against the canyon wind.

And then the stone began to crack.

Hairline fractures laced out from his feet, glowing faintly like veins of molten ore. The cracks spread wider, deeper, until the entire circle seemed to pulse with a heartbeat that wasn't its own. Dust rose in slow spirals. The air thickened, heavy as though the mountain itself bent toward him.

"Eliryn—" Garrion's voice was tight. Warning.

But she couldn't look away.

Druven raised one clawed hand—and the ground answered. Pillars of stone erupted, jagged and raw, lancing upward like spears torn straight from the earth's marrow. With a twist of his wrist, they shattered outward, fragments hanging in the air for a breathless moment before slamming back into the ring with a force that made the stands quake.

The arena gasped as one.

But Druven wasn't finished.

His storm-gray wings unfurled, and the fractures in the stone widened, light flaring brighter until it seared white. For a heartbeat, Eliryn thought he might lose control, that the whole arena would split apart beneath him—

And then he closed his fist.

The light died. The cracks sealed as if they had never been. Only a faint tremor lingered in the earth, a memory of power that refused to vanish entirely.

The silence that followed was different this time.

Eliryn's chest tightened. "He wasn't showing off," she whispered. "That wasn't spectacle. That was warning."

No, Vaeronth corrected, his molten gaze fixed on Druven. *That was restraint.*

Her stomach dipped. *Restraint. If that had been restraint, then what did it look like when Druven didn't hold back?*

Eliryn thought she understood him in that moment. Not reckless. Not careless. Just a blade honed too sharp for anyone to dare hold.

Her palms stuck damp to her thighs. She knew the ache of holding too much power without the strength to contain it. She knew what it was to be dangerous simply by existing.

Then the light changed.

At first it was only a flicker—one rune along the arena's rim flaring too bright, its glow swallowing the sunlit hue. Then another. And another. In the next breath, the whole circumference of the fighting ring ignited at once, lines of ancient script blazing gold-white in violent succession.

The crowd's murmur died. Even Garrion froze.

A heartbeat later, the realm *screamed*.

The runes shattered into motion, slashing light across the stands as the sound hit—a deep, resonant bellow that wasn't a horn or chant but something older, carved into the mountain's bones itself. Every gargoyle in the arena went rigid. Wings snapped open. Heads turned toward the horizon in perfect, terrible unison.

Eliryn's pulse stumbled. "What—"

She never finished. A thunderclap split the air. Above them, the banners of the Kin twisted in a wind that hadn't existed seconds ago.

Garrion's head snapped toward the outer wall, wings flaring. "The wards—"

The rest was swallowed by the roar of magic tearing free.

Runes along the cliffsides flared red, one after another, cascading like falling stars. The air itself seemed to recoil. Gargoyles surged to their feet, stone bodies coming alive, talons scraping against marble.

Eliryn's hands clutched the edge of the dais. Her breath came shallow. She didn't know what the alarm meant—only that every protector in the sanctuary was moving.

Vaeronth's mind crashed into hers, molten and vast. *The border is breached.* His voice was pure flame, iron and wrath in equal measure. *The sanctuary reels. Stay with Garrion. I will fly with the Kin.*

Vaeronth's roar split the air, echoing from the cliffs. One mighty beat of his wings sent dust spiraling across the dais, and with him the Kin rose—a storm of stone and fire exploding into the sky.

Garrion barked orders to the sentries still on the ground; runes along the walls pulsed red, warning sigils spilling light across the stone.

Then Vaeronth's voice struck her mind—hot, urgent, frayed by distance.

Eliryn.

She caught her breath. *I'm here.*

The wards bleed with corruption, he said, the words edged with iron. *I know this magic. The same stench that filled the air when the king's assassin came for you.*

Her stomach dropped. *You mean—*

Malric. The name burned across the bond like a brand. *It is his mark. The same twisted pulse. He is here—pressing at the wards.*

The world narrowed to the pounding in her ears. She turned toward Garrion, voice low but steady. "Vaeronth feels it—the same magic that came with Malric when he tried to kill me. He's here."

Garrion's head snapped toward her, granite eyes widening. "Malric? Is Vaeronth sure?"

"Yes," she said, her throat tight. "If Vaeronth says the magic feels the same, he's certain."

Garrion straightened, shoulders squaring, his voice hard as struck stone.

"Then we protect you first. Your dragon can meet the threat. Our duty is to keep you breathing."

Above them, Vaeronth's roar ripped through the mountain again, a sound of warning and promise both.

Eliryn drew in a breath that tasted of smoke and fear and iron.

He was coming for her.

Interlude 1: Malric

"What cannot be caged is all the more coveted." —Attributed to the Mad King Aerath

Time blurred after the uprising.

Malric no longer counted in days or nights. The rebellion had shattered any rhythm the world had once carried, leaving him with only a gnawing urgency that pressed harder than hunger, sharper than thirst. He remembered blood—his own, his enemies'—and smoke clogging the sky. He remembered

Eliryn vanishing like a wisp of shadow, leaving his grip empty.

She ran from me. Slipped from me.

The thought should have soured her worth. But it hadn't. Defiance was fuel; it made her luminous. Untouchable. And if she could not be held by the chains of death, then she was a prize only he could claim.

The city of Vireth had broken open in her wake. Guards torn down for treachery, rebels dragged screaming to the dungeons, the stone foundations slick with the cost of betrayal. He had seen dragonrider sympathizers flooding the cells, commoners and courtiers alike—ordinary faces suddenly painted as threats. She had sparked it. Eliryn had left before she ever witnessed the fire she lit, but Malric had walked through the embers.

And when it had ended, when the screams dulled into silence, he had stood beside Thalen and Vraxxis, the ruin of the citadel at their backs. He had watched the impossible: the Flame returning, gold fire sliding into Thalen's eyes like an old god reclaiming its throne.

That moment was supposed to be the end. Eliryn dead, her power reclaimed by the king. The empire had its story, a tale of sacrifice and survival to hush the people. Vraxxis crowned in her place. The world lulled back into the shape they wanted.

But Malric had known better.

The Dragonrider lives.

The certainty had crawled into his marrow that day and refused to leave. And then he had seen the dragon.

It had been a flicker across the horizon, just before dawn—vast wings breaking the sky, scales catching firelight. Too large for myth, too real to dismiss. He had followed that shape ever since, through mountains and forests, through ash and snow. Always just behind, always hunting.

Now the forest pressed close, a cathedral of pines and stone. The air grew heavier the deeper he went, thick with something he could not name. Every step was work, as though the mountain itself resisted him. Roots snared his boots. Branches clawed at his arms. The silence was too complete, as if no bird dared cry here.

He felt it in his blood before he saw it. The wards.

The air shivered where the tree line broke, heatless but dense, a barrier that thrummed against his chest when he drew near. He reached out once, testing the invisible wall with his palm. The sensation jolted through his arm, sharp as frostbite, and he snatched back his hand with a hiss.

Old magic. Older than anything the citadel's scholars had whispered of.

He bared his teeth, circling the invisible line, searching for a fracture, for some weakness. The world beyond it seemed blurred, as though the mountain itself had wrapped its secrets in smoke.

And then the sky split.

First one shadow, vast and unmistakable: wings like a storm, scales like burnished dusk.

The Endbringer.

Malric's breath caught in his throat. There was no denying it now, no story he could feed himself to blunt the truth. The dragon lived, which meant so did *she.*

But it was the others that froze him where he stood.

Shapes followed in Vaeronth's wake, wings hewn of stone, talons gleaming like onyx blades. Dozens of them, their silhouettes jagged against the sky. Malric's chest tightened, his mind flinching to old stories—nursery tales, soldier's warnings, legends of the Kin. Guardians carved of the mountain, oathbound and eternal.

Stories. Myths.

Except they were real.

He stumbled back a pace, the wards thrumming at his spine, the forest dark at his heels. For the first time in years, disbelief gripped him, clawing against the marrow-deep certainty that had always steadied him.

Impossible. And yet...

His pulse quickened. The stories had lied. Or perhaps they had always been true, buried under centuries of fear. Either way, Eliryn was among them. Hidden in the last bastion of oaths and stone.

He pressed his palm to the ward again, ignoring the burn this time, forcing his teeth into a smile.

There would be no breaking this barrier. Not today. Perhaps not ever. But capture didn't frighten him.

Let them drag him inside. Let them bind his hands, chain his throat, cage him in stone. None of it mattered.

Because capture meant entry. Entry meant proximity. And proximity meant he would see her again—with his own eyes, breathing, alive.

That was all he needed. No plan. No escape. Just the confirmation that she was still his to find.

Malric leaned his forehead to the invisible wall, the mountain's hum thrumming against his skin, and whispered to the silence, almost tenderly:

"I'll see you soon, Eliryn."

CHAPTER 14: THE ENEMY WITHIN REACH

"Chains do not bind only the captured. They bind all who must decide what to do with him." —from the Sepulcher of Oaths.

Eliryn's breath caught in her throat. The arena, the Kin, the dust rising from the ring—it all blurred to nothing.

Behind her, a shadow shifted. Druven. He had been keeping his distance, lingering at the edge of the dais. But now—now he stepped closer, each stride deliberate, until the line between guardian and ward was erased. He placed himself within reach, shoulders squared, storm-gray eyes fixed outward.

Garrion noticed. His wings shifted wider, tension sharpening every line of his body. But he did not order Druven back. Instead, his hand brushed Eliryn's elbow, firm, guiding. "Down. Now."

Eliryn's legs wobbled as he pulled her from the dais. Druven fell in step without being asked, his talons rasping softly against stone. He said nothing, but his presence pressed against her like a shield too close to ignore.

The corridor swallowed them quickly, torchlight flickering across stone walls etched with the Kin's runes. The roar of the crowd dimmed behind them, replaced by the heavy thud of Garrion's strides and the measured scrape of Druven's claws.

Eliryn's chest ached. The words tumbled from her lips before she could stop them:

"He killed me."

Her vision blurred—not with tears, but with the memory: the citadel's stone cold against her cheek, the burn in her chest as life slipped away.

Garrion's jaw worked, stone grinding stone.

Druven's shadow lengthened against the wall beside her. He did not speak, but the subtle shift of his stance—the way his talons flexed, the way his shoulders braced—told her he had heard.

They reached a turn in the tunnel, the air cooler here, leading deeper into the sanctuary's belly. Garrion slowed only enough to check the chamber ahead, then gestured her inside. "Here." His tone left no argument. "Safer ground."

Eliryn stepped in, the chamber broad and hollowed. A safe room, meant for warding. Its runes hummed faintly as she crossed the threshold. Druven entered last, positioning himself with quiet finality between her and the hall they had left behind.

She barely had time to steady her breath before Vaeronth's voice slammed into her thoughts.

Alive. The word shook through her like a strike of thunder.

Her heart seized. "What?"

We have him. The bond throbbed with the dragon's pulse, wings beating in rhythm with the message. *Malric. At the wards. Captured. Alive.*

The world seemed to tilt. Eliryn pressed a hand to her chest as though she could keep her heart from leaping out of it. Malric. Here. Breathing.

Her throat worked soundlessly before she managed, "Vaeronth says they've captured him. Malric. Alive."

The silence that followed was heavier than any roar of battle. Garrion's features darkened, his jaw locking like bedrock shifting under strain. Druven's stance stiffened, talons biting into the floor as if the stone itself might break beneath him.

Garrion's voice came first, low and absolute. "Alive is more dangerous than dead."

Eliryn's breath hitched. Her fingers curled into fists at her sides. "But it means he can be questioned." She met Garrion's gaze, her own words trembling but unyielding. "If he found me here—then how? Did someone tell him? Is he alone? What if more are coming?"

The thought made her stomach knot so tightly she had to press a hand there. The Sanctuary was supposed to be hidden, sacred, untouchable. If Malric had breached its wards... the others could, too.

The bond rippled with Vaeronth's reply, sharp as a blade drawn in the dark. *Better to cut out the rot than let it spread. He dies now, Eliryn. A clean end, before his poison seeps further.*

Her heart hammered. "You would kill him without even asking what he knows?"

I would burn him where he stands. The heat of her dragon's fury flared so hot it singed her mind. *He gutted you. There is no justice in letting him breathe.*

Her knees went weak. The memory slammed into her—the flash of Malric's blade, the searing agony in her chest, the helpless collapse. Her voice cracked as she pushed back through the bond: "And yet, I'm still here. He failed. Why shouldn't we question him and gain more information?"

Garrion's gaze narrowed, unreadable, but there was something like approval in the weight of it.

Druven, silent as ever, shifted half a step closer, his storm-gray eyes steady on her, as if bracing himself for a command that had not yet come.

Eliryn dragged in a shaking breath, the words spilling faster now, desperate. "If Malric hunted me, he'll keep hunting. If he found me, others can too. We need to know how he did it, who else he's working with. If we kill him now, we lose all of that."

The silence stretched.

Finally, Vaeronth's rumble returned, darker, reluctant. *You would speak with him?*

Eliryn's hands trembled, but she steadied her jaw. "It could help us."

Or you invite venom into your veins.

She closed her eyes. "Or I stop it from spreading further."

The chamber held its breath around her. The runes hummed faintly, pulsing with the same rhythm as her heart.

Alive. Malric was alive. And she would face him, not as prey, but as the dragonrider he had failed to kill.

The bond thrummed suddenly, a pulse so sharp it made her flinch.

They bring him now, Vaeronth said. His voice coiled low, edged with the heat of a forge about to roar. *The guardians hold him bound. He bleeds, but he breathes. They will question him first.*

Eliryn's stomach twisted. The image unspooled in her mind unbidden—Malric in chains, his face tilted up with that same cold, cutting smile she had seen in the citadel. Her chest ached at the thought of being anywhere near him again.

But Vaeronth wasn't finished. *Tell Garrion: I have called for the Elders. You are to come. The matter of his capture is not for stone alone to decide.*

Her breath caught. "He wants me there," she said aloud, her voice thinner than she intended.

Garrion turned his gaze on her, granite-solid, waiting. Druven shifted closer still, a silent wall at her side.

"He says the guardians are bringing Malric." Eliryn forced the words past the tightness in her throat. "They're going to question him... and Vaeronth wants me to come. To meet with the Elders first."

The silence that followed pressed against her ears. Garrion's jaw flexed once before he inclined his head, slow, deliberate. "If the dragon calls, the Kin listen."

Eliryn's pulse thundered. To face Malric again, even at a distance, even behind chains—it made her skin prickle with dread. Yet beneath it, like a second current, was something fiercer. She *wanted* answers. She wanted to look him in the eye and demand why her blood had been worth spilling.

Her hand curled unconsciously, nails biting her palm. She lifted her chin. "Then let's go."

Chapter 15: The Elder's Verdict

"The last rider will stand where others would bow. That is her curse, and her crown." —Vision of the Sightless One

The corridors of the Sanctuary were hushed as Eliryn walked between Garrion and Druven. Their footsteps rang hollow against the carved stone, the sound swallowed quickly by the weight of the mountain pressing in around them. Every arch they passed was lit with a faint blue rune-fire.

Ahead, Garrion's silhouette was an unyielding wall of discipline. His voice, when it came, carried the resonance of someone who had walked these halls for centuries.

"The Elders are the marrow of the Kin," he said, not looking back. "Their eyes do not miss, and their judgment does not falter. When you stand before them, Dragonrider, you must speak truth. Nothing else will serve."

Eliryn's throat tightened, but she lifted her chin. "You make it sound like they're going to weigh my soul."

"They will," Garrion replied, without hesitation. Then, softer—almost a reassurance, though it rumbled like granite grinding together: "Do not fear. They are not your enemy. Their oaths are bound to you as much as mine. Whatever you have endured, whatever shadows you carry—they will not turn against you."

The reassurance only pressed the weight deeper into her chest. She caught herself twisting her fingers in the hem of her tunic and stilled them quickly.

Behind her, Druven's presence was a quiet thunder. He hadn't spoken once since they left the dais, but she could feel him closer than a shadow. When Garrion finally slowed at the carved threshold of a high, rune-lined archway, he turned, his gaze cutting first to Eliryn, then to Druven.

"You will wait outside," Garrion told him, the words clipped, final.

Druven's storm-gray eyes didn't so much as flicker. He didn't bow his head. He didn't nod. He simply stood there, as if Garrion's command had passed over him like wind.

Eliryn reached out before Garrion could bristle further, her fingers brushing against the cool ridge of his forearm. The stone there was unyielding, but the gesture halted him.

"Let him stay," she said quietly. Her voice surprised her with its steadiness. "If these Elders are going to judge me, if they're going to ask questions I can't answer... then I want him there. He's already chosen to stand closer to me than any of them."

Garrion's jaw tightened, his gaze narrowing at Druven as though measuring the risk in that choice. The silence between the three of them stretched.

Vaeronth's voice slid through her thoughts then, low and certain: *He will not bend to another's word. Only yours. He is already loyal to you.*

Eliryn straightened, meeting Garrion's stare with her own. "Please. He remains."

For a long, grinding heartbeat, Garrion didn't move. Then—finally—he inclined his head once, sharp as a blade cutting stone.

"So be it," he said. "But know this, Dragonrider: the Elders will see him as clearly as they see you."

The massive doors ahead began to shift, yawning open with the groan of ancient stone, their carved faces splitting along a seam that hadn't moved in some time. Runes pulsed brighter along the arch, sending veins of cold blue light crawling outward until they licked the walls of the passage beyond.

The descent began.

The corridor tilted downward, each step echoing hollow and slow. The air thickened the deeper they went, weighted with the musk of earth and magic. Light flickered faintly along the walls, caught in carved reliefs of battles Eliryn didn't recognize: Kin standing unyielding against shadowy figures, wings mantled, talons lifted. *Oaths in stone,* she realized. Promises pressed into the mountain itself.

Eliryn's pulse thrummed harder with every step. She smoothed her damp palms against her thighs, then caught herself and balled them into fists. *Steady,* she told herself. *This isn't combat. This is just a formality.*

"You walk in the Sepulcher of Judgment," Garrion intoned, his voice reverberating in the cavernous space. "Do not think to withhold the truth here."

She winced faintly. "You really know how to calm a girl down, Garrion."

A rumble of dry amusement drifted from behind—Druven. He hadn't spoken, but she felt it. She glanced back. His expression hadn't changed, but his proximity had.

Garrion noticed too; his gaze flicked back, narrow, assessing. The tension sharpened between them like flint and steel.

Her boots slipped once on damp stone, and Druven's clawed hand was there instantly, steadying her arm before she'd even realized she was off-balance. The touch was brief, practical.

She pulled her arm back gently. "Thanks."

He said nothing. Just stepped closer, as if the very air between her and the shadows wasn't safe without his presence.

The passage widened into a vast antechamber. Pillars carved like talons curled upward to meet a ceiling lost in shadow, runes burning cold in their grooves. A heavy door loomed ahead, its face etched with circles of oaths so dense the lines tangled like constellations.

Eliryn's heart stuttered. She pressed her palm to her chest as if to slow it. *No hiding now.*

Vaeronth's voice curled through her mind, low and steady: *Breathe, Little Flame. You are not stone—but you are fire. And fire belongs even in the deepest dark.*

She drew in air, steady, and lifted her chin as the final doors began to open.

Eliryn stepped forward between Garrion and Druven, her boots soundless against the stone floor.

The chamber stretched longer than it had any right to be. Its walls curved in a great circle, each stone block veined with silver light that pulsed faintly.

At the heart of the chamber rose a dais carved from a single column of obsidian. Upon it sat seven thrones, hewn not from wood or metal, but from the mountain itself. They were not chairs. They were monuments. And upon them sat the Elders.

They were not like the other protectors.

Eliryn had thought some of the gargoyles she'd seen at the Rite of Choosing were ancient—their stone-veined skin marked by the weight of centuries, their wings ridged like mountainsides. But those, she realized now, had only been veterans. These were something else entirely.

These were time itself given form.

Their faces bore the cracks of centuries, yet those cracks glowed faintly from within, veins of light seeping through the stone as though their very bodies couldn't contain what lived inside. Horns crowned their brows like spires—some sweeping back in elegant arcs, others jutting forward like the tips of scythes. Their eyes were molten coals in pools of shadow, every gaze a weight that pressed the breath from her lungs.

The air thickened as their wings shifted. Even folded, they filled the chamber like walls closing in, draped in ceremonial cloth so dark it seemed to drink the runes' glow. Chains of silver hung heavy at their throats, etched with ancient circles of oaths that caught and reflected the faint light. They were less individuals than living pillars—seven anchors of the Kin's will.

And they were watching her.

A shiver traced Eliryn's spine. The beings before her looked as though they had remained in these thrones for decades, unmoving, unbothered by the slow crawl of time.

Only now had they stirred.

Only now, with the sanctuary's wards breached and Malric's shadow clawing at their borders, had the stone gods chosen to wake and speak.

Eliryn swallowed, her throat dry. The silence was unbearable; thicker than a battlefield's pause before steel met steel. Every instinct screamed to look away, but she forced her chin high.

"Dragonrider."

The voice came from the central throne, a male Elder whose horns curved like a crown. His voice was deeper than thunder, yet clear, each syllable shaking the runes beneath her feet. "You walk in the Sepulcher of Judgment. Here, history has been made. Here, the mountain commands truth."

She nodded, not trusting her voice.

Another Elder leaned forward, her face a lattice of glowing cracks, her eyes sharp as shards of glass. "You carry death and remnants of Flame in your bones. You walk with sight that is not your own." Her wings rustled, stone grinding on stone. "The last of your kind."

The words were a measure, a reminder that what had happened was not a miracle, but a debt.

Beside her, Garrion dipped his head low, his wings folding tighter. Druven didn't move. He stood straight, talons flexing once, as though daring the scrutiny to land on him instead.

The crown-horned Elder's gaze swept to him, then to Garrion, before burning back into Eliryn's. "Speak, Dragonrider. Our wards have been discovered. It is time we heard the truth of your death from your own mouth."

The chamber seemed to tilt beneath her. Her palms dampened. Vaeronth's presence pressed close through the bond—solid, steady, unyielding.

Tell them, Little Flame, he rumbled, the words rolling like magma.

Eliryn's tongue stuck to the roof of her mouth. Words swam there, but none that she wanted to spill into the charged silence.

Her mind flashed back—not to the triumphs of trials or the weight of prophecy—but to that moment in Vireth when she had trusted her gut. Trusted the wrong man.

Her stomach clenched, anxiety thickening in her chest.

She had been raised on stories of dragonriders who had stood against the impossible, who had bent flame and sky to their will. And what had she done? She had been gutted. Not in some honorable clash of blades, but by betrayal—her blind faith turned into a weapon. She wouldn't have even seen the strike coming had it not been for Vaeronth.

The shame of it burned hotter than any wound.

The Elders' eyes bore into her as though they could see the memory replayed inside her ribs. Garrion shifted faintly at her side, but he did not speak. He would not shield her from this. Druven was closer now, too close, his storm-gray gaze fixed forward, as if to absorb the weight should she falter.

Her breath rattled. *What if they see weakness? What if they decide I am unworthy because I failed, because I bled?*

Through the bond, Vaeronth's voice came easily. *You lived, Eliryn. Speak it. Do not let shame silence you. The stone does not scorn the fault—it remembers and learns from it.*

Her hands trembled where she clenched them at her sides. Still, she forced her chin higher, though her throat burned with the effort.

"When I died," she began, the words scraping out raw, "it was not in battle. It was not in glory. It was because I trusted someone I should not have. He used my weakness, my blindness, to put a blade through me. I never saw it coming. Not because he was strong, although he is that. But because I believed him when I shouldn't have."

Her voice faltered, but she held.

"I tell you this because I won't lie—not to you and not to myself. If I am to stand here as the Last Dragonrider, wanting to use this man as a means to gaining an advantage, then you should know the truth of my fall."

The silence stretched, long enough for Eliryn's pulse to begin thrumming in her ears. The Elders' eyes did not blink, did not soften. They sat in judgment, their eyes tracking Eliryn with a scrutiny that stripped her bare. She had expected something else... But what she felt under their stares felt like a judgment she was already failing.

One of them spoke, his voice rough with centuries. "You are not what the riders once were. They were tempered in skill. You..." his gaze flicked to her sightless eyes, "...come to us broken. Blind. Untrained."

The words landed like stone to her chest. She forced her face to remain unchanged, but heat crawled along her skin.

Then, as if the taste of her weakness wasn't enough, their attention shifted. To Druven.

"And him," another said, talons clicking against his chair, "the Oathless one. A danger left untethered. Should he even be permitted this close to you?"

Another Elder leaned forward, granite eyes narrowing. "We remember what his strength cost. We remember the blood he shed."

At her side, Druven stood immovable. Only the curl of his fists betrayed him—stone palms closing until black blood welled between claw and skin, dripping thick to the floor.

Something inside Eliryn snapped.

"I will decide who stands near me. Myself and my dragon." She said, her voice louder than she intended, but she didn't back down.

The chamber stilled. For a moment, her words rang in the vaulted stone like an oath.

The Elders exchanged looks, unreadable, before one finally spoke again. "And what of the human who hunts you? The one clawing at our wards. Why should he live?"

The shift made her stomach flip. Malric. His name wasn't spoken, but the weight of it pressed in all the same.

"He gutted me," Eliryn said, voice steady though her hands curled tight. "He killed me. I should want him dead, but..." She drew in a breath, forcing the storm inside her into words. "...we need to know what he knows. Who holds the Flame. Why the realm is still bleeding magic. Killing him outright gives us nothing."

Murmurs rose around the chamber. Some nodding, others bristling. The air thrummed with divided judgment.

Then one Elder snorted, dismissive. "You speak like a fledgling. Dragonriders of old would never have hesitated to kill those who stand against them."

The barb dug deep. Too deep.

Her breath came sharp as she surged to her feet. "Maybe I'm not the Dragonider you wanted. But I'm the Dragonrider you have. And I'll do what must be done, whether you sneer at me or not."

She turned on her heel before they could strip more from her, the scrape of her boots against stone echoing in the heavy silence.

Gasps and mutters rippled at her dismissal, but Eliryn was already moving, boots slapping against stone as she stormed for the chamber doors.

The sound of heavy steps followed immediately—Druven's. He caught up in three strides, falling into place beside her as the doors thudded shut behind them.

"You should not have done that, Dragonrider," he said, voice rough but even. "Standing against the Elders will make your life harder."

She shot him a glare, her chest still heaving. "My life has never been easy, Druven. I'm very used to being uncomfortable."

For a moment, his lips twitched, so faint she might have imagined it

They walked in silence until the corridor opened wider, the stone air cooler. Eliryn dragged a hand down her face, her heart still racing.

Vaeronth, she whispered through the bond, needing him like breath.

His rumble answered instantly, hot and grounding. *I felt it. You were very quick to react. Your disrespect won't earn you favor with the Elders, Eliryn. Even if I understand why Malric's presence has put you on edge, they won't tolerate brash decisions that involve their people. They woke when we arrived and they woke again when they felt their wards being tested. They deserve more than your dismissal.*

I stormed out, she admitted, sinking against the wall for a moment. *But they see me as weak and childish. They see Druven as dangerous. We can't just... wait to be judged and found lacking. We need a plan.*

The bond pulsed steady in her chest, his voice coiling low and sure. *We will plan, but we should not freeze them out.*

Eliryn closed her eyes, steadying herself against the stone.

She didn't just feel the weight of prophecy pressing her down.

She felt the fire of choice burning up through her bones.

For a long moment, she stood there against the wall, breathing. The stone still thrummed faintly with the pulse of the Kin below—their quiet voices, their judgment. Her reflection in the dark marble of her vambrace looked like a stranger: dirt-streaked, hollow-eyed, too young to be what they needed her to be.

You're right, she whispered through the bond.

A faint, approving rumble. *Then act like it.*

Eliryn pushed off the wall, Druven tight behind her without question. Her legs were heavy, but the kind of heavy that meant she'd stopped running. The corridor opened again ahead of her, the muted glow of the council fire spilling through the cracked doorway. Voices carried—Garrion's low rumble, one of the Elders' gravelled tones in answer. Vaeronth's shadow moved against the far arch, vast and still, the faint heat of him bending the air.

When she stepped through, the conversation stopped for the second time that night.

Garrion turned first, his face unreadable. The Elders did not blink. Their eyes, carved from the same age-worn stone as the walls themselves, waited.

Eliryn swallowed the lump in her throat and made herself walk to the center of the chamber. Her palms itched to fidget. She didn't let them. When she spoke, her voice was steadier than she felt.

"I owe you all an apology."

The words hung there.

Not groveling. Not prideful. Just true.

"I shouldn't have left the way I did. It was—disrespectful. And that's the last thing I want to be to the people who saved my life."

One of the Elders shifted—a scrape of stone on stone—but said nothing.

She pressed on.

"I'm... on edge. You know why. You can feel it. Malric's presence—everything he's touched—sets my skin on fire. But running from that doesn't help anyone. I know I'm not enough to save this realm alone. But maybe—" she drew in a breath, made herself meet those unblinking eyes, "—maybe with your help, I can be."

Garrion's gaze softened just enough to show approval.

Druven stood near the far wall, arms folded, silent but listening.

"If we keep Malric alive," Eliryn continued, "if we use what he knows instead of throwing it to dust—then maybe we can start making the right kind of progress. I'm not asking for forgiveness. Just... time. Time to prove I can learn. That I can do better."

A silence fell heavy and deep. One of the ancient Kin—broad-shouldered, half his skin veined with the pale glow of stone—glanced toward Vaeronth's shadow.

The dragon's voice filled the chamber, low and vast, the kind of sound that lived in the marrow of things.

"She speaks with intent now," he said. "That is all I ask of her. That is all any of us should ask."

The Elders conferred in low tones, their language more vibration than word. At last, the eldest among them inclined his head a fraction.

"Intent is not enough," he said, voice deep as bedrock. "But it is a start."

Eliryn bowed her head—not deep, but enough. "Then let me try."

The elder's gaze lingered a heartbeat longer. Then he nodded once.

Vaeronth's approval brushed her through the bond—a spark of warmth, bright as sunlight through storm.

Better, he said. *Now we begin.*

Interlude 2: Malric

"Beware the one who wears bone for a crown; for in his hand, ruin sleeps, and in his hunger, ruin wakes."
—Fragment of the Warden's Lament

The chamber smelled of stone and old dust, the kind of silence that remembered oaths sworn long before he was born.

Malric studied everything. The way light bled through fissures in the walls. The faint glimmer of wards crawling like veins across the floor. The guardians stationed at the archway, still as statues until their eyes caught light.

Gargoyles.

He almost laughed aloud. Legends, he had always thought. Old wives' tales whispered in shadowed halls about creatures carved from stone who had walked beside dragons in ages long dead. But they were real. They breathed. Their wings stirred the air. And they had captured him.

Strangely, he didn't care.

Now that he was close to her—closer than he'd been since the citadel, since she had slipped from his grasp in fire and blood—his mind felt sharp again. The fury that had consumed him, the wild hunger that had sent him scouring forest and mountain alike, dulled into something cleaner. A razor's edge.

She is here.

He savored the thought like wine on his tongue. Somewhere beyond this chamber, Eliryn drew breath. Alive. Exactly as he'd always known she was.

Not gone. Not lost. *His.*

Malric sat chained to a block of basalt, iron biting into his wrists and ankles, the rune-light catching the dried blood on his skin. Around him, the gargoyles came to stand in a half-circle—hulking silhouettes with wings half-furled, talons flexing and scraping against the floor as though itching to carve truth out of his flesh.

They were not men; they were something older. Their eyes glowed faintly in the gloom—emerald, amber, violet—light burning from within like coals in a furnace. They watched him without blinking, stone lips grim, shoulders hunched forward as though the act of breathing was unnecessary to them.

Malric studied them in turn. He should have been afraid. Any sane man would have been. Instead, he marveled. *So the legends were true,* he thought. *Stone come to life. Dragons' wardens. Kin of the old oaths.*

And yet, for all their bulk and menace, he thought them... brutish. Not gods, but tools. Heavy, simple, inevitable. He had faced worse in the Thalen's pits. He had carved through worse on the battlefield.

When they asked him who he was, he didn't hesitate.

"Malric," he said, his voice carrying evenly across the chamber. "Right hand of King Thalen, Sovereign of Vireth. Commander of the Royal Guard. And more powerful than you can imagine."

Their stares sharpened. A growl rumbled low in one chest.

He leaned forward slightly, chains clanking. "That is why I had no trouble finding you. Why your wards did not keep me away. You thought yourselves hidden, but nothing can hide from me. Not her. Not this place."

The words burned as he spoke them, because even he knew they were not quite true. His strength alone had not led him here. It was hunger. Obsession. That pull he could not name but never escaped. A need to be near Eliryn that had consumed every thought since she fled.

And beneath it all—the ring.

Bone-white against his bloody hand, it had been with him since the day Thalen pressed it into his palm. Forged with his blood. Bound with words Malric hadn't understood, but that had burned into his marrow all the same. He had worn it for centuries, never once removing it. And since meeting the Dragonrider it had sunk into him, whispered to him, twisted every thread of want inside him tighter around a single, inescapable axis: *her*.

He thought it was simply him. His desire. His obsession. But the truth was far darker.

The gargoyles circled him with questions, their voices grinding like stone on stone. Why had he come? Who had sent him? Did Thalen know where the Sanctuary lay? What right did he think he had to live, after raising a blade against the Last Dragonrider?

He smiled at their fury. Gave them pieces of himself—yes, he had hunted her, yes, the crown was behind him, yes, he carried strength beyond a mortal's. But the rest? He let silence answer.

Until one of them saw the ring.

Its pale gleam caught the rune-light. Their voices faltered. Heads turned. A ripple passed through them like a quake.

One barked something guttural, and claws like hooked knives seized his wrist, wrenching it forward. Pain flared as skin split under their grip, blood smearing the bone-white band. They shoved his hand beneath the glowing runes.

The chamber thickened with silence.

The gargoyles muttered to one another in a tongue older than kings. Malric caught fragments—words rough as gravel, tones sharpened with fear. Their unease was new. It made him lean back, pulse quickening.

At last, one turned to him, voice a rasp of granite. "Do you know what it is you wear?"

Malric blinked at the ring, then at them. "It was given to me. Forged in old magic. It sharpens me. Keeps me alive where others fall." He smiled faintly, lips curling. "Why? Do you envy it?"

A growl shook the circle. Another elder stepped forward, wings spreading. "That is no gift. That is desecration."

That word and the way it was spoken gave him pause. "Desecration?"

One voice rose, making a declaration: "Dragonbone."

The word cracked through the chamber like a bolt of lightning. Some recoiled, snarling. Others flared their wings in fury, claws striking the floor. The rune-light seemed to burn hotter, throwing stark shadows across their faces.

Malric tilted his head, caught between shock and fascination. *Dragonbone?* The bone of a dragon, carved and worn like jewelry. He almost laughed at the audacity of it. Of course Thalen would do this. Of course the king he served would hollow out legends and turn their hide into weapons disguised as jewelry.

"Remove it," one growled, stepping closer. "Now. Or we will cut it from you."

Malric's lips curved into something colder. "You think to strip me? This ring is mine. It was forged for me, with my blood." He lifted his chin, defiant despite the chains. "Do you truly think your claws can take it?"

They didn't argue. They seized his hand again. Talons dug in, prying, forcing, even as the ring burned hot enough that Malric hissed.

And then—

The band tore free.

Pain lanced his hand, his blood sizzling against the stone floor. The gargoyles staggered back, some snarling, some looking away as though they had witnessed something unspeakable.

"Dragonbone," one spat again, voice shaking with fury. "The bone of the slain, bound in dark magic. A crime against every oath ever sworn."

Their words echoed, and Malric's pulse hammered. Desecration. Dragonbone. He had never known. But then again, he had never asked.

The gargoyles stood in their half-circle, wings spread, their glowing eyes fixed on the pale ring clutched in a warrior's talons. Some hissed like fissures venting steam, others murmured curses that sounded older than language.

The absence of the ring left Malric's hand feeling naked and wrong, as though part of him had been torn away.

Then—

A roar split the sanctuary.

It came not from the chamber but from the sky above, rolling down the mountains like the voice of the gods themselves. The stones trembled. Dust sifted from the ceiling, the runes along the walls flaring as though braced against the sheer force of it.

Vaeronth.

Malric's head snapped up, heart hammering. Through the carved arches of the chamber, a shadow blotted out the light—vast wings spread, scales catching the sun like molten bronze. The roar hit again, closer this time, the sound so enormous that it tore through Malric's ribs and rattled his bones.

The gargoyles staggered. Even they—ancient, carved, unflinching—bowed their heads at the weight of it. Some pressed claws to their chests, others snarled in answer, fury braided with mourning.

And in Malric's mind, the truth crystallized:

The dragon knew.

Vaeronth had felt it the moment the ring came free. The desecration that had clung to Malric for centuries was laid bare now, undeniable. The bones of the dragons' brethren, slaughtered and twisted into a relic of power, bound to the blood of a mortal.

The dragon's outrage thundered like a storm at the edge of ending.

The chains cut into Malric's wrists as he leaned forward, laughing hoarsely even as the sound quaked around him. "So that's what it is. That's what I've been carrying all this time." His lips pulled into a smile, wide and terrible. "Thalen really did it, didn't he? He broke your beasts down to the parts."

The gargoyle holding the ring growled, wings mantling wide. "Silence, desecrator."

Malric only bared his teeth. Of course Thalen would crown his closest killer with a relic made of sacrilege. And of course Malric—faithful Malric—had worn it all these years, its poison fusing with his blood until he no longer knew where the ring ended and he began.

Another roar split the air—closer, louder, the fury of it tearing cracks through the stone floor. The rune-light guttered, struggling to hold against the dragon's rage.

Malric's laugh broke into a rasp, then softened into something else. A whisper. "And still... it brought me to her." His eyes gleamed, fever-bright, as he raised them to the chamber doors. "It led me straight to the Dragonrider."

Chapter 16: The Dragon's Lament

"When dragons wept, the sky itself split. Their grief was not a sound, but a wound the world could never mend."
—Fragment from *The Songs of the First Flame*

Eliryn walked the corridor in silence, her thoughts turning over like stones in a riverbed. The air still smelled faintly of the council fire—smoke, metal, and the weight of things left unsaid.

She wasn't proud of how she'd reacted earlier. Storming out had been childish; she could admit that now. The apology had cost her pride, but the Elders had deserved it. They'd seen something steadier in her afterward—or maybe she just wanted to believe they had. Either way, the heaviness in her chest had lightened, a little.

Vaeronth's steady presence brushed against her mind—warm, approving. *Now we begin,* he'd said, and she'd felt that rare pulse of satisfaction through the bond, old and certain as the mountain itself.

She almost smiled at the memory.

Then the bond snapped tight.

Her breath hitched. The warmth vanished, replaced by a sharp, searing pressure that stole the air from her lungs. Pain speared through her chest—jagged, merciless, alive.

Eliryn staggered, a hand braced against the wall as the world blurred.

"Vaeronth—"

The connection pulsed once, hard and wrong, and her knees nearly gave.

Vaeronth!

She screamed his name through their link as the corridor spun. Her knees buckled. She clutched at the wall but missed, palms slamming against cold stone as the floor rushed up to meet her.

Her runes flared, sudden and violent. Silver fire scorched along her skin, glowing through the fabric of her tunic, painting the corridor in a ghostly light. The heat seared her, but it wasn't hers. None of it was hers.

Grief. Rage. Horror.

It all came flooding through the bond, drowning her. She gasped like she was the one suffocating, as though her lungs were being crushed beneath a mountain's weight. Her vision blurred, doubled—the corridor overlaid with flashes of wings, fire, broken stone. Vaeronth's memories, his anguish, bleeding into her senses.

"Dragonrider!" Druven's voice cut through, sharp as steel. He was crouched beside her in an instant, claws biting into her shoulders. "What is this? Where's the enemy?"

She shook her head, words breaking against her teeth. "Not—enemy—" Another wave slammed into her chest. She arched off the floor with a strangled cry, hands clutching her ribs as if she could cage the hurt.

The runes along her arms blazed brighter, each line of script burning like molten metal. Her pulse faltered, skipped, staggered. For one horrifying heartbeat, she was sure her heart had stopped.

Druven gripped her tighter, hauling her half into his lap as if that would hold her together. "Talk to me, Dragonrider. What is happening?"

She forced the words out, broken and gasping. "It's—Vaeronth. Pain—too much—"

The bond howled again, his roar echoing in her bones. Her skin felt as if it would split open from the force of it, every vein and nerve set alight with anguish that was not her own.

She pressed a trembling hand to Druven's chest, desperate, her nails scraping against the thin fabric over his stone skin. "Get me—" She coughed, choked. "Get me to him. Now."

Druven's strides were relentless, each one hammering through the stone corridors like the beat of war drums. Eliryn's body jolted with every step, her runes still blazing so fiercely that the light painted his chest in pale fire where she clung to him.

Her breath hitched, her lips trembling against the weight of the bond. Druven's arms tightened around her as though daring the realm to try and take her from him.

"It's not my pain— It's him. It's Vaeronth. He's—" The bond surged again, ripping the rest from her throat in a soundless gasp.

Druven's jaw flexed, fangs flashing briefly as his expression hardened. "Then your dragon is bleeding through you. And if he bleeds, you bleed."

Her nails dug into his tunic, helpless.

His wings snapped once behind him, grazing the walls as he stormed through another archway.

The bond surged again, harder, white-hot. Eliryn choked, the agony tearing through her chest until she could barely breathe. "It's too much—I can't—"

Druven leaned his head closer, his words pitched for her alone. "Then let me bear some of it. Grip harder. Anchor yourself. Don't drown alone."

Her trembling fingers fisted his tunic, clinging like a lifeline as he barreled on. She let herself lean into the steady weight of his strength, even as her vision blurred and the bond threatened to drag her under.

The corridors bled into open air, sunlight striking like a blade across the stone. Druven didn't slow. His wings flared once, catching the canyon wind, and then they were spilling out onto the wide platform that overlooked the sanctuary's heart.

Vaeronth was there.

The dragon's bulk loomed like a mountain of living obsidian, his wings mantled wide against the sky as though he might tear the sun itself from its perch. The air throbbed with heat, with fury, with a pain so vast it shook the marrow of the stone. Runes carved into the dais flared and guttered under his weight, unable to contain the raw storm surging from his chest.

Eliryn's breath tore out of her, ragged. "Vaeronth—" The bond pulled her forward even from Druven's arms, a magnetic drag that screamed of desperation. She had to reach him. She had to *touch* him.

Vaeronth's eyes, those Molton gold furnaces, snapped to her. The bond slammed harder, doubling her agony, doubling his. For a heartbeat she thought her bones might splinter just from looking at him.

Druven staggered under the force of it, but did not release her. He crouched low and set her onto unsteady feet, though his hand hovered at her back ready to catch her if she crumbled.

Eliryn swayed, her knees buckling, her chest aching with every pulse of Vaeronth's torment. "What—what is happening to you?" she gasped through the link. "Tell me—please."

But Vaeronth's thoughts were a wildfire, half-formed, jagged with grief and rage. His roar ripped through the Sanctuary, shaking dust from the cliffs and sending a scatter of gargoyles wheeling overhead in alarm. The sound wasn't for her, not entirely. It was for the entire realm. For the horror that had woken in him.

Eliryn flinched, covering her ears though it did nothing to dampen the bond's scream inside her skull. She dropped to her knees, palms pressed against the stone that shuddered with his rage. Her runes blazed brighter than they ever had, veins of silver fire racing over her skin in frantic counterpoint.

"I can't—" Her voice broke, strangled. "Vaeronth, you're—burning me alive."

For the barest instant, his fury wavered—just enough for his voice to press into her mind, cracked and low.

They mutilated us, Eliryn. Desecrated us.

The words rattled her ribs, her spine, her teeth. She could barely breathe around them.

She repeated the words out loud without meaning to. "Desecration?"

Druven bent close, his stone-rough voice cutting through the firestorm. "What does he mean?"

Eliryn dragged in a shaking breath, eyes locked on Vaeronth as her dragon loomed above, wings blotting out the sky. "I—I don't know. But I have to stay with him. Whatever it is… he can't face it alone."

Her knees scraped raw as she tried to crawl closer. Druven's claws flexed at his sides, torn between pulling her back and shielding her from the fury pouring off the dragon. At last, with a wordless growl, he fell into step beside her, his shadow covering hers as they moved into the space beneath the dragon.

Chapter 17: Echos of the Fallen

"Sorrow can break the body before it breaks the soul."
—Fragment of *The Kinstone Codex*

The world was noise and heat and a hurt that didn't belong to her.

Eliryn clung to Druven's shoulder as if the stone of him could anchor a sky that had come loose. The bond roared with a blinding rawness, Vaeronth's grief pouring through her like fire down a dry gully. Her ribs felt strung too tight; every breath was a dragged blade. Talons hammered somewhere—no, boots—no, her own heartbeat. She couldn't sort the sounds. Only the ache.

"Breathe," Druven said, voice a low gravel. He didn't jostle her. He moved with a predator's economy, a steady, brutal grace. "In. Out."

"Trying," she rasped, though the word scraped wrong in her throat. Her dragonmarks throbbed in answer to an older pulse—the one that lived in the hollows of Vaeronth's bones. The pain wasn't hers. But the bond didn't care whose name it wore.

Eliryn reached through the pain the way a hand reaches through flame for a dropped blade. *I'm here.*

The bond bucked; then it turned, like a storm's eye finding shore. His attention found her—not gentle, but *there*—and for one suspended heartbeat the pain didn't crush so completely.

"Tell me," she whispered to the air between her and the dragon. "Please."

Instead it was Garrion who answered, his form appearing at the edge of her sight.

He came like a shadow thickening, straight-backed, wings half-mantled, the carved planes of his face set in a severity she had not seen before. Two Kin flanked him, both older than the canyon, both wearing matching expressions she could not decipher. One carried a wrapped bundle.

"The prisoner is contained," Garrion said. "We questioned him in the Subvault. He gave us truth enough, or what he believes truth to be. And then..."

His glance cut to the bundle. The elder to his left unwound the linen with hands that didn't tremble, though the cloth made a whisper like a shroud.

Eliryn's stomach lurched.

A ring lay in the folds. Simple. Bone-pale. No jewel. No flourish. The light slid across it with a dull, porous sheen.

Every hair on her arms rose.

"The king's hound wore this," Garrion said.

Eliryn's mouth went dry. "What is it?"

Druven's jaw worked once. He didn't look away from the ring.

"Dragonbone," Garrion answered. The word fell like a bell dropped from a height. "Carved and bound in blood."

Heat punched the air. Vaeronth didn't move, but the temperature *spiked,* the faintest vibration running along the terrace stones.

Eliryn shook her head once, as if she could rattle the meaning out of the word. "That can't—"

"It can," Garrion said, and anger finally cracked his tone. Not a flare. A fault line. "Long ago. Quietly. Hidden behind crowns and ceremony and the signs of dying magic. They harvested magical creatures far before the fall of the dragons. But this, we could have never predicted."

A wind she could not feel sheared through Eliryn's chest. She tasted metal. "Thalen."

"And those who bent the knee for him," the elder said. "Bone for blades. Bone for fetishes. Bone for rings. They call it relic, reliquary, inheritance. We call it desecration."

Vaeronth's head lowered by a fraction. Smoke snaked from his nostrils, thin and constant. *Relic.* The word ground through the bond. *They name theft with worship to hide the rot in their mouths.*

Eliryn swallowed. Her mind snatched at images—Malric when she had met him, Malric as he held her as she fell apart... She had never paid attention to his hand, not really.

"We removed it by force," Garrion said. "He refused. The moment it was separated from direct contact, the air turned wrong. Your dragon felt it."

The bond answered with a pulse that hurt.

Eliryn found her voice in tatters. "Is... is it the ring? Is the ring *why* Malric found us?"

"Partly," Garrion said. "We keep wards for men and magic. But dragonbone answers the old currents. It longed for the Sanctuary. A hunter wearing such a thing could find us."

Vaeronth's wings shivered once. Not a tremble. A contained violence. *He wore us like jewelry.*

Eliryn staggered a step. Druven's hand ghosted at her elbow, then stayed. He was silent, but not empty. The set of his shoulders promised murder, slowly leashed.

"What did he say?" she asked Garrion, and hated the rasp in it. "Malric. What does he know?"

"That Thalen keeps more secrets than the realm could imagine," Garrion said. "That rebellion still simmers in the city, but its leaders are chained beneath it. That a woman crowned and burned in the same breath can make men make rash choices." His gaze cut to her, unreadable. "He knows you live. He insists he has always known it."

Eliryn's throat worked. *Always.* The word carried too many other words inside it—possession, obsession, a kind of worship that made her skin crawl. "And the ring?"

"He did not know," one of the other gargoyles answered—no softness in his voice. "He thought it *old magic.* It is *old* and it is *magic*—but it is ours. Our dead forced to serve the hands that killed them."

Vaeronth's roar strangled the air.

It was the guttural, strangled refusal of something too large for a throat—rage damned by a will that did not want to hurt what was near. The terrace trembled. Far below, a waterfall lost its pattern for a breath and then found it again.

Eliryn stepped forward before she could stop herself. Her palm met scale hot enough to sting. "I'm here," she said, though her voice shook. "I'm here, I'm here."

The bond surged, then banked. He let her touch be a gate the fury could move through without flooding. *Little Flame,* came the thought, rough as a mountain path, and then nothing else for a long while but the feel of him not moving so he would not destroy.

Druven shifted minutely, putting his body between Eliryn and the open edge of the terrace without making a cage of it. If Vaeronth leaped, if the stone broke, if the sky turned on them—he would be the thing that met all three first.

At last, Vaeronth's head lowered again, the heat easing from blast to blaze. "Take it away from me," he growled—not to Eliryn but to Garrion.

Garrion bowed in full, the kind of bow that spoke to a sovereign grief. He wrapped the ring in the linen, bound it twice, and handed it off to one of the others with a spoken word Eliryn didn't know. The moment it left their sight, the air lost a bitter flavor she hadn't realized it held.

Eliryn's hands had stopped shaking. Her knees hadn't. She breathed around it.

"What now," she asked, to no one and to everyone. "Because if that thing helped him find this place, others can do the same—right? Who else wears—"

"Too many," Garrion said. Honesty, like a blade laid on a table. "But the ring is a beacon we can learn from. Wards know their own. We will braid a warning into the Sanctuary's bones—let the mountain spit the taste of it back at anything that carries the same stain."

The remaining gargoyle inclined her head. "We can do it before dusk."

Eliryn nodded. "And Malric?"

"He will be questioned again," Garrion said. "By those who make questions an art. He will be kept from you. He will—"

"No," Eliryn said.

The word surprised even her. It came out clean. Not loud. But a line drawn nevertheless.

Garrion's eyes narrowed the smallest degree. "No?"

"I want to speak to him," she said, and the words spilled out of her before she could cauterize them. "I need to know more. He betrayed me. He hunted me. He wore that—" she couldn't say ring; her mouth wouldn't frame it—"*thing*. He's been taking orders from Thalen and whatever passes for a court there. If he knows who else wears dragonbone, if he knows which of the citadel's veins are still open—then I need his answers. From his mouth."

Garrion studied her. "You would put yourself within arm's length of the man who killed you." He didn't even phrase it like a question; it was more like a statement that questioned her sanity.

"Under guard," Druven said before she could speak. It wasn't a request.

Eliryn didn't look at him, but she felt herself stand straighter against his surety, as if his promise made her request valid.

Vaeronth's silence pressed hard on her thoughts. Not refusal. Not consent. A coil of heat and memory and something like smoke over water. *I don't know if this is the right decision,* he said at last.

"I am not afraid," she said. "And I would not go alone."

A slow beat. Then, grudging as a mountain ceding an inch to a river: *You will not go alone.*

Garrion's mouth flattened. "The Subvault has wards that knot a man's magic and keep his strength at bay," he said. "He can't shadow-step, can't draw on whatever edge that ring gave him. Even so—two guards. And myself."

"Three," Druven said.

Garrion's gaze cut to him, a small iron smile that wasn't warmth and wasn't not. "You do not ask."

"I do not," Druven said.

Something in Eliryn *eased.* Not relief. There was no room for that. But her ribs felt less like glass.

She stepped closer to Vaeronth until her hip brushed heat and scale. The bond rose, met her. She gentled it with her palm, the way you tell a warhorse with your body that the battle line is not this *yet.*

"I'll go now," she said. Not an order. A decision her mind had already made.

Eliryn looked up into eyes that had seen civilizations rise, fall, and turn to ash—eyes that now burned like a storm trapped in amber.

"I can feel it," she said, her voice barely holding. "What they did—it's wrong in ways I don't have words for. I can't fix it, I know that. But I need you to know I *feel* it. The grief. The fury. All of it. I'm so sorry, Vaeronth. For them. For you."

For a long moment, he didn't answer. His gaze was distant—somewhere far beyond the chamber, beyond the mountain, as if he were listening for voices that would never rise again.

When he finally spoke, it was low and rough, the sound of stone giving way under the weight of years.

I did not mean for you to carry it, he said. *The pain of my fallen should never have touched you.*

He lowered his head slightly, breath hot enough to tremble the air.

But... I find a kind of peace in sharing it. For so long, I thought I would bear everything alone. Yet you— his voice faltered, just for a heartbeat, *—you are the only family I have left.*

The words landed like a vow.

Eliryn pressed her forehead to the curve of his chestplate. The metal was hot, alive beneath her skin. For a moment, the whole world smelled like rain that would never touch earth—grief too vast for the sky to hold.

"Let's move," Garrion said quietly.

They went.

The way to the Subvault dove under the Sanctuary proper, beneath training yards and barracks, past storage caverns and the low, humming rooms where the Kin wove wards into rope and stone. The air cooled in increments. Runes shifted from bright to deep to a color that wasn't color at all.

Eliryn walked between Garrion and Druven. She didn't speak. She catalogued what could be catalogued instead: the scrape-kiss of her boots against old stone; the echo of wings overhead, a rhythmic hush as Vaeronth paced them from above along the cliff's skin; the way Garrion's shadow moved like a second sentinel; the way Druven didn't seem to move at all and yet was always nearby.

When they reached the iron-banded door, Garrion lifted his hand to the sigil set in the lintel. It looked like a spiral at first, then like a knot, then like a circle of mouths. "This place is ancient," he said. "It has held far worse than a king's knife."

The door opened on a chamber carved straight from the mountain's throat.

Not a dungeon—too clean for that. Too intentional. The walls gleamed smooth as riverstone, runes circling their base in an unbroken pulse of dull gold. Containment, not cruelty.

At its center waited a single obsidian chair, fitted with padded restraints. The kind made for holding storms, not prisoners.

Malric sat within it.

He looked smaller without a sword, without his rank, without the weight of command to make him seem taller than he was. But there was no softness in him, only focus. Every part of him was drawn tight, as if even stillness were a form of weaponry.

When he lifted his head, his eyes found hers immediately. Not Garrion. Not Druven. Just her.

And for one impossible heartbeat, the memory returned: his breath near her ear, the steel's flash, the sound of her name breaking on his tongue before the pain had taken everything else.

"Eliryn," he said softly. Too softly. Like he was afraid to break something that was already dust.

It hit her harder than a shout.

"Malric." Her voice came out steady, though the name felt like iron on her tongue. "You've lost something."

His mouth curved, not in shame but in memory. "It wasn't lost. It was stolen."

Druven's talons scraped stone. "The relic was never yours to wield," he rumbled. "You desecrated what you could not understand."

Malric's gaze flicked to him, then back to her, dismissing the gargoyle as if he were furniture. "And yet it listened to me," he said, staring at Eliryn. "As you once did."

Something in her chest twisted, sharp and old.

"I listened," Eliryn said quietly, "until you drove a sword through me."

For a moment, silence held. Even the runes dimmed, their pulse shallow.

Then Malric's tone shifted—gentle, almost affectionate. "And yet here you are. Breathing. Talking. Wearing borrowed divinity like it's always belonged to you." His smile didn't reach his eyes. "Tell me, Eliryn—when they saved you, did you stay the same?"

Garrion stepped forward, voice hard as a closing gate. "Enough. You will answer what is asked of you, or you will answer to the dragon above."

Malric didn't look at him. His eyes stayed on hers. "He won't burn me," he murmured. "She won't let him."

Eliryn's hands curled, but her voice stayed level. "If fire finds you now it would be a mercy."

The bond flared, heat and a warning that felt like a talon drawn across slate. Eliryn did not step back. She let the anger move through her, pick up her spine, lay it back down straight.

"You hunted me," she said. "You brought whatever rot sits in Thalen's court to the edge of the only place in this realm that still feels clean." Her voice did not rise. It didn't need to. "So you are going to tell me what you know. Not for your life. Not for your comfort. For mine."

He laughed once, low and surprised. A genuine sound, and somehow that made it worse. "There you are," he murmured. "I wondered if you would still hold the same fire as before."

"Names," Garrion interrupted.

"Routes," Druven said.

"Thalen," Eliryn directed. "Start there. Start with where the Flame sits and whose hand it burns."

The questioning began.

It was not the cruel kind with knives and magic. It was the more patient kind with truth and time. Garrion asked like a man who had built rooms for answers. Druven stood like an answer to a different question entirely. Eliryn watched, and when Malric tried to turn a story into a mirror, she refused to look.

Piece by piece, a map uncurled. Rebels chained under the castle, not killed because example is louder than absence. Courts split—those who worshiped Thalen because he still breathed the Flame's breath, those who longed for anothers' rule, regardless of who that might be with the Dragonrider believed dead. Merchants who traded rumor like coin. Names. Houses. Corridors.

Eventually, Garrion lifted a hand. Enough—for now.

Eliryn hadn't realized the ache in her jaw was from clenching her teeth. She released her molars one by one until she could taste the iron of her own mouth again.

Malric looked at her like a man looks at a horizon he means to cross. "You will come again," he said. Not a hope. An arithmetic.

"Not because you asked," she clarified.

Something like satisfaction flickered, then shuttered. He sat back as far as the straps let him and closed his eyes, as if he had worries at all.

Garrion touched Eliryn's shoulder. The weight was permission and question both.

"Done," she agreed. "For now."

They left him under the mountain where the runes ate power and the stone gave nothing back.

On the climb up, the world felt thinner, like the mountain had lost air. At the terrace again, the wind met them like a blade that had been cooled. The Sanctuary beyond moved as it always did—wings along walks, voices in the halls, the taste of iron and resin singing in the light. And yet everything felt... edged.

Eliryn stood with her palms on the low wall and watched the canyon take sun like a cup takes water. She did not speak until the quiet stopped bucking inside her.

"We harden the wards," she said. "We find out who else wears bone and we make a plan." She blew out a breath that tasted like old ash and new iron. "And I will choose a protector soon."

Garrion inclined his head. "Say it and the arena opens."

"Not yet," she said. "Soon." Her gaze slid to Druven without her permission. He didn't flinch from her attention. He didn't ask to be chosen. He didn't promise her anything. He simply *was*.

She turned back to the canyon.

There—hugging the stone where magic met earth—blooms of impossible purple lilies unfurled, their petals drinking starlight, their glow soft as breath. Fragile things, rooted in the line between safety and ruin.

Eliryn's chest tightened.

She wondered if the flowers were omen or promise.

Chapter 18: Training for Vengence

"Two weeks may temper steel; two years may temper men. But prophecy tempers only through trial, and it cares little for the measure of time." —From the Oracle of Ashfall

The Sanctuary woke before the sun.

And for weeks now, so had she.

Eliryn rose in the thin gray light, before the fires stirred and before the Kin's wings shadowed the sky. It had become ritual—sleep, train, eat, train again.

When her muscles burned, she trained through it. When her mind wandered to Malric, she hit harder. It was the only rhythm that made sense anymore.

The days since that first meeting had blurred into motion and silence: Garrion's relentless drills; Vaeronth's wordless approval and equally wordless challenges; the high, cold air that stripped her lungs clean as they flew through the sky. There had been no second audience with the traitor beneath the mountain. She'd avoided it. Not out of fear, but because the fury still lived too close to the surface, and she refused to give him the satisfaction of seeing it.

She braided her hair tight, pulling until her scalp ached. The sting grounded her. She had learned the ache was proof of progress; pain made into purpose. She dressed in the training garb the Kin kept leaving for her, dark fabric scuffed and mended in places now that it was hers, no longer just borrowed.

You're awake early, Vaeronth murmured through their bond, his voice a lazy curl of smoke.

Earlier every day, she thought back.

A low rumble of approval rolled through her chest. *Good. The realm won't wait for you to feel ready.*

"Then it will have to keep up," she muttered, and stepped into the corridor.

The air outside carried the taste of stone and cold metal. The Sanctuary hummed faintly with the sounds of distant wings, the clatter of weapons, and the steady rhythm of a place that had never known idleness. She passed a handful of Kin already sparring under torchlight; their movements were shadows caught between heartbeats. None looked her way. Respect, or indifference—she couldn't tell, and maybe didn't need to.

By the time she reached the training court, the sky was only beginning to pale. Garrion was already waiting, as always, as if he'd never stopped. His presence was gravity; silent, immovable, and absolute.

"Dragonrider," he greeted. The title still landed heavy, a crown she hadn't learned to wear without wincing.

"Morning," she said.

He handed her the training pole without ceremony. "Let's begin."

The stance came easier now. Feet rooted. Shoulders loose. Breath steady. Her body knew what to do before her mind caught up. Garrion's strikes weren't as merciful as they once were; they carried the weight of expectation now. He didn't train her as a fledgling anymore. He trained her as someone who might soon be *followed*.

"Again," he said when she faltered.

"I've done this a hundred times," she panted.

"Then do it a hundred and one. Rulers don't stop when it hurts."

"I'm not—" She bit the word back. *Not yet,* she thought instead.

When she finally found rhythm again, something clicked. The poles met with clean, resonant sound. The runes on the floor flickered brighter, then held their glow. Garrion's nod was subtle, but it felt like victory.

He lowered his weapon. "Sky."

The word no longer filled her with dread but it still woke something deep and electric in her chest.

Vaeronth's shadow cut across the courtyard a moment later, wings outstretched against the dawn. He landed with surgical precision, the impact shuddering through the stone.

We go easy, he said.

Eliryn smiled despite herself. "Which means what it always means."

Hard enough to make you wish you'd stayed in bed.

She laughed—short, sharp, and real—and climbed the ladder of his foreleg. The air bit cold, the wind sang high in the bones of the mountain. For the first time in weeks, she let herself breathe deep.

Above the Sanctuary, the world opened wide, light spilling over endless stone and sky. Below her, the Kin moved like a living tide. Every one of them preparing. Watching. Waiting.

For her.

Eliryn's grip tightened as Vaeronth spread his wings. The world tilted. The air rushed past, fierce and bright.

She wasn't ready. Not yet.

But she was learning what readiness felt like.
And this time, she would not falter.

Interlude 3: Malric

"Even stripped of shadow, obsession does not fade—it only waits for a new shape to fill." —Unknown

He had learned to measure time by the breath of the mountain.

It sighed in these corridors—long, low exhalations that threaded through the seams of stone and the joints of the ironwork. Sometimes the sound was a rumor, sometimes a weight. Down here it was a patient pressure that made the torches waver and the skin on his forearms tighten.

Malric stood rather than sit. The bench was too low and too damp; the chill took to the bones and lingered. He preferred the wall, shoulder pressed to it, hands loosely bound in front so the guards could tell themselves he was contained. Across the passage, two of the stone sentinels, creatures he'd once filed under fable and folklore, watched without blinking. Their eyes weren't quite like gems or fire. They were... mineral. Depth caught in a hard body.

Gargoyles, his mind supplied, tasting the old word with a new, involuntary respect. Not statues. Not temple dogs. Something that had never belonged to the stories the citadel sold to children.

He flexed his fingers and felt, again, the ghost of a ring that was no longer there.

Silence where there should have been a hum. No percussive throb of borrowed strength. The absence thrummed so completely it almost made a sound of its own.

How long has it been?

Time had blurred in the way it always did when he had nothing to hunt. He had slept in shards. He had eaten when a tray slid through. He had cataloged the way these stone people moved. He had tracked boot-falls and torch changes and the faint metallic whisper of runes along the corridor's spine. None of it added up to days. Time had no shape here.

It was easier to count by the afterimages: the moments since she'd last come.

She'd spoken like someone balancing a blade on the tip of a finger—careful, steady, aware that one breath too much would topple everything. He had watched her without the ring's fever scalding his gaze and it had unsettled him, the way clarity did after a long hallucinatory night. He had seen the faint glow of the markings along her throat and wrists, the defensive wit she wore like chain under silk, the way she braced herself not against him but against the world that had repeatedly tried to unmake her.

She had looked strong.

You did that, the ugliest part of his mind said, toneless. *You made her stronger by breaking her.*

Malric shut his eyes until breath was the only thing left. In. Out. The stone's cool surface against his back, the leather of his bindings creaking when his wrists subtly turned. No ring. No extra pulse. Just his own heartbeat.

The guards across from him shifted their stance together, a minute adjustment that most men would have missed. Malric filed it. The way their weight went to their heels said readiness, not boredom. The way their chins lifted said someone important was moving nearby. He could have smiled.

Old habits: build a map from what others show you without meaning to.

He opened his eyes and found the cell's world exactly as it had been: the runed lintel, the bars that looked ornamental but were not, the seam in the floor where water had once found a path and worn it smooth. Even here, in the belly of a fortress built into mountain bone, there were signs of flood and ebb. The world was always trying to move.

He rolled his shoulders once to ease the ache.

Without the ring, his body felt lighter and more honest about its pains. The healing wasn't so immediate; the bruises announced themselves. His ribs remembered the last time he'd met a winged fist, his knuckles the last time he'd repaid it. The clarity wasn't a mercy, but it was... true. The ring had been a lie he'd mistaken for a promise. A power he'd thought he had earned because he had carried it so long.

Decades of influence, he corrected himself.

He could still see it when he closed his hand: bone-white, the grain like fossilized lightning frozen in a circle. Thalen had pressed it into his palm the way a priest pressed a relic into a supplicant's. *Wear this. Serve the realm. Be more than a man.* Thalen's smile had been the shape of a blade sheathed in velvet.

He had not questioned it because the ring had done what it promised and more. His shadows grew longer. His footsteps became less than whispers. He could strike through a man and be gone before his blood graced the floor. Hunger had become philosophy: the clean belief that ends justified means if the ends were written by his hand.

So why does breath feel simpler now?

Because the hum has stopped. Because the compulsion is gone. Because there's space where there was pressure, thought where there was only need. Because for the first time since he could remember, he wanted something and it did not immediately turn to obsession.

His mind turned inevitably towards her. *Eliryn.*

He did not say her name aloud. He wasn't sure it was a name men were meant to speak often. He thought it instead, and the thought didn't come like claws. It came like a hand he could almost take.

The guards across the corridor angled their heads at once. There—the sign. Footfalls, two sets: one heavy, deliberate; the other lighter, matching it for pace. Not a march. Not a rush. A procession that did not need to announce itself louder than the runes already would.

He turned his face slightly toward the corridor, showing the sentinels that he could hear what they heard, that he wasn't pretending ignorance. One of them—broad across the shoulders, the mineral sheen of his skin threaded with pale veins—met Malric's gaze for the first time. Not a challenge. A test.

Malric did not look away.

In another world, he might have marveled at their nature. In this one, he was their enemy.

The step-pattern shifted as the approaching pair rounded the last turn. The torchlight changed character with them—less flicker, more steady presence, as if the flames knew who moved beneath them.

She came first into view.

Not an apparition in a doorway, not a recollection realized. A woman in dark, practical clothes whose braids hung damp against her shoulders, whose runes pulsed at a low, unhurried rhythm beneath her skin. Her blindness had not receded from her eyes, but it did not hollow them. There was something in their set—calm, direct—that made the word sightless feel like a child's insult for a god.

The air in the corridor seemed to lift when she stopped.

Behind her, the big one—stone-carved and severe, the one who moved like he meant to outlast weather—took up his place a half-step back and to the right. *Protector*, Malric thought.

"Eliryn," Malric said out loud, not needing the ring to feel her name drag a little at his ribs. He forced a smile, crooked and practiced, something that could be mistaken for courtesy if you'd never seen him use it to wound. "You look evolved."

Her head tilted, listening past the words for the blades inside them. He felt the old reflex—press, press, keep pressing until you learn the soft parts—but the reflex didn't take. He let the space be.

"You're different," she said simply.

"Am I," he countered, and this time it wasn't deflection so much as invitation. *Was he?* Had he changed, or had a fever broken and left him exactly what he'd always been?

Her gaze held him without flinching. The runes at her throat kindled slightly, like stars catching a wind. "Yes."

The guards slid the door aside. The iron sang once against stone and then stopped, an old sound that knew its place in a ritual. Malric did not lunge. He did not even step forward. He stood where he was and let the weight of her presence reset the room like the first stillness after a storm.

He did not reach for the ghost of a relic that was no longer on his finger.

Malric inclined his head. "Then I will try something I have not tried in a very long time," he said, the words feeling wrong even as he shaped them. Like testing his tongue on a nearly forgotten language. "Honesty."

The stone warrior behind her didn't relax. Of course he didn't. Malric hadn't expected him to. Good. Let the sentinel weigh every breath he took.

She stepped closer to the threshold, into the strip of light where torch-flame met rune-glow. She didn't shrink from the bars or from him. She didn't reach for them either. She simply stood, framed in that strange, fractured brightness. "All right," she said. "Begin where you think you should."

He didn't know if he could. The silence that had replaced the ring's hum pressed in, sharp-edged and restless. Yet it didn't feel like emptiness. It felt like space. Room enough, perhaps, to try.

The bars looked decorative, but he knew better. The runes layered into the iron could hold things far older, far stronger than him. Still, the sight of himself behind them made something sour twist in his gut. She was seeing him clearly now—without fever, without obsession clouding the edges. He wondered what she saw.

He leaned closer, shadows draping around him like a cloak. "You're disappointed," he said, voice low, laced with the dangerous charm that came to him too easily. "You thought I'd be broken in here. Hollowed out." His mouth curved. "I'm not."

Her answer came flint-sharp. "You tried to kill me, Malric."

The words cut. His eyes closed for a beat, as if that small mercy could dull the truth. When he opened them again, the storm-dark in his gaze was unguarded. "Yes." Nothing more. No excuse. Just the weight of stone.

"You should be dead," she pressed. "The Kin wanted to tear you apart the moment you were dragged through their wards. Vaeronth wanted it too."

He remembered the dragon's fury, the way its rage had licked across his skin like fire when he was discovered outside the wards of the Sanctuary. Malric should be ashes by now for that alone. "But you wanted me here," he said, voice soft as confession. "They listened to you. Even the dragon bent, because you—" His words snagged in his throat. "You said I could be useful. You gave me another breath."

She looked at him like the act had been a mistake. He almost agreed. Still, he tilted his head and let a slower smile edge across his mouth, one that felt unique in its fragility. "Because you know I won't lie to you twice."

"Then tell me what I want to know," she said at last. "What brought you here?"

The old mask slid into place, bone-deep hunger and sharpened cruelty carved into his features. But only for a heartbeat. Then it cracked, and the truth bled raw.

"You."

Her face tightened. He knew what she was thinking. That it was obsession, not answer. She wasn't wrong. His hand twitched against the bar where the ring had once gleamed. "It was an obsession," he admitted, the taste of ash in his mouth. "The ring burned it into me. Twisted what I felt until it consumed me. I couldn't breathe without your shadow pressed over mine. I couldn't think past wanting to own you. It was a sickness."

The admission scraped him hollow.

"And now?" she asked.

He let himself really look at her. The clarity stung. "Now I see. Without it, I can finally see. And what I see is this: you are more than a girl who escaped my blade. More than the dragon who chose you. You are the prophecy they whispered about in the old halls. The one they thought would never come."

She shook her head, defiance cutting sharp in her voice. "You don't get to decide what I am."

Malric leaned back, spreading his hands in mock surrender. "No. But I can recognize what stands in front of me." His mouth twisted, haunted. "And maybe I can tell you what hunts you, because I know it better than anyone. Thalen doesn't only want control. He wants what he's already begun." His gaze caught on her runes, and something ugly flickered in his chest—guilt, maybe even envy. "And you'll need more than dragons and stone guardians to stop him."

The words rang with a truth that cost him to speak.

Her silence dragged, weighted. At last she said, "If you want me to believe you, Malric, you'll give me every name. Every plan. Every hidden piece you know."

He almost applauded her, but instead he felt his face shift into a grim smile instead. "Then you'll have to keep me alive."

Chapter 19: The Edge of War

"When the realm forgets, it is the few who remember that must carry its fire." —The Testament of the Last Watcher

The Sanctuary had grown quieter since Eliryn's last meeting with Malric.

Quieter, but not calmer.

Gargoyles spoke in low tones when she passed. Sentries on the heights straightened as she walked beneath them, eyes tracking not only her steps but the dark shadow that circled endlessly overhead. Even the wind seemed tauter, its whistle through the canyon sharper, edged with expectation.

Eliryn had thrown herself into training to fill the silence.

Mornings were for flight—hours spent high above the peaks, the thin air burning in her lungs as Vaeronth drove her through maneuvers until she could feel every shift of his wings like her own heartbeat. Afternoons belonged to Garrion and the courts, the crack of poles against poles ringing through the air until bruises bloomed beneath her sleeves. Evenings were for magic—her runes glowing in rhythm with her pulse, her breath a thread of focus as she tried to master the vast, unpredictable power that waited just beneath her skin.

Eat. Train. Breathe. Sleep.

Repeat until the ache became the only thing she trusted.

But no matter how many hours she gave the mountain, her thoughts always circled back—to Malric's face, to the blade that had ended her, to the prophecy whispering that her death had only been the beginning.

She walked the outer path that traced the Sanctuary's cliffs, the wind tugging at her braids, the canyon yawning below like a wound carved into the earth.

Morning light caught in the runes etched along the walls, making them flicker faintly as she passed.

Have the scouts returned? she asked, her voice half in thought, half aloud.

For a moment, there was only wind—the rush of air over scales, the distant thunder of wings cutting through thin sky. Then Vaeronth's reply settled into her mind, heavy as heat and just as steady.

Some. The city shifts like smoke. Each day brings new banners; each night, new fires. There is still a lot to be learned.

She frowned, scanning the distant haze where the horizon blurred. "So the rebels might still be alive. Or gone."

Both possibilities are dangerous, he answered. *Hope breeds recklessness. Despair breeds surrender. Until we know which remains, we hold our ground.*

"Waiting doesn't win wars," she said quietly.

No, he agreed. *But neither does striking blind. The gargoyles mark their paths and listen for the hidden voices. The moment we know more, we will move. Not before.*

His voice was calm, but beneath it she felt the same pulse that lived in her own chest—a hunger for motion, for action, for something other than endless preparation. The kind of restlessness that came from knowing what needed to be done but not yet being allowed to do it.

She stopped at a bend in the path that overlooked the canyon. The world below shimmered with distance, the far-off city of Vireth little more than a smudge beyond the horizon. She imagined its towers, the gilded citadel, the empty marketplaces. All of it still under Thalen's heel.

"What does it even look like?" she murmured. "Taking back the crown. Saving what's left of the realm's magic. I know what we're training for—but I don't know what it *looks* like."

Vaeronth's shadow rolled over her, swallowing the light. His reply came low, deliberate.

It looks like blood on stone. It looks like choosing who survives and living with the names of those who don't.

Her throat closed around the words. "So I become an executioner."

You become a ruler, he corrected. *And sometimes, those are the same thing.*

She turned her gaze skyward, toward the jagged peaks. "I was raised to heal, to study. Not to cut throats and call it mercy."

And yet you exist to do what others could not, he said. *Every strike Garrion drills into you, every scar you earn—it is not to delight in killing. It is to ensure that when death is the only path forward, you will walk it without flinching. That is the price of leadership.*

The wind whipped harder, flinging her braid against her shoulder. "You sound certain."

I am certain of you. His voice softened like a sigh through her bones. *You have already chosen to fight. The rest will come when it must. When you act, you will not hesitate. And afterward, you will grieve. That is what it means to lead and not to rule.*

Her chest tightened. She wanted to argue, but there was a steadiness in his conviction she couldn't break. "Then we stay the course," she whispered.

Always.

The scrape of claws on stone interrupted their conversation.

Two gargoyle scouts descended from the cliffs above, wings folding close with practiced ease. Dust rolled in small clouds around their feet. Behind them came Garrion, his stride slow but certain, the weight of his presence cutting through the morning calm.

"Eliryn," he said, the title that followed a stone in his mouth. "Dragonrider."

She turned, pulse quickening. "What is it?"

The first scout bowed his head, voice rasping from the wind still caught in his throat. "We bring news—from beyond the Sanctuary walls."

Every instinct in her body went still. "What news?"

"An announcement from Vireth," the gargoyle said. "Sovereign Vraxxis, speaking for King Thalen. A public execution, to be held within the week."

The words dropped into the canyon like stones, and her world tilted after them. "Who?"

The second scout hesitated. "A prisoner. The name was... Stonewell? Stonefell? Something like that."

For a moment, she didn't understand what she was hearing. Then her breath vanished.

"*Garic.*"

The name scraped free of her throat, half prayer, half disbelief. The air around her seemed to collapse.

She hadn't allowed herself to think of him in quite some time. She had remembered how he had stepped in between herself and certain death. She had buried that memory in the dark places where she kept her grief.

Now it clawed its way out.

"He's alive," she whispered. "He's *alive?*"

The words cracked open something she hadn't realized she'd sealed shut. A sound echoed above—a roar so massive it shook the cliffs. Vaeronth's fury thundered across the canyon, his wings cutting arcs through the sky. Dust shivered loose from the heights; the gargoyles around her lifted their heads, eyes flaring gold.

"Eliryn." Garrion's voice was steady but hard as forged metal.

She shook her head, breath trembling. "He should've died that night. I thought he *did* die. He—he stood between me and the blade. In front of Malric's blade." Her voice broke. "If he's alive, then he's been suffering. He's been suffering all this time."

"Not because of you," Garrion said, sharp and certain. "Because of a crown that devours its own. Because of a king who cannot stand against the weight of his own sins."

But the words didn't stop the guilt from bleeding through her ribs. Garic—her friend, her ally—rotting in a cell while she trained in secret.

Her knees threatened to give, but before she fell, a shadow appeared beside her. Druven. He didn't touch her, didn't speak. But his presence—solid, silent, immovable—anchored her back to herself.

"They'll kill him," she whispered. "They'll make a spectacle of it. They'll hang him before the people, call him traitor, and then call it justice."

Garrion's gaze turned to the horizon, stone-hard. "Then we remind them what justice truly is."

Vaeronth's voice filled her again, molten and unyielding.

Do not let grief scatter you, Little Flame. Grief scatters armies before blades ever touch flesh. If he lives, if he has endured, then it was not so you could drown now.

Her hands curled into fists, the ache grounding her. She lifted her chin, breath steady.

"Garic stood between me and death once," she said, voice low but sure. "Now it's my turn to do the same for him."

Garrion inclined his head. "We have less than a week."

Eliryn looked toward the sky where Vaeronth circled—dark and vast and waiting.

"We'll bring him home," she said.

The vow left her soft, but the cliffs carried it, echoing back through the canyon like a promise forged in fire.

For a long moment, she stood there, listening to the mountain breathe—the distant clang of forges, the murmur of wings, the pulse of runes alive beneath the stone. The Sanctuary felt like her home now.

Not because it was safe, but because it had made her strong enough to leave it.

She drew one more breath of cold, clean air and lifted her chin to the wind. Whatever waited beyond these cliffs—blood, war, prophecy—it would meet her on her own terms.

Chapter 20: Ashes of Resolve

"There is no cruelty sharper than memory, no weight heavier than regret." —The Codex of Ash and Flame

She tried to sleep. She couldn't. The chamber felt packed too tight—bed, chest, walls, the sound of her own breathing sitting heavy in her throat. After the third time she turned her pillow over and stared at the ceiling, she got up, pulled on boots and a plain tunic, and went to the balcony.

Cold air hit the heat in her face and did what it could. She braced her hands on the stone rail and tried to slow her thoughts. That didn't work either.

Above, Vaeronth turned in a slow, wide circle. He didn't speak at first. He knew when silence did more work than words. When he did reach for her, it was steady, like someone reaching out a hand.

You are awake.

"Can't stop thinking," she said. Her voice sounded rough, as if she'd been crying. She hadn't. "It keeps starting over. The Rite. The rebels. The panic and confusion as Malric tried to kill me. And then Garic appearing when I needed him most."

He is a noble man, Vaeronth said.

"I know," she said. "I still can't—" She stopped. "I keep hearing the fight from that night. Steel and the scrape of boots as I tried to get outside the corridors, tried to get to a space where you could be free. In that moment it felt like the only thing I could do, but—"

There was a long beat where the only sound was the wind moving past the cliff. When he spoke again, it was quiet.

You did not know. That does not make you faithless. It makes you human.

She let out a breath and felt it shake apart halfway through. She steadied it on the next one. "I keep thinking if I had asked different questions, earlier, I might have learned this sooner." She rubbed her thumb along a chip in the rail. "I keep thinking I abandoned Garic."

At the time, he gave us the only escape, Vaeronth said. *You were dying. There was no going back if we were to survive.*

She swallowed. "Malric knew. He could have told me the first day I walked into that cell and spoke to him. He didn't. He sat inside silence and counted how I reacted to not knowing."

He uses silence as a tool.

"It still feels like a kind of cruelty," she said.

It is a cruelty.

She nodded once. For a while she listened to Vaeronth's wings above her, not loud at this height, just present.

"I don't know how to look at Malric and not—" She ran out of words. It wasn't rage exactly. It was bigger and messier than that. Anger, yes. Hurt. Embarrassment. Relief so sharp it felt like it would cut through her if she gave it room. And under all of it, the same hard fact: whatever she felt, he had information she needed, and Garic's time was being counted out by other hands.

You do not need to be empty to act, Vaeronth said. *You only need to be able to carry feeling and still move your feet.*

"That sounds like something you say to fledglings who think waiting to be fearless is wisdom," she said.

It is something I say to anyone who bleeds and keeps going.

She made a sound that might have been a laugh if there had been humor in it. There wasn't. She was grateful for the steadiness of his tone. She kept her eyes on the far dark where Vireth would be; she tried to hold it at a distance, just a place on the horizon.

"Tomorrow," she said. "I have to go speak with Malric again... though I don't want to."

But you will.

She closed her eyes at that, just for a second, like the words put a hand to the center of her chest. "I will." She agreed. "Garic saved my life. I can't leave him to die for it."

The reason is simple, Vaeronth agreed.

She set her arms on the rail and let her chin rest there a moment. The stone was cold and it helped. "When I walked into Malric's cell last time, he watched me like he was measuring out pieces. Just taking stock. Without the ring, the fever was gone from his face. He looked... not harmless. Just more human."

Because you don't want to find anything about him redeemable, Vaeronth said.

She didn't answer. He was right, and admitting it wouldn't change anything tonight.

A breeze lifted hair from her cheek and laid it back. She felt very awake. Not frantic anymore. Just awake and exhausted in the same breath. There was no place to put the guilt that made it lighter. It would ride with her.

"Do you think I'm being foolish, trying to use him?" she asked.

No, Vaeronth said. *But I want you to be prepared for more hurt where he is concerned.*

She let out a breath she hadn't realized she was holding. "I won't trust him this time. That should cure any additional hurt."

Vaeronth's presence moved higher, then lower, catching a different current. He never went far enough that she lost sight of him.

They didn't speak for a while. The night had a hinge in it where everything felt like it was holding breath. She stood in it and tried to match it.

"I need to say something out loud once," she said, keeping her eyes on the far dark. "Then I'll be done for tonight."

Say it.

"I'm angry at Malric for knowing," she said. "I'm angry at myself for not asking harder. I'm ashamed I trained and ate and slept while Garic was in a cell, even though I didn't know. I feel like my life got bought with his and I spent it, and now I have to account for what I bought. And I am afraid of walking into that cell and seeing the way Malric looks at me when I say Garic's name."

All valid things, Vaeronth said. *But none of that stops you.*

"No," she said. "It doesn't."

She let her hands fall from the rail and rubbed warmth back into her fingers. *Enough.* Talking had taken her as far as it could.

He circled once more, a slow turn. *I will be where you can reach me.*

"I can always reach you," she smiled. Their link had become the one steady thing that didn't ask for anything before it gave back. It still scared her sometimes.

She stayed on the balcony until the raw edge of the cold dulled enough that she could feel her fingertips again. Then she went inside. She splashed water on her face, then stood with the towel in her hands a long time before dropping it over the chair. She retied her braid tighter, not because it needed it but because the small, exact motions gave her back a kind of control.

She didn't lie down. The bed had turned against her the minute she'd tried to close her eyes. She sat on the edge with her feet flat on the floor and her hands on her knees. She let her breath get as even as she could make it. This wasn't rest so much as preparation. It was enough.

She made herself think through the morning: she would go to Malric and stand where the torch couldn't throw his face into shadow; she would ask for routes and bells and doors and drains; she would ask where Vraxxis liked to stand; she would ask who the guards checked and who they ignored; she would ask why he held back the truth of Garic's survival; she would not argue; she would not apologize. She would leave with what she needed.

A thin gray showed at the edge of the balcony door. Dawn was not here, but it was on its way. She stood, because she had promised herself she would when she saw that light. She pulled on her leathers and the heavier boots.

She opened the balcony door a hand's width to feel the change in the air. It had that early cold that thinks it might be kind and then isn't.

She looked down once toward the lower levels, toward the row of cells two floors below. She pictured the path. She pictured the way Malric's head tilted when he was listening to himself think.

She didn't look at the bed again. She waited in a chair by the wall instead, back straight, palms open, counting slow until the gray at the sill shifted toward pale. When it did, she stood.

It would not be enough to be brave.

It would be enough to be honest and precise.

Interlude 4: Malric

"The line between ruin and salvation is not strength, but choice." —Veyra Stoneblood, Protector in the Age of Fire

The cell had no windows. A slit high in the stone let the mountain push cold air through. Malric counted the hours by that draft—thin at dawn, heavier at night. The rest of time slurred. The day she left could have been yesterday or a week.

Without the ring the noise in his head quieted. Thoughts came straighter now; they did not coil until heat behind his eyes forced him to act without thinking. Clarity brought new things: guilt that had not fit before, the names he could not pull from memory, a small, sharp emptiness where certainty used to sit.

He thought about Eliryn. Not how she had been in the citadel—blood-gray and bent under a blade—but how she stood the last time she'd come: the runes along her skin steady, voice even. That steadiness had not made the mark she left any lighter. If anything, it made him more aware of the wound.

The draft changed. He felt it more than heard it—a shift in the corridor outside, boots measured and single. His chest tightened without permission.

She came alone.

That surprised him. Guards usually walked with her. That she came without a protector made the visit real in a way rank and ceremony never could.

She stopped at the bars. Rune-light made angles on her face. She did not look smaller for being alone; she looked sure.

"You came back," he said.

"Yes." She didn't soften. "I came to ask questions and to get what I need."

He watched her. He could have made himself sharp—sardonic, measured, the soldier who habitually wore malice like armor. Instead he let his voice be plain. "Ask what you need to."

She folded a scrap in one hand. "Routes, bells, guards that will look and won't see. The square. Vraxxis' position. If you help me, we might get someone out of that place."

He let that land. The word someone struck him the way knives used to: precise, immediate. "You want to use me," he said.

"You have information I don't," she answered. "I need it faster than I need to punish you."

The honesty in that was worse than any barbed question.

She folded her arms. "Do you know why Thalen did what he did—using dragonbone in his rings?"

"No." He did know more than he had before, but not that. "I knew he butchered things to get their power. I smelled it in the lower halls. I heard the machines they kept down there, the sounds that do not belong in any hall that holds people. I didn't know he turned bone into band."

"Do you think there are living things under the citadel?" she asked.

"Yes." He felt the answer in his ribs like an old bruise. "Old things with magic the crown thinks is useful."

She wrote the single word he said and kept her eyes on him. "Can you draw where they might be kept?"

He thought of lines in dust and of stairs that did not follow on a map. "I can mark what I remember.

Wards, traps, rooms that drink light. I don't know what's changed, but I'm sure the bones of it are the same. I can point you where pressure gathers."

She didn't soften. "Why help me this willingly?"

"Because if enough breaks, the tool Thalen made me into becomes useless. So that maybe I can be free."

She listened like a ledger being balanced. "Selfish reasons," she said. "Your own utility."

"Yes." He let the word be stark. "I don't seek forgiveness. I seek to be of use in a way that stops him."

She asked for practical notes, not the map of every alley. He pared what he gave her down to what would matter in the first hours: where the scaffold would be likely placed, where visibility narrowed, which parts of the square would be kept open to feel free but actually be corral. He spoke of how the city staged spectacle and where guards habitually left blind patches because routine made them blind.

She wrote. She asked the sharp questions about exits and where the plan would likely fall apart.

When she paused, watching him, he said something she hadn't asked for.

"I want to go with you."

He watched the movement of her face. She was careful—measured—before she answered. "You want to be there when we advance on the citadel?"

"Yes." The admission was small and fierce. "I can read the guards in ways you can't. I know where someone will step to check a street because I used to be the man who put them there. I know the corridors under the citadel better than anyone who walks it for the king. I want to see him fall. I want me to be the witness that I once was not."

She did not say no immediately. That steadied him and scared him. He pushed on, honest in a way he hadn't allowed in a long time.

"I know I am a risk," he said. "I know what I was. I am not asking out of bravado. I am asking because I believe I can make a difference where planning and experience meet chance."

There was more under that: a plea not to be left to sit and fester in his shame if he could actually act. He imagined the taste of doing something that helped, instead of only thinking about what he had taken.

Finally she spoke.

"I'll consider it," she said.

They worked through smaller things—timing windows, where to test signaling, possible choke points—enough to make a plan take its first honest shape, not a thousand details that would trip them up in confusion. He kept the specifics brisk; he'd learned that too many facts could drown a plan just as easily as too few.

At one point she looked straight at him. "You almost killed me," she said. Plain. "I remember how it felt to die because of you."

"I know," he said. "I am ashamed of it. I am ashamed that I let a man like Thalen tell me what to be. I do not ask you to forgive me." n

"Then be useful," she said. Simple as that.

When the list thinned, she closed the scrap and folded it into her sleeve. She looked at him with a concentration that felt like weight. "Garic is alive," she said.

The name pushed the air out of him. He had held it like a hot thing and wrapped shame around it. "He is," he said. "I knew that he might be useful later, because of his connection with you."

"Is his execution a trap?" she asked.

"Yes," he said. "But it's a trap shaped to look like law and order. He will count on people to show. He won't count on you showing up on the day it's supposed to happen. That's the advantage you can take: move on them when they least expect it."

She folded her hands. "If I get him out and he's alive, we bring him home. If he isn't—"

"You'll take it out on me," he assumed.

She looked at him like she was measuring a new line on her list. "Yes."

He hesitated, then added what he had been holding back. "If I go with you, I do it because I want to see what I can do to undo what Thalen made me. Not for absolution. Not for thanks. If I fail, I accept the consequences."

She was quiet a long moment. Then she nodded once. "Then we understand each other."

She stood and backtracked from the bars. The draft shifted around her as she moved. Dawn hadn't come, but it pressed at the edge of the sky. He heard the weight of her steps recede.

He sat and, because the motion steadied him, traced lines in the dry dust of the floor—turns, doors, stairs that did not belong on simple maps.

When he was done he leaned his head back against stone and touched the empty groove on his hand—the place the ring had sat. "Different," he said into the dark, the word a promise to himself more than anything else. "Not absolved. Not better. Different."

Chapter 21: The Rite Resumes

"Two strengths shape a shield: one unyielding, one unwavering. Together, no blade can break them." —Saying of the Kin

Eliryn had delayed long enough.

Through firelit nights and sleepless councils, she had weighed her path. She had spoken with Garrion, who pressed duty like a blade, and with Vaeronth, whose mind brushed hers with the weight of stone and storm. It was time.

So she called the Kin.

The summons rolled through the sanctuary like thunder, pulling stone and flesh alike into the arena. The warriors came, magic thrumming in their veins, eyes bright with the hunger to prove themselves. The Rite had been halted once by Malric's breach, but it would not remain unfinished.

The stands filled with the dark shimmer of wings. The ward-runes glowed around the ring, steady and pulsing. Eliryn stood on the dais, every breath sharp under the weight of hundreds of gazes. The air itself seemed to hum with expectation.

The Rite waited.

The Kin waited.

And she would choose.

The herald raised his staff. Runes climbed its shaft like veins of fire. "Kin," he called, "the Third Phase begins of the Rite begins. Strength has been proven. Magic has been shown. Now the bond will be tested. No illusion. No mask. The truth of what lies within."

A low rumble moved through the tiers.

Vaeronth stepped forward onto the dais, wings arching wide, scales reflecting light in shades of molten silver. He lowered his neck toward her.

With me, he said.

Eliryn swallowed, fighting the urge to glance back at the gathered crowd. "In front of everyone?"

You practiced this for battle, not ceremony, he said, amused. *All the better that it serves both.*

"Right," she muttered. "Let's hope I don't face-plant in front of them."

You won't. You never do.

She climbed to his shoulders, muscles remembering every movement they'd drilled over weeks of training. His wings swept down, and the ground fell away. The roar of the crowd blurred into a single, living sound.

They circled once over the arena, the runes glowing brighter beneath them. Then Vaeronth banked low. Eliryn shifted her stance, heart hammering, and leapt.

The drop stole her breath for half a heartbeat. She hit the sand hard and clean, knees bending, landing solid. Straightening, she lifted her chin as the crowd's murmurs rippled through the space.

Graceful, Vaeronth murmured in her mind.

"Thank the gods for practice," she replied, forcing her heartbeat to slow.

The herald's voice carried again. "Dragonrider," he said. "To test the bond, you will extend your hand and your power. Each contender will do the same. The meeting of magics will reveal the truth. You will feel what is right. You will know."

Eliryn nodded once. "Understood."

The staff struck stone. "Step forward."

The first contender—a gray-skinned male with veins like molten iron—lifted his hand. His eyes glowed faint blue. Eliryn extended hers, letting her silver-blue power flow across her palm. When the magics met, the feel was distant—cool, smooth, without spark. She felt nothing stir.

Another came, eyes green, wings nicked from a dozen old fights. His power hit like warm air, pleasant but heavy. She met it, let it touch her, then drew back. The connection faded at once.

The next gargoyle's magic was jagged, rough-edged, smelling faintly of ozone. It scratched against her power and died there, like sparks in rain.

One by one, they came forward. She greeted each with the same calm precision—her face still, her voice silent. No one in the stands could see the faint tremor of light under her skin as she held her magic steady. It wanted to surge, to rise like a tide through her veins, but she kept it locked behind her breath.

To everyone else, she was composed. In control.

Only Vaeronth knew the truth.

Keep it centered, he warned, steady and low.

"I am," she answered. "Barely."

Barely is enough.

A dozen passed before the first female stepped forward—a dark basalt gargoyle whose name Eliryn couldn't recall. Her aura was sharp, violet-tinted, her eyes pale lilac. Their magic met in a hiss of heat, bright and fleeting, gone before Eliryn could form a thought. The female bowed and withdrew.

Then Meyra stepped into the circle.

Her gold-green skin caught the light. She didn't waste motion—just a clean step forward, eyes steady. When she lifted her hand, her magic spread like sunlight over water. Eliryn matched her, silver-blue meeting gold. The two energies twisted together for a breath—warm, sure, deeply alive.

Peace sank through her. Confidence. A steadiness she hadn't realized she'd been craving.

"I will not waver," Meyra said simply.

Eliryn believed her. She could see this woman as an ally, a confidant. A friend.

You like her, Vaeronth said, tone calm but knowing.

She's... solid. Good. The kind who would stand beside me and keep me grounded. Eliryn answered him through their bond.

It is one thing to be friends with someone, Vaeronth said, *another to trust them with your life. Meyra has skill, heart, and discipline—but she lacks a killer's edge. She will seek mercy first. And mercy, in battle, is a wound waiting to open.*

Eliryn didn't answer aloud, but the truth rang in her chest. She didn't doubt Meyra's strength—only whether it would always be enough.

More contenders followed, their magic swirling in every flavor of heat and cold, sweet and bitter. One's power was sharp as glass. Another's heavy as river stone. Each met her silver-blue briefly, flared, then dimmed.

And then—Druven.

The crowd fell silent the moment he stepped forward. He didn't bow. Didn't speak. Just extended his hand. His skin was darker than basalt, eyes the color of tempered steel.

Eliryn lifted her own. Their magic met in the space between.

The impact wasn't gentle. It felt like gravity locking into place—stone finding its fault line and settling. No heat. No spark. Just that instant, solid *fit*.

The ring's runes flared once, white-blue, then steadied.

His voice came, low and even. "I will do whatever it takes to ensure your survival. No matter the cost—to myself, to others, or to the realm."

The silence afterward was heavy. It wasn't boast or threat. It was fact.

Eliryn didn't answer. She only nodded once. Druven dipped his head in return, then stepped back into the line, every motion controlled, every breath deliberate.

Vaeronth's presence filled her mind again. *He would burn the world for you.*

"I know," she thought.

And he would not regret it.

She said nothing.

The last contenders stepped forward one by one, each extending a clawed hand, each meeting her silver-blue power and finding no purchase. A few had presence, one or two even confidence, but nothing *fit*.

The runes around the arena dimmed as the final warrior withdrew, and the herald's staff struck stone once more.

"The test is complete," he intoned, voice echoing through the ring. "The time to choose is now."

The crowd shifted, wings rustling. The sound was low, collective—expectant.

Eliryn stood in the center of the circle, hands still faintly aglow, heart beating a deliberate, measured rhythm.

Vaeronth's shadow moved along the dais above, a living mountain watching over her. His voice reached her mind—deep, coiled, steady as ever.

You have your answer.

She didn't speak aloud. *I have two.*

Two?

Yes. Her gaze slid between Meyra and Druven. *One who feels calm in the storm. And one who is the storm."*

Vaeronth's mind hummed in quiet thought.

Eliryn's pulse thudded in her ears. *Both of them would die for me,* she thought. *But only one would make sure I lived, no matter the cost.*

Vaeronth's tone softened. *Then you already know what you must say.*

She drew in one long, steadying breath. The weight of the choice settled across her shoulders.

She looked up at the herald, her voice carrying clear and even.

"It has been an honor," she said. Her silver-blue eyes caught the runelight, turning pale fire. "And I know what my decision is."

The sound that followed wasn't silence—it was the breath before a storm.

The Kin leaned forward as one.

Vaeronth's wings spread wide above her.

Eliryn stepped forward to speak her choice.

The decision settled into her bones like a key into a well-made lock. She tucked it there, secret for a breath longer, and when Vaeronth tasted it through the bond, he made a pleased, lethal sound that promised trouble for anyone who thought to argue.

CHAPTER 22: BEYOND TRADITION

"Second chances are the fire in which true loyalty is forged." —*The Songs of the Riders*

The arena thrummed with stillness.

Not the fragile kind that comes before applause, but the heavy, breath-held quiet of something about to change. Every gargoyle in the colonnades had gone motionless, obsidian claws biting faint grooves into the stone benches. Wings hung half-spread and unmoving. A thousand eyes—gold, ember, silver, onyx—fixed on her with a collective focus that burned.

Even the mountain seemed to listen. The carved arches loomed like witnesses of an oath older than speech. Rune-light guttered and caught, passing in ripples along the ring as though it, too, waited to record her choice.

Eliryn stood tall though her knees trembled. Her pulse hammered in her chest, the sound of her own blood too loud in her ears. It would have been easy to reach for Vaeronth through the bond—to let his steadiness shore her up—but she didn't.

This choice had to come from *her*.

When she spoke, her voice carried not only on the air but on the strange, terrible current that had lived inside her since death failed to claim her.

"I see you. All of you—the last of a people who should have passed into legend. Yet here you stand: unbroken, unyielding, willing to give your lives for mine. For a prophecy promised long ago, to save the realm's dying magic."

The words rang against the walls, echoing through the tiers.

Her throat tightened. She shook her head, caught her breath, and pressed on.

"You call me Dragonrider," she said softly, "but I have not earned that name. I am untested. Unworthy of your loyalty. And still, you offer it. That means more than I can say."

The hush deepened. Wings rustled. Stone shifted. A murmur like the grinding of distant cliffs rolled through the crowd.

She let the sound pass and lifted her hands, the faint light of her runes brightening with each word.

"Whoever stands at my side will not only guard me. I will guard them. Their oath will be mine, and mine theirs. More than duty. More than breath. It is bond. It is vow."

Silver-blue light coiled down her arms and through her hair. Though her eyes saw no color, their glow reflected in every watching gaze. The moment stretched, taut with expectation.

"Meyra of the Gold Vein," she said at last, her tone clear as struck steel.

The reaction was instant. Gasps, then cheers. Meyra stepped from the line, gold-green skin gleaming, braids swinging forward as she entered the ring. She didn't preen or falter; she dropped to one knee, palm to earth, head bowed.

"By watch and wing, by stone and oath—I will protect you," Meyra said, her voice rich and sure.

The Kin roared their approval. Dust rained from the high arches, the mountain answering in thunder. For a breath, Eliryn's chest eased. *She had chosen well.*

Beside her, Garrion leaned close, his tone a low rasp almost lost in the uproar. "You've made an excellent—"

She lifted a hand. Not harsh, but final.

"I am not finished."

The sound sliced clean through the noise. The uproar faltered, then collapsed into an echoing hush.

Eliryn drew a long breath. Heat rolled through the bond where Vaeronth waited—steady, immense, a living drumbeat.

"I am also choosing the one who has already acted as protector, even without the title. Druven."

She did *not* use the title they had branded him with.

For an instant, even the air seemed to recoil. Then the silence cracked open.

Gasps. Shouts. Outrage breaking like a storm. Gargoyles surged to their feet; wings snapped open in violent rhythm. Claws gouged the stone. Elders leaned forward, their carved faces split by disbelief.

"You would bind yourself to a murderer?" one bellowed.

"He is cursed!" cried another. "He brings death wherever he stands!"

The fury struck her from all sides, but she didn't flinch. Garrion moved on instinct, stepping before her, granite frame ready to block anything that came close. His jaw worked once, torn between fear and pride, but he supported her nevertheless.

Storm-gray wings folded tight, shoulders squared, he stood as though the uproar didn't touch him. Only his eyes betrayed anything—steel flashing, not with arrogance, but stunned disbelief.

As if it had never once crossed his mind that she might choose him.

Eliryn met that gaze. She thought of his brutal precision, his restraint misread as violence, the way his people had turned fear into condemnation. She thought of her own power—the way it could unmake as easily as it could save.

Perhaps that was why her decision felt so inevitable.

The Elders shouted again, demanding explanation, demanding reversal. Before she could answer, Vaeronth's voice slid through her chest like liquid flame.

Well done, Little Flame.

His pride filled her like heat, solid and grounding. It wasn't gentle; it was fierce, protective, and absolute.

The uproar raged on. Garrion stood beside her now, silent but firm. Meyra, still kneeling, lifted her gaze and rose—not in jealousy, but steady understanding, a quiet nod that said she would follow Eliryn's will wherever it led.

Eliryn drew one final breath and smiled—not small, not meek, but full and certain.

The mountain would remember this day; the moment the old oaths cracked, and a new kind of bond was born.

Interlude 5: Malric

"A knife may cut the hand that wields it, but in the right moment, even a cursed blade can turn a battle." —Fragment from *The Siege of Emberfall*

He heard them coming before he saw them.

Three sets of steps. One heavy enough to make the chains hum, one slow and even, one light but steady. He knew who each belonged to before they reached the cell. Druven. Meyra. And Eliryn.

Even in the depths of the mountain, whispers carried. *She chose two.* No one had believed it at first. Two protectors sworn to a single dragonrider. It went against everything the Kin had ever done.

Keys turned. Iron scraped. The torchlight shifted as they stepped into view. Malric stood.

Eliryn came forward first. Her runes glowed faintly, steady instead of wild now. Strength sat differently on her—less fury, more control. Druven followed, solid as a fortress wall. Meyra took position slightly behind her, posture calm, eyes sharp and watchful.

"Malric," Eliryn said.

"Dragonrider." He dipped his head slightly.

"I brought my protectors," she said. "You'll need to meet them properly before we take another step."

He glanced between the gargoyles. "So this is the part where I'm judged?"

Eliryn crossed her arms. "The Kin swear oaths when they're chosen. Magic binds those vows between rider and protector—it's how trust is kept. Since you're asking to stand with us, I want them to see you for themselves, and decide whether it's worth the risk to involve you further."

Druven's stare didn't shift. "If you lie, we'll know."

Malric gave a short nod. "Fair enough."

Eliryn stepped aside slightly. "Meyra, can you start with the plan?"

The gold-veined gargoyle nodded once, turning to Malric. "We've briefly gone over the maps you drew. The entry tunnels make sense, but we'll need more than a crawlspace if we're bringing a full strike team. The Kin can't move quietly through a hole meant for one man."

"You won't be bringing a full strike team," Malric said. "The citadel's not built for that kind of breach. The patrols overlap every seven minutes on the southern wall. You time it wrong, and they'll close the gates before your wings hit the courtyard."

Meyra frowned. "Then what do you suggest?"

"Three inside, no more," he said. "You, Druven, Eliryn. Small, fast, unseen until it's too late to stop."

Druven grunted. "You mean reckless."

"I mean possible," Malric said. "You want to move an army, fine. Just be ready to bury it under Vireth's walls when they collapse."

Meyra studied him for a long moment. "You sound certain."

"I spent years in that city. I know how it breathes. I know how its guards get lazy when they think the king's watching someone else."

She glanced toward Eliryn. "He's not wrong. Small teams move cleaner."

Druven's eyes narrowed. "Clean doesn't mean safe."

"Nothing about this will be safe," Eliryn said quietly.

The silence that followed carried weight. Even the torches seemed to burn slower.

Meyra refocused on Malric. "If we take your route, how do we reach the cells?"

"There's an old maintenance stair between the cisterns and the chapel vaults," he said. "No guards posted there anymore. They assume no one knows it exists."

"And you'll guide us?"

"Yes."

Druven shifted, stone grinding faintly. "And if this is another trap?"

Malric met his gaze. "Then you'll kill me before I take another step. I'd rather die here than under Thalen's leash again."

That landed heavier than he meant it to. For the first time, neither gargoyle looked ready to speak.

Druven's voice broke the silence, his tone clipped. "The same magic that ties us to you could hold him too. A vow, sealed by the Kin. He wouldn't be able to harm you, or act against your command. Not without the binding turning on him."

Meyra considered that. "It's possible. The Sanctuary's old magic still answers to blood and intent. The runes could take his promise."

Malric's brows drew together. "You're talking about a magical leash."

"Not a leash," Druven said. "Insurance."

Eliryn looked at him, calm but firm. "Would you agree to it?"

Malric didn't answer immediately. He thought of the ring—of what it had done, how it had chained him from the inside out. And now, here she was, offering another binding.

But this time, he could choose it.

"What would it do?" he asked. "Exactly."

Meyra answered. "It links your life to hers. If you act with the intent to harm her, or the mission, it will turn magic inward on you. Painful, but fast. It's old law—never meant for humans, but it can hold."

Druven's gaze was steady. "It's the only reason I'd walk beside you outside these walls."

Malric nodded slowly. "Fine. I'll do it."

Eliryn studied him. "You'd agree that easily?"

"Easily?" He let out a short, humorless laugh. "You think this is easy? I've lived half my life bound to something worse. At least this one's clean. I know what it's for."

Meyra's voice softened a fraction. "It's not meant to punish you."

"I know," Malric said. "It's meant to keep her alive. That's reason enough."

Druven's jaw flexed once, as if deciding how much of that he believed. "You'll take the vow at dawn. The Sepulcher is strong enough to hold it."

Meyra glanced between them. "The risk is worth it," she said at last. "If he's telling the truth, we gain more than we lose."

Druven gave a low grunt but didn't argue.

Eliryn stepped closer to the bars. "Then it's settled. At dawn, we go to the Sepulcher. You'll swear the vow, and the stone will judge the rest."

Malric nodded once. "Good."

"Good?" Meyra asked.

He met her eyes. "I'm tired of everyone guessing what I am. This'll make it clear."

The words hung there a moment before Eliryn turned to leave. The gargoyles moved with her, shadows folding back into the torchlight's edge.

When they were gone, Malric sat again on the stone bench. The silence closed in. He flexed his hand, still half expecting to feel the ring's bite.

This time, there was nothing. Only the weight of what he'd just agreed to, a weight he'd chosen himself.

Chapter 23: The Sepulcher of Oaths

"Not all betrayals end in ruin. Some are only the beginning of a better allegiance." —fragment from *The Book of Ash and Flame*

The cell doors shut behind them with a sound that echoed up the mountain's spine.

Eliryn didn't look back. The echo chased her anyway—iron, cold, and far too familiar.

Druven and Meyra flanked her in silence, steady as carved guardians. Their steps carried the faint grind of stone on stone as they climbed toward the upper galleries.

Garrion waited at the overlook, arms folded, his face half-cut by shadow. The runelight from the open arches painted his features in gold and ash.

Above, Vaeronth's shadow slid across the cliff face, vast and restless. *You are certain?* his voice rumbled through her mind, edged with heat.

Certain enough, she answered, though the idea of it scalded her.

Vaeronth's reply was a growl, low and molten. *You bring him into this again? After what he did?*

Eliryn stopped short of the steps. "He'll be bound," she said quietly. "The magic will hold him."

He killed you once, Little Flame. You think I forget the moment your heart stopped? Vaeronth landed silently beside the group.

The words struck deep, but she made herself meet the glow of his golden eyes. "I haven't forgotten either. That's why the vow matters. If he breaks it, the stone will end him before he ever reaches me."

He can hurt you without touching you.

The truth in that sat heavy in her chest. *Then I'll handle it. This isn't about trust—it's about the mission. We need him.*

Meyra spoke, her tone even and deliberate. "We've just come from his cell," she said to Garrion.

"He'll take the vow at dawn. The binding will anchor through the Sepulcher—same as ours. Once sworn, he won't be able to act against her or the mission without the magic itself turning on him. It's the safest path forward, given what he knows of the Citadel."

Garrion's gaze flicked between them, stone-still but thoughtful. The faintest muscle moved in his jaw, the sound of stone under strain.

Then his voice cut through the tension. "If the vow binds true, the risk is tolerable. The mountain's magic has never lied."

Meyra inclined her head. "He'll be under watch. The binding answers intent, not words. If he turns, it'll turn on him."

Druven's tone was level, but his eyes were flint. "Binding or not, I'll be watching him."

Eliryn gave a brief nod. "Then it's settled."

For a long moment, none of them spoke. The air between them pulsed with old magic, old grief.

Finally, Garrion broke the silence. "Dawn comes quick. The Sepulcher will be ready."

The night bled away faster than it should have.

By the time the first light spilled over the peaks, the air smelled of frost and stone and the faint metallic hum of awakened runes.

Eliryn stood near the cliff's edge, cloak tight around her shoulders. Vaeronth wheeled overhead, a great silhouette against the paling sky. His presence in her mind was quiet now, coiled but constant—ready if she needed him.

Behind her came the clank of iron. Garrion approached, flanked by two guards. Between them walked Malric.

He was without restraint, and his steps were steady, expression unreadable.

"The guards have gone over the words with him," Garrion said as they drew close. "He knows what he's to say. The Sepulcher won't tolerate mistakes."

Malric's gaze lifted. "Then I won't make any."

No one answered him.

Together, they made their way toward the arched passage where the mountain's heart waited. The runes carved into the stone flared softly as they neared, their light spilling across the floor in gold and white.

Garrion halted at the threshold and turned to face them. His voice carried, calm but weighted. "The Kin know their vows. They were born with the words in their throats. When they speak, the mountain listens. And it remembers."

He looked to Eliryn. "You are not required to speak. You are there to witness, to accept what is given. The Sepulcher records what is spoken."

Eliryn nodded, though something in her chest tightened. She knew her part, but it still felt wrong to give nothing back.

Druven and Meyra moved into position behind her, wings half-raised, eyes bright in the glow, and Malric remained where the guards placed him.

The runes at the door pulsed brighter, like a heartbeat beneath stone. Garrion pressed his palm against the carved sigil at the center. The magic answered, the great doors parting with a deep, resonant hum.

Light spilled out, alive and warm.

Eliryn stepped forward first. The others followed.

The Sepulcher opened before them like the inside of a living sun.

Runes crawled across every surface—some faint and old, others bright and raw. They spiraled up the curved walls to the open dome where dawn spilled in unbroken. The air shimmered with quiet power.

Vaeronth crouched above the rim of the dome, wings folded tight, eyes burning gold.

Eliryn walked to the center dais, her footsteps whispering over etched sigils. Every mark here was a memory, every line a promise carved into eternity.

The hum of magic rose as Druven and Meyra stepped forward. The sound of their wings opening filled the chamber, heavy and slow. When they spoke, their voices resonated through the stone itself:

"By stone unbroken, by wing unbowed, by fire that forges and flame that binds,
we swear our lives to the Last Dragonrider.

Her flesh is our charge, her spirit our shield,
until eye darkens, until wing breaks,
until the mountain itself is ash and dust.
So we are bound. So let it be."

The words struck the runes like hammer on steel. Light burst upward, racing along the walls in burning threads. Eliryn's breath caught at the weight of it—the vow wrapping around her, through her.

Tradition said nothing more was required. The guardians gave, the rider received. But she couldn't let it rest one-sided.

She lifted her chin and spoke, her voice steady but bright with feeling:

"By breath and blood, by flame and sky,
I swear to stand beside the Kin.
Not as shielded, but as sister.
Not as master, but as sworn comrade.
Your strength is my strength, your burden my burden,
until my last breath carries me to ash.
So I am bound. So let it be."

The chamber *answered*.

Light erupted across every surface, white and gold and fierce enough to blind. The runes surged, rearranging into a single sigil above the dais—a dragon's eye crowned with a starburst and crescent moon. The air vibrated until it hurt to breathe.

Above, Vaeronth let out a low growl that rolled through the chamber like thunder answering flame.

Then, as quickly as it had come, the brilliance faded. The runes settled. Three new marks glowed among the thousands—Druven's, Meyra's, and hers.

And then Malric was brought forward.

He looked smaller beneath the light. His eyes met hers briefly, and for an instant, she saw it again—the way he had looked at her in Vireth. Sword in hand. Eyes wild with devotion twisted into violence. The moment before everything went black.

Her heart stumbled, but she didn't step back.

Malric drew a long breath and began to speak. His voice wasn't ceremonial—it was bare, scraped clean of pride:

"By the blood I have left, by the breath still mine, I swear to stand with the Dragonrider and her Kin. I'll mend what I can. I'll pay for what I can't. If I break this vow, let the stone take me. Let it end me before I betray her. So I am bound. So let it be."

The Sepulcher listened.

The runes answered, but their light was muted—a smaller mark etched into the stone beside hers, jagged and uneven. Accepted. Not exalted.

Eliryn said nothing.

She gave him no mirrored vow, no absolution. The silence between them was heavier than any blade, and he bore it without protest.

The chamber stilled, holding the weight of all that had been spoken.

Garrion bowed his head. "The mountain has heard," he said quietly.

Eliryn's chest ached, but her voice was calm. "Then it's done."

Vaeronth's growl echoed faintly from above—displeasure, but acceptance too.

And for all of them, the weight of dawn had never felt heavier.

The light faded from the runes at last. The air was thick with the scent of stone and something faintly scorched—magic still burning off the edges of the vows.

They stepped back into the open air, the cold morning cutting through the lingering heat of the Sepulcher. The horizon had shifted from gray to gold; dawn had arrived in full.

But waiting at the cliff's edge were three scouts, cloaked in the dust of hard travel. Their wings twitched with exhaustion. Garrion stiffened at the sight of them.

The lead scout dropped to one knee before Eliryn, breath misting in the cold. "Dragonrider," he rasped. "Word from the valley."

Eliryn's pulse tightened. "Go ahead, Protector."

"The Citadel has moved the execution forward." The scout's voice was hoarse, scraped raw by the climb. "Garic of Stonefell is to die at midday tomorrow."

For a heartbeat, no one moved. Even the wind seemed to pause.

Meyra's wings lifted slightly, instinct more than thought. Druven's jaw flexed, stone grinding faintly in his throat.

Eliryn felt Vaeronth's presence snap sharp in her mind—rage and warning in equal measure. *They mean to draw you out.*

"Then they'll get what they wanted," she said quietly. Her voice was low, but it carried, steady and cold. "We move tonight."

The mountain seemed to shiver around them, as if the stone itself knew what that meant.

Interlude 6: Malric

*"A man cannot undo the path he walked in shadow, but
he can choose where to set his feet when the sun returns."*
—From *The Book of Flame and Ash*

Malric lay on the slab of stone they called a bed,
staring up into the dark that pressed close as breath.

Rest wouldn't come. The echo of the Sepulcher
still rang in his bones—the sound of vows binding, of
runes answering light with light.

He had spoken the words and made a vow.

Not under command. Not because a king demanded it.

Because he had chosen to.

That difference sat heavy in his chest—not a burden, but an anchor.

He drew a slow breath, remembering how the air in the chamber had tasted: iron and dust and the faint hum of power older than memory. The gargoyles' voices had shaken the stone, their oaths striking the walls like hammers. Then Eliryn's voice—steady, unflinching—had joined them, binding herself to the Kin as they bound themselves to her.

And then she had turned her eyes on him.

No hate. No mercy either. Just expectation.

Show me who you are now, her gaze had said.

He had done the only thing left: spoken truth. A vow made not from pride or fear, but from will.

It wasn't glory. It was gravity.

And he welcomed it.

He rolled onto his side, hands free for the first time since his capture. The skin of his wrists was still raw, faint red bands where the metal had lived for too long.

They had come for him before dawn.

The scrape of iron on stone had cut through sleep and memory alike. Malric had been awake before they reached the cell, his back stiff, his body cold to the marrow.

Two Kin guards filled the doorway, shoulders broad enough to block what little light the corridor offered. Their eyes caught the torchglow and threw it back in molten gold. He'd seen that look before—divine judgment dressed in mortal patience.

For a long time, neither spoke. The silence was a verdict in itself.

Then the larger of the two stepped forward, his voice a low, grinding thing that carried the weight of the mountain.

"Chains will not follow you into the Sepulcher."

Malric had lifted his head, uncertain if it was a threat or mercy.

The Kin's expression didn't change.

"The mountain will bind you instead. Defy your vow, and you'll beg for the weight of iron again."

The lock had turned. The cuffs had fallen.

He remembered staring down at his hands, pale and unfamiliar, the skin marked by years of restraint. Freedom felt like something borrowed. Dangerous.

When the other Kin shoved him toward the corridor, he hadn't resisted. The mountain itself seemed to hum with awareness, its stone veins whispering of old power and older promises.

"No need to fear his escape," one guard had murmured. "If he breaks faith, the mountain will unmake him."

And Malric had believed it.

Now, hours later, that vow sat deep in his bones.

It had settled something inside him—not peace, exactly, but a line drawn through the chaos.

It was strange how simple it felt: no oaths to a throne, no lies about destiny.

Only a promise to her.

Eliryn.

She was the shape of everything Thalen had tried to erase: fire, magic, hope. The sight of her standing beneath the runes, the dragon's shadow sweeping across the open dome—it had been enough to make even a man like him believe in beginnings again.

He had watched her as the power took hold, the runes blazing to life, her expression steady and solemn. He'd seen the small flicker of pain when his mark appeared beside hers. She hadn't looked away. She had accepted his vow without flinching, even knowing what he'd been. That alone was enough to unmake a man—or rebuild him.

He wondered which he would be when the sun rose.

The mountain's hum still lingered under his skin, steady as a heartbeat. The Kin said the stone remembered every promise ever spoken within its walls. If that was true, then the mountain itself now carried his words—the first he'd ever spoken in his own name.

It was a strange kind of freedom, to belong to something honest.

He sat up, elbows on his knees, the chill of the floor biting through his palms. The cell around him was carved with faint sigils that pulsed every so often, like the mountain was breathing. The silence was heavy but not hostile—watching, waiting.

The vow didn't erase what he'd done. It couldn't.

But it gave him something clean to build on. A single truth: he would protect her—and through her, the fragile thread of magic still holding this realm together.

He thought of the others.

Meyra, solid as gold-veined stone, eyes sharp enough to cut lies in half.

Druven, quiet and deliberate, strength coiled under silence.

Garrion, disciplined to the bone, his stare sharp enough to flay a man's pride.

They didn't trust him—not yet. Maybe not ever. But they didn't have to. The vow would hold where faith could not.

He had spent so long serving the wrong master that he'd almost forgotten what choice tasted like. Now, with the vow thrumming quiet and alive beneath his skin, he found himself wanting to use it—not for conquest, but to mend what was left.

Maybe that was what atonement really was: not apology, not punishment, but work. The slow, brutal work of standing where it matters and refusing to move.

He pressed a hand over his chest, as though the pulse of the vow still lived there. Maybe it did.

He couldn't pretend it was redemption. Not yet. But it was direction.

And that, for once, felt like enough.

Tonight they would march on Vireth.

Tomorrow the world might burn again.

But this time, he would walk into the fire for the right reason.

He looked toward the slit of light bleeding through the narrow window—the faint, early promise of dawn. The shadows of the bars fell long across the floor, but they didn't look like cages anymore. They looked like markers. Boundaries he meant to step past.

He exhaled, the breath shaking loose something he hadn't realized he still held. When he spoke, his voice was low; not a plea, but a promise.

"Let me do one thing right."

The stone took the words and carried them down into the mountain's heart.

Malric felt the realm answer back—a low, steady thrum, like the world itself acknowledging the vow of a man it once condemned.

CHAPTER 24: THE EVE OF WAR

"To wait is often wisdom. To act is often folly. But sometimes, to wait is to let the world burn." —The Codex of the First Riders

Eliryn didn't rest .

Runelight crawled across the ceiling in slow pulses, counting out the hours she refused to waste. The vows thrummed under her skin, steady as breath. When she finally pushed up from the narrow bed, the mountain air slipped cold along her arms, sharpening the edges of everything.

At the foot of the bed, the Kin had left her leathers: black, silent, built to move. No crest. No ornament. Purpose, stitched into every seam. She dressed, tied her hair back, strapped the last buckle, and felt her body settle into readiness like it had been waiting.

Vaeronth brushed her mind. *We gather.*

Already? she asked.

The sooner we begin, the sooner we end this, he said—simple, certain.

She took one last look around the room. It felt like a pause, not a home. Then she stepped into the corridor and followed the runelight to the Council Hollow.

The chamber opened wide at the mountain's heart, an arc cut for dragon wings and war. Runes etched along the walls fed a soft glow into the space. Wind pushed through the high arch and tugged the torchflames sideways. A long table of dark stone anchored the center, its surface carved with a map of the valley and the city beyond.

Garrion stood over the map with his hands braced, jaw tight. Meyra and Druven flanked him in full armor—quiet, coiled. Malric lingered in the shadow of a pillar, unbound but watched, posture easy in a way that never quite relaxed.

And between them all stood a Kin giant Eliryn had only ever heard of in passing, a name dropped with respect like a title. Kaelith.

He was taller than the others by half a head, gray stone shot through with deep-gold seams that glowed faintly even at rest. His wings folded high and tight, the edges nicked from centuries of use. Scars webbed his forearms. His face was all hard planes—cut by time, not vanity—and his eyes held the kind of patience only battle teaches.

When Eliryn stepped into the light, he turned and bowed, palm pressed to chest. "Dragonrider." His voice filled the chamber without strain.

Garrion straightened. "Eliryn, Commander Kaelith, High Captain of the Kin armies."

"General," Eliryn said, then lifted her chin. "And—just Eliryn, please. We are here as one. No titles needed."

Something almost like surprise sparked in Kaelith's eyes. Then he inclined his head, the respect in the motion clean and unapologetic. "Then hear me, Eliryn," he said. "The Kin stand as an extension of your will. The strength of our generations is yours. We will fly where you point and strike until the work is done."

"Thank you," she said, and meant it. "I'll strive to be worthy of that."

Vaeronth's shadow darkened the arch. He descended to the stone with a gust of heat, claws kissing rock, wings folding in a rolling ripple of scale and sinew.

"Let's begin," he said.

Garrion tapped the map. "The scouts were right. Executions moved to noon. Vireth is locked. Gates shut. Patrols doubled. Sentries on the roofs. If we want Garic, we move tonight under the stormbank."

"Yes, we need to move while the castle staff are sleeping and the civilians haven't arrived yet for the execution," Eliryn said.

Malric stepped closer to the table. "Western kitchens. Runoff tunnel. The stench keeps men away. It returns to the cisterns and the lower halls. It's narrow but solid. Half the ward-lines are old, the rest patched in a hurry. If we keep low, we'll slide under most of it."

Garrion's eyes cut to him. Malric didn't flinch. "We used it when the kitchens flooded," he added. "It's still there."

"How long from entry to the holding cells?" Meyra asked.

"If we move fast—ten minutes," Malric said.

"And if we don't?" Druven said, dead even.

"Then the rest of this conversation won't matter," Malric said.

"Then we move fast," Garrion snapped, not bothering to hide the edge in his tone. "Kaelith?"

Kaelith drew a claw along the line of hills skirting the city. "Two dozen wings will ride the eastern cloud bank. We light the sky where they want it dark. We draw the roof bows to us. The rest hold high and wait. When your signal rises, we descend."

"What signal?" Meyra asked, eyes on Eliryn.

"Mine," Eliryn said. "You'll feel it."

Vaeronth's head lowered until his gold eyes met Malric's. "You know these halls because you hunted her through them."

"I do," Malric said, unblinking.

"And now?"

"I'll use what I know to get her in and out alive." No softness in his answer. No appeal. Statement, clean and bare.

"Your word is ash," Vaeronth said.

Malric's jaw ticked. "It isn't my word alone. I swore in your mountain."

The line held between them until Eliryn set her palm on the table. "Enough. The vow binds. We use it or we waste time we don't have."

Vaeronth's gaze shifted to her. Heat pressed against her skin, but she didn't look away. After a long breath, he scraped his claws once against the stone—unhappy acknowledgment. "Say what you're thinking," he told her, already guessing at her plan.

Eliryn nodded. "We need a distraction inside the lower levels. We have to pull guards and ward-keepers off the cells or the Kin will spend precious minutes fighting iron and sorcery both. I'll do it."

"No," Garrion said at once.

"Absolutely not," Meyra said, almost at the same time.

Druven didn't speak. His attention sharpened like a blade edge.

Kaelith folded his arms. "You won't be alone in that pit," he said. "That's not a place for a Dragonrider."

"But it needs to be done," Eliryn said quietly. "No one expects me in the halls alone. They'll be looking for a guarded path. I won't give them one. I'll crack the floor above the lower cells, make enough noise and light to split their attention. If it goes wrong, there's no one next to me to get burned by my own magic."

"Except you," Vaeronth said.

She held his gaze. "You've trained me not to go too deep into my Well. Trust that."

"Distracting a fortress isn't a training yard," he said. Less anger now. More worry.

"Agreed," Garrion said. "We do not split our strength unless we're certain the gain is worth the risk."

"It is," Malric said, eyes still on the map. "The lower wards are pinned by men. Pull them, and the cages are only stone and script. Your Kin can break stone. If she drags enough bodies and bowstrings upstairs, the cell block clears. It's the best trade you have."

No one liked that he said it. But it was true, and the room knew it.

Meyra looked to Eliryn. "Where do we meet you after?"

Malric tapped a small, unlabeled crosshall on the map. "Here. Under-transept stair. It sits behind the old chapel. Guards favor the other corridor because this one creaks in winter. The floorboards are still bad. You can hear them coming and step around it."

"And if the chaplain's hall is manned?" Druven asked.

"I'll take care of it," Malric said.

Meyra's eyes narrowed, weighing him and discarding the parts that didn't serve the plan. "We move fast, we keep low, we don't engage unless forced. Free Garic. Meet at the under-transept. Then?"

"Then we get out," Garrion said. "Kaelith drops a second wave to cover retreat. We burn the gate pivots from inside so the doors won't close clean. We pull back to the storm line and make them chase us into the sky. None of their kind can fly."

Kaelith inclined his head. "Done."

"Contingencies," Kaelith added, turning to Eliryn. "If you miss the rendezvous, if the hall collapses, if the cell block is gone—"

Eliryn shook her head. "No. We're not leaving without him."

"Eliryn," Garrion warned.

"This isn't a debate," she said—quiet, absolute. "He stood between me and death. He gave me time I used to live. I am not leaving him to the block. If the walls fall, we pull him through rubble. If the citadel swallows us whole, we cut a throat and make a door. I am not flying away and calling it fate."

Silence held, not empty but solid.

Kaelith studied her a long moment, then bowed again, lower than before. "Then the Kin will make the path," he said. "If a wall is in your way, it will not be for long."

Vaeronth's tail scraped the rock. Pride rolled through the bond, bright and hot even as worry coiled under it. *You're stubborn,* he said.

I learned from the best, she answered.

He huffed, which might have been a laugh.

Garrion exhaled. "All right. Assignments." He pointed—clean, efficient. "Meyra and Druven, you're with Malric on the tunnel and the cell. Get Garic out. Eliryn, you take the upper corridors. Make it loud, then disappear. Fall back to the under-transept. I'll ride the parapet line with Kaelith's second flight and break whatever tries to cut you off."

"And me?" Vaeronth asked, mildly offended to not already be at the top of every plan.

"You're the sky," Eliryn said. "You keep the roof bows looking up, not down. If they field mages, take their breath away before they finish a word."

He bared his teeth, pleased.

Meyra stripped one gauntlet and reached across the table. "Let's make the meeting place clean. No confusion." When Eliryn set her hand down, Meyra's cool stone palm closed over it once—brief pressure, a pact. Druven followed, covering both their knuckles with a hand vast and scarred. Garrion set his hand last, human among stone and dragonfire.

Malric stayed where he was.

He didn't reach in. He didn't belong there. He looked at Eliryn instead. There was nothing pleading in his face, nothing crude. Just the sharp assessment of a man counting exits, risks, and what it would cost to carry another body when he ran out of breath. He gave one tight nod. "I'll get him to you," he said. "Don't be late."

She nodded once.

Eliryn looked around the table—at Garrion's hard focus, Meyra's quiet strength, Druven's controlled violence barely held behind the stillness, Kaelith's patience hammered into shape by centuries, Vaeronth's heat banked hot and steady. Even Malric at the edge of the light, dangerous and soul-bound and watching.

She stepped around the table and faced them all.

"I don't know if I've earned any of you," she said, voice low but steady. "But I know what I owe. You call me Dragonrider. That word isn't a crown—it's a promise."

She looked around at them—Garrion with his jaw set, Meyra's hands steady on her blade, Druven's calm like thunder before a storm, even Malric watching from the edge of shadow. "I won't ask any of you to do what I wouldn't. We're not strangers anymore. I haven't known you long, but in my chest it feels like something older. Like family."

Her next words came sharper, purpose rising behind them. "What we do tonight—it's more than breaking chains. It's the first strike in a war Thalen doesn't yet realize he's already lost. We'll bring Garic home, and we'll burn a hole through his fortress so deep he'll never forget it. Every guard we draw, every ward we crack, every secret we steal—it all leads to the same end: freeing the Flame, taking down Thalen, and restoring magic to the realm he's been bleeding dry."

The silence that followed felt like breath held by the mountain itself. The torches burned blue. Even Vaeronth's eyes gleamed brighter, molten with approval.

"If we fall, we fall together. If we stand, we stand because the one beside us refused to yield." She drew in a breath that trembled with power and grief and something older than both. "We go tonight. We come back with Garic. And when the dawn rises, let the realm remember—this is more than vengeance."

Her gaze lifted, the runes along her arms igniting like stars.

"This is prophecy answering at last."

No cheers. No theatrics. Just a hard, quiet yes in the room that sounded like armor cinching.

Garrion clapped the table once. "Gear up."

They moved. The next minutes were noise and detail—straps tightened, blades checked, spare runes tied to belts and forearms, water skins filled, a small wrapped pack of burning-paste set aside in case doors refused to admit they were doors. Kaelith's lieutenants came and went with reports tapped out in low tones, then disappeared again to ready the wings.

Meyra crossed to Eliryn and adjusted a strap at her shoulder without comment. "When you signal," she said, "make it bright enough I can see it with my eyes closed."

Eliryn smiled once. "You'll feel it in your teeth."

Druven studied the map one last time, then erased a small mark with the side of his hand. "They'll block this corridor when the alarm sounds. We'll go under." He didn't explain under. He didn't need to.

Malric watched the three of them and kept his mouth shut. When Eliryn glanced his way, he said, "There's a portrait hall on the upper ring. You'll want to break line of sight. The paint is warded to report what it sees."

"Noted," she said. "Anything else?"

"Don't take the second spiral. The steps are slick. Men slip there when they run. Bodies pile."

"Good," she said.

Vaeronth dropped his head to her shoulder. She put a hand to his jaw and pressed her forehead to the warm ridge above his eye. He didn't speak into her mind. He didn't need to. The bond filled with a steady, unyielding presence: *I'm here. Lets make this count.*

"We will," she said.

Kaelith rolled his shoulders, then turned to his officers at the arch. "Wings one through four, with me on the eastern bank. Five and six hold high. Seven on reserve. Eight on the valley mouth. No one descends without my roar or hers." He nodded toward Eliryn. "If she burns, we flood."

They answered with stone fists to chests and took off into the wind, one after another, vanishing into storm-dark like arrows gone clean to their targets.

Garrion looked each of them over a final time. "This is the part," he said, voice low, "where we breathe."

They walked together to the outer ledge. Night was pulling its hood over the peaks. The storm had come in heavy and low, the kind that smothered moonlight and broke archers' lines. Lightning jumped behind thick cloud, lighting the world for a heartbeat at a time: the city's black silhouette, the river like a piece of steel, the long wall where men would stand tomorrow if she failed tonight.

"Make peace within yourselves," Kaelith said.

She did the opposite. She sharpened.

Vaeronth crouched for her, and she climbed up, the heat of him grounding. Meyra and Druven took the air on silent wings, turning toward the valley mouth to disappear into the dark. Garrion stepped to the lip with them, eyes on the stormbank like it was something he could measure and cut. Malric drew his cloak tight, face unreadable, then looked up at Eliryn one last time.

"Under-transept," he said.

"I know," she answered. "Don't be late."

"I won't," he said.

Vaeronth gathered himself, six tons of power leashed and ready. He looked back at Kaelith. The general lifted his chin. It was permission and promise both.

"Ready?" Vaeronth asked Eliryn.

"Always."

They dropped from the ledge as one. Wind punched her chest; the mountain fell away. Behind them, wings unfolded and caught, caught, caught—Meyra a dark arrow, Druven a moving wall, Garrion a shadow skimming the stone like a sentinel. Ahead, the storm opened enough to make a road.

Vireth waited—hard lines, hard men, hard lies.

Eliryn set her teeth and reached for the power under her skin.

Tonight, they'd make the city remember who they were.

The air hummed, alive with the promise of ruin. Eliryn drew a breath that tasted like storm and steel. Above, thunder rolled like a verdict.

The storm was coming—because she was bringing it.

Chapter 25: The Storm of Vireth

"Every victory is a theft: of time, of breath, of tomorrow. The wise count the cost before the cry is loosed." —Anonymous battlefield maxim

The storm came fast.

By the time Eliryn reached the launch ledge, the sky over the Sanctuary had turned iron. Wind hauled at the banners until the cloth snapped like whips. The Kin lined the rim in two tight wings of shadow and stone—helms low, armor sealed, runes breathing steady on their throats and wrists. Garrion moved along the line with quiet orders. Meyra checked the laces of her gauntlets. Druven said nothing at all.

Vaeronth crouched and lowered his neck. Heat poured off his scales.

With me, Little Flame.

She swung up and settled into the grooves behind his skull, fingers finding the holds they had practiced a hundred times. The leather of her gloves squeaked against warm scale. For one beat she looked back into the Council Hollow—the map table, the ash still clinging to the torches, the faint gold of wardlight along the walls—and then forward into the dark.

Go.

Wings thundered. The ledge fell away. Cold punched her lungs, and then there was only speed.

They cut through cloud like a thrown blade. Rain struck her face in sharp points. The Kin kept formation on either flank—two long chevrons of living stone and runelight—silent as a single thought. Below the Sanctuary, the valley unspooled: pines bent under weather, the river swollen, the old road a pale scar. At the far end, the city of Vireth smoldered with watchfire—a ring of orange around a black heart.

Hold to me, Vaeronth said, and dropped.

Her stomach lurched. The wind screamed past. Lightning stitched the horizon; thunder followed like a hammer across mountains. Vaeronth's body flexed under her—a rhythm she knew as well as her own pulse. Every tilt, every pull. She leaned with him without thinking.

In the bond, his presence was a furnace—steady, contained, deadly when opened. It steadied her.

They're ready, she sent. *We all are.*

We are more than ready. This is what we've been waiting for.

The city rose, closer, bigger. Outer farms lay drowned in shadow. Closer still, the citadel pushed up from the city center like a black tooth—walls thick, towers cut sharp, wardlight webbed like veins across stone. Alarm bells hadn't begun yet. The storm helped. The Kin had timed it well.

Vaeronth banked left. The Kin mirrored him, two wings bending in perfect accord. Eliryn's palms tingled as her magic rose to meet what waited.

On my call, Vaeronth said.

Ready.

Now.

The formation broke like a storm-snap. Vaeronth folded, dove, and the world became rain, slate roofs, the blur of a tower face rushing up to meet them. A spool of chain arced overhead as Garrion's unit flung anchors into a crenellated parapet—the iron bit, runes flared, and a whole guard tower yanked sideways with a shriek. Stone sheared. Men tumbled with it, their shouts lost in the gale.

The first line of Kin hit the outer turrets. Stone fists smashed loopholes into open wounds; wings scissored, bodies pivoted, throws drove armored guards into rock hard enough to dent it. Ward-fires woke late—red bars flared across rooftops, then blew out when Druven's squad tore their sigils up by the roots. The bells finally began—one, two, then a ragged choir—and were drowned under the second wave's impact.

Vaeronth skimmed the rooftops. Heat rolled off him in a rolling tide that turned rain to steam. Eliryn saw sentinels sprint along a high catwalk, saw Meyra sweep through them with a blade stroke that took three men quiet and clean, saw Kaelith's banner flash once on a lower roof—gold veined through black—before the banner vanished into smoke and shadow.

Vaeronth dropped past the western wall. The stench of the runoff slick punched up—a thick gutter smell, rot and old ash—just as Malric had promised. Eliryn rose to her feet, knees flexed against Vaeronth's movement.

You have one heartbeat to tell me this is not a mistake, Vaeronth said, dry and furious at once.

It's not a mistake.

Then jump, Little Flame.

She jumped.

Cold hit like a slap. She landed on the west wall, rolled, and came up with her hands already charged.

No steel. No hilt. Only the tight, controlled surge of power at her command.

The first pair of guards barreled through the stair arch. She lifted one hand and pushed. The air convulsed. Both men flew back, hit stone, and stayed down. A third came screaming with a spear. She cut left, slid, and touched his wrist with two fingers. Blue cracked. The spear went dead in his hand and he folded.

"Move!" she shouted to the squad ghosting from the opposite parapet.

Meyra landed beside her in a slide of grit. Druven hit stone like a falling hammer. Malric swung over the merlon from the shadowed side—soaked, hair dripping, expression level.

"We're in," Eliryn said, already moving.

They dropped to the catwalk. Kin swept the opposite angle, clearing it one rung at a time. The city below was a smear of torch and rain and bodies sprinting. She felt Vaeronth carve a wide circle overhead—his presence pressed her ribs in from all sides.

The runoff grate squatted behind a charred cistern buttress, half-buried under rubble and slick with a film that made the air sting. Druven knelt, touched it, and snorted.

"Warded."

"Not for long," Eliryn said.

She pressed her palm to the grate.

Blue burst through rust. The runes braided into the metal hissed like fat on a pan and went black. Druven wrapped both hands around the iron bars and ripped. The grate tore free with a scream, metal bending like wet reed. Heat rolled out of the dark.

"Down," Malric said, almost conversational, as if they weren't at war. "Right fork for the dungeons. We split at the drain arch."

Meyra slid first. Druven followed. Eliryn took the edge, felt the rough of the stone under her palms, and dropped.

Rot. Heat. The hiss and slap of runoff against brick. They landed ankle-deep in slurry that tried to pull their boots off. The tunnel ceiling hunched low. Meyra lit a sliver of glyph-light with a thumb press. It drew a thin pale line down her cheek; her eyes glowed in the blue.

"Left to kitchens," Malric said behind them. "Right to cells. We're quiet from here."

They moved. The rounded ceiling beaded with moisture that dripped at a steady pace, so regular it turned seconds into a clock. Eliryn kept the power wound tight across her knuckles—enough to answer, not enough to flare.

Ahead, a rusted gate leaned crooked in its frame. Druven braced one hand on the ceiling, one on the bar, and slammed it sideways. Old iron protested, then gave. They slid through into a cistern wide enough for boats, if the water hadn't been black. Runes crawled under the scum in faint red.

"This whole place is fed with magic," Meyra whispered.

"It's diseased," Malric replied. "Thalen drains the Flame through the bones of the city. The wards drink it and spit it into towers."

Eliryn felt it too—the wrongness. Magic wasn't supposed to taste like metal and mold. It was supposed to run clean. She set her jaw and pushed faster.

They reached the drain arch, slick and low. The noise of the city above came down in muffled strikes—bells, shouts, the roar of a dragon. Eliryn glanced back at them all in turn.

"This is where we split," she said, voice even. "I go up and pull the patrols off the cells. You get Garic and move for the inner gate on the south transept. We meet there."

Meyra clasped Eliryn's forearm—solid, quick. "We'll bring him."

Malric didn't touch her. He didn't need to. "Two patrols on the low hall, three on the upper stair," he said, factual as weather. "Ward posts every twenty spans."

"Understood," Eliryn said, and meant it. "Go."

They split.

She took the climb alone, hands and feet on narrow stone, damp grating under her palms. The stair corkscrewed. At the first landing, a pair of sentries rounded the angle, swords already up. She lifted her palm. The air hit them like a wall. Both dropped in a heap. She didn't look twice.

Up.

The tunnel breathed heat. The smell changed—less rot, more oil and torch smoke. Her magic nudged at her skin, eager, a living pressure that wanted to leap. She kept it on a short chain. *Not yet.*

Vaeronth, she sent, the thought a strain to keep steady around her breathing, the climb, the focus. *How's the sky?*

Holding. Sentries down on the east turrets. The western wardline tries to crawl—Druven's wing is cutting it. Your ten counts begin now.

Copy.

The upper corridor opened into a long run lined with narrow slit windows. Rain knifed through them. Half a dozen guards sprinted left to right toward the bell stairs. She let them pass, then turned the opposite way, right hand trailing the wall, left hand tight to her chest, eyes on the floor where hair-thin wardlines were inked into the grout.

At the next corner, she stopped dead.

A full wardbar flowed across the hall. Not one of Thalen's usual bars—a thick pulse, more like a rib than a line, pale red under the wet. Someone had re-inforced it after the first bell.

She pressed her hand to the floor, exhaled slow. The blue under her skin answered. She fed a controlled surge into the stone and watched the red lace with it—two colors fighting, then twisting, then snapping. The bar guttered. She stepped through and kept moving.

Voices rose ahead. A trio of guards stood at a door bound in iron. One had a keyring. One watched the stair. The third braced his foot on the wall and tried to kick the lock. Someone trapped inside screamed for help.

Eliryn didn't think. She shoved her palm forward. The first man flew backward, keyring rattling, skull cracking stone. The second lunged. She caught his blade on her forearm bracer and hit him with a short pulse at the base of his throat. He gagged and went down. The third—faster than he looked—recovered from the kick and slashed. She slid under it and let the magic roll out of her like a tide upending a skiff. He hit the opposite wall and didn't get back up.

"Open!" a woman's voice cried from behind the iron. "Please—"

"Quiet," Eliryn hissed, and took the ring. The fourth key turned the bolt. Six women spilled through—cooks by the look of their dress, though she didn't recognize them.

"South transept stairs," Eliryn said, shoving the door wide. "Down one flight, left at the window with the cracked sill. Stay low. Do not run in the open. If you see a gargoyle, get behind it and do not grab its wings."

Blank stares. Then fast nods.

"Go."

They fled, bare feet slapping wet stone.

She pushed on. The corridor kinked, then opened into a square of open roof under the tower's belly. Rain ran in sheets across slate. She felt the lattice hum overhead where the tower wards braided into a net. This was it. The feed point.

Eliryn planted her boots on wet stone, planted her hands flat, and dropped her shoulders like a fighter settling into stance.

Ready, Vaeronth murmured. No flourish. No praise. Just the weight of him at her back even from the sky.

Ready.

She drew breath, full and slow, and let the power rise.

It came hard. All at once. Not a flare—a tide. It pressed her bones from the inside, ran like current along her arms, threaded her hair, curled behind her eyes until the edges of the world went white and then settled into a color she had never truly **seen**, only understood: the blue she had carried since the day the dragon chose her.

Hold, she told herself. *Hold*.

She pushed both hands into the stone and pulled the ward down.

The net above them screamed. Runes went from red to white to a cracked, ugly gray. Lightning chose that moment to rip the clouds—and the flash fused with her light until there was no telling storm from sorcery. The net tore.

The blowback hit like a kick to the chest. She went to one knee, braced, forced air into her lungs, and kept the power leashed. *Do not flood. Do not drown the hall below. Precision.*

The tower gate thunked as the rune locks died.

Through the bond, Vaeronth's roar rolled like a second heart. *The skies are ours. Go.*

She pushed up. Hands shaking. Vision edged with spark. She turned on a heel and ran.

The corridor back toward the south transept smelled of ozone and hot iron now. She crossed bodies who'd been knocked sideways by the ward collapse. Some moaned. Most didn't. She stepped over a dropped spear and kicked another aside before it could trip her.

Down a narrow flight, across a fishbone of hallways, and into the low passage that bent toward the under-transept stairs. A pair of guards burst from a door on her left and stopped cold when they saw her runes lit to the bone. She gave them one warning look and neither tested it. They backed away, hands up, faces white. She moved past without wasting a breath.

Eliryn swung right where the plaster on the wall had split in a long hairline fissure. She pressed to it, found the hidden seam Malric had described, and shouldered through into a service passage that stank of lamp oil and old soap.

She took the stairs two at a time. The air down here was hotter; the ward collapse had sent a surge through the tower belly, and the detritus of it reeked. She rounded the final bend—and kept running.

The corridors bled heat and smoke. The torchlight bent strange against the walls, flickering over runes that guttered in and out like dying stars. Every breath burned, every sound blurred into the storm's rhythm above—the groan of stone, the scream of wind, the endless echo of wings.

Eliryn's boots splashed through water that ran red from the upper floors. Her pulse matched Vaeronth's thunder. She didn't let herself think about the bodies she stepped over or the shadows she left behind.

She pressed a blood-slicked hand to the wall, steadying herself as another shockwave rattled the tower. The heat of her magic still hummed under her skin, raw and heavy, begging to be used. *Not yet,* she told it. Not until she saw them.

Not until she saw him.

The corridor ahead forked into darkness. One way led down toward the cells. The other bent toward the south transept and the promise of air. She turned toward the smoke and ran harder, every step a prayer flung into the fire.

Let them be there.

Let them be alive.

Let me not be too late.

Above, Vaeronth's shadow swept across the stained glass, blotting out the lightning for half a heartbeat.

Eliryn didn't look up. She only ran faster—toward her allies, toward the place where she prayed the gods still listened, and where, if mercy had any meaning left, Malric, Druven, and Meyra would be waiting with Garic.

Interlude 7: Garic

"Better to fall unbroken in spirit than to live bent beneath another's crown." —Proverb of the Northern Clans

Garic of Stonefell had learned to tell time by the dungeon's sounds.

A guard's boots scuffed from heel to toe when he was sober, toe to heel when he wasn't. The drip by the second torch took seven breaths between falls unless the pipes above were clogged, and then twelve.

Chains sang when the night was cold. Tonight they didn't sing. They hummed.

He pushed his back harder into the wet wall and sat up straighter against the pull of the manacles. His wrists burned where rust had eaten skin to meat. He drew his legs under him, slow, so the cuffs wouldn't clatter. The humming in the iron wasn't a sound you heard with your ears. It was a pressure—like the air before lightning.

Two guards passed, whispering about noon and spectacle and the way fear fed a city. He filed it away, set his jaw, and lifted his chin. He would meet dawn on his feet.

Then the humming changed.

Not the iron. The stone.

The floor took a breath.

A long, low groan moved through the corridor like a beast turning over in deep sleep, and dust shivered off the vaulted ribs. Far above, something roared—huge, alive—and the dungeon shivered again.

Garic stared into the dark until his eyes watered. A draft slid under his cell door, cold and thin, with the clean bite of outside air.

Footsteps. Not the lazy shuffle of bored men or the stomp of a changing watch. Weight. Purpose. Three sets. One heavy as a falling gate. One even, measured. One silent enough that it shouldn't have had weight at all.

Keys clinked once. Stopped. The lock didn't turn. The door didn't open. It left the hinges.

The iron slab lifted straight up, bars and all, and set itself aside with a sound like boulders grinding.

Garic surged to his feet on instinct, chains jerking him short. He braced for torches, for sneering faces, for the drawling voice of a captain he'd promised himself he'd kill with his teeth if he had to.

He got wings.

They filled the doorway—shadows cut to edges. Stone skin veined in faint light. Eyes that caught the torchglow and turned it to metal. One stepped in, taller than any man, shoulders built like the buttress of a keep, skin the color of storm rock. Another followed—sleeker, gold-veined, her movements as precise as a blade being laid flat against a whetstone.

Gargoyles.

His mouth went dry. He'd told himself, in old taverns and colder fields, that the Kin were stories. Prayers with names. He watched them breathe.

The big one—storm-gray—looked once at the chains bolted into the floor and walls and then at the rune-cages sunk into the iron cuffs. He didn't speak. He reached for the left manacle and closed his claws around the bracket.

"Stop," said the gold-veined female, quiet and cutting.

The big one stilled. She crouched, put two fingers to the etched sigils, and hummed—not a tune, a tone.

The runes flickered. She hummed again, shifted the note by a hair's width. The lines guttered out like candles pinched between wet fingers.

"Now," she said.

The big one pulled.

Iron shrieked. The bracket tore, bolts shearing in a spray of rust. Garic bit his lip until he tasted blood rather than cry out. The second cuff went a heartbeat later, and the weight left his arms so suddenly he swayed.

He staggered forward on numbed legs, heart hammering like it wanted through his ribs. He would have gone to his knees, but the big one's hand hit his shoulder and kept him upright like a wall does.

"Easy," the gold-veined one said, straightening. Her eyes tracked his face once—calculating, not unkind.

"Who—" Garic tried, voice breaking into gravel. He swallowed. "Who sent you?"

"Eliryn," said a third voice from the doorway.

He knew that voice. He knew it like you know a wound that never closes.

Garic didn't think. He moved.

He lunged across the small space—blood-slick feet finding purchase on stone—and hit the man in the doorway with his full weight. His shoulder cracked into ribs. He drove him back into the corridor wall hard enough to make the torches ring in their brackets. His hands were empty, but the chain on his right cuff wasn't long—he wrapped it around the man's throat and hauled.

The man didn't fight back.

Garic didn't care.

He dragged the chain tighter, forearms and biceps knotting with old muscle memory, that raw mur-der-heat flooding him for the first time since the ring had carved him open in front of a crowd. He brought his face close enough to see what he was doing to the bastard and made himself look. Storm-gray eyes. Calm. Too calm.

"Breathe now," Garic snarled, "and I'll take that too."

The big gargoyle was there before the last word left his mouth—one arm across Garic's chest, the other hand closing around the chain between Garic's fists. He didn't rip Garic off. He just stood there like a cliff and leaned a fraction. The chain slipped. Garic's grip failed under the kind of strength that didn't brag.

"Stand down," the gold-veined one said. Not loud. Final.

Garic tore free of the big one's hold and swung.

His fist connected with a cheekbone. He felt the skin split over his knuckles and had the savage satis-faction of seeing blood on the other man's face. The man took the hit and didn't lift his hands.

"Again," Garic panted, chest heaving. "Take an-other one. You owe me more than teeth."

The big gargoyle slid a foot between theirs. "Enough."

Garic ignored him and swung again—an old soldier's hook, short and mean. The man let it land. Blood slicked his lip. He blinked once. That was it.

"Fight back," Garic spat. "Or is it only fun for you when you're trying to kill an innocent woman?"

The man wiped his mouth with the back of his hand and met Garic's eyes through the torch-shadow.

"I'm bound," he said, voice even. "Not by iron. By vow. If I move to harm her, I die."

"Good," Garic snapped. He wanted to believe it. He wanted to break his hand on this man's face more. He stepped in until their foreheads almost touched. "Say her name."

"Eliryn," the man said, no heat in it. No plea. Just fact.

"Say what you did."

Garic's snarl still echoed in the cell when one of the stone creatures caught him by the shoulder. The hand was massive—warm despite its hardness, strength leashed beneath restraint.

"Enough," it said, voice low and resonant, like a boulder shifting underwater. "This isn't the fight."

Garic jerked free, chest heaving. "Do you even know what he's done? You think—"

The other creature stepped between them, wings folding close, eyes like molten gold fixed on him. "We think," it said evenly, "you want to live long enough to see him answer for it."

That stopped him. Just for a breath.

Malric stood a few feet away, blood streaking his jaw, saying nothing. No defiance, no remorse—just silence. That was worse somehow. Garic's grip tightened on the length of chain he'd meant to use as a weapon, but he didn't move.

The first creature inclined its head toward the corridor, the glow of its runes dimming. "Our Dragonrider is drawing the guards away. She'll meet us at the stair that cuts through the mountain's spine. If we stay here, her risk means nothing."

Garic's pulse stumbled. *Dragonrider.*

It couldn't mean—

"Eliryn?" he asked before he could stop himself.

The creature's eyes flicked to him. "She lives," it said simply. "Now move."

The world seemed to tilt. Garic's breath left him in a harsh exhale. He had imagined hearing those words a thousand times in the dark, but never like this—not with monsters speaking them as truth.

Still, he moved.

The corridor beyond the cell was narrow and slick with damp, the air heavy with old blood and torch smoke. Two bodies already lay cooling near the door, their armor crushed as if by falling stone.

He fell into step behind the winged figures, every sense sharpened by disbelief. The creatures moved like predators, silent despite their size, their runes faintly pulsing beneath armor that looked grown rather than forged.

The man—Malric—kept between them, unarmed but dangerous even in stillness. Garic watched him with the wary focus of a man who'd once crossed blades and nearly died for it.

They ascended through winding tunnels, the mountain alive around them. Each vibration felt like a heartbeat—slow, vast, deliberate. Far above, the echo of shouting filtered down, joined by something deeper. *Dragonfire*, Garic realized. He felt it more than heard it, a pulse of pressure in his chest.

A flicker of movement ahead—two guards rounding a corner, lanterns raised. The first creature didn't break stride. It caught the nearer man by the collar and slammed him against the wall hard enough to send stone dust raining down. The second tried to shout, and a wing swept through him like a hammer. Silence followed.

Garic's stomach twisted. He had seen death, given it, carried it—but this was different. Efficient. Ancient.

He didn't know if he was walking beside allies or something far older that simply shared his enemy.

They reached the first stair—narrow, winding, slick with water. One of the creatures went first, testing the way. Garic followed, his breath loud in his ears. His body protested every step, old wounds flaring with each jolt. But he didn't stop. He couldn't.

Halfway up, they met resistance—three soldiers, drawn by the noise below.

Garic reacted before thought could interfere. He grabbed the nearest fallen sword, stepped into the open, and drove it through the gap in a man's armor. Blood sprayed his hands, hot and real. He pivoted, blocking another strike. The creatures moved beside him, wings unfurling with bone-shaking power. The sound filled the stairwell like thunder.

In less than a minute, it was over. The guards lay scattered like broken puppets.

Garic stood breathing hard, his grip shaking on the sword hilt. One of the creatures looked at him—not unkindly. Its expression was unreadable in the shifting torchlight, but there was something like acknowledgment there.

"Keep that," it said, nodding to the weapon. "You'll need it."

Garic wiped the blade clean on a fallen cloak and fell in behind them again.

The higher they climbed, the louder the world became. Shouts, explosions, the low rumble of shifting stone. The citadel was under siege.

They reached a landing where half the ceiling had collapsed, exposing a sliver of open sky. Smoke rolled through the gap in black waves, tinted gold by firelight. Garic stepped forward before he could stop himself.

The city below was a storm of flame and shadow. A large dragon wheeled above the rooftops, their fire lighting whole districts in sheets of orange and gold. The air trembled with the beat of wings, with the echo of something greater than war—a reckoning.

Garic's throat tightened. He had fought in dozens of battles, but he had never seen anything like this. He had thought magic dead. He had thought the Flame itself gone cold.

"She's out there," one of the creatures said behind him, voice almost reverent. "Holding the guard's eye while we went to you."

Garic didn't look back. His fingers clenched around the sword. "Then she's doing what she was born for."

A low rumble answered, half approval, half grief.

The creature nearest him turned its gaze toward the mountainside. "She will meet us at the stair's crest," it said. "We move until then."

Garic nodded once. He looked out over the burning sprawl of Vireth, the towers crumbling, the sky alive with the last living dragon, and felt something stir inside him that he'd thought long dead.

"If this is how the world ends," he said quietly, "then let me see it standing."

The creatures said nothing. They didn't need to. Together, they turned and vanished back into the tunnels, the light from the burning city chasing them into the dark.

CHAPTER 26: GARIC OF STONEFELL

"It is not the sword that frightens kings, but the loyalty they cannot buy." —Garrion

The upper corridors burned blue.

Eliryn burst into them like a storm given shape, her breath raw, her magic still singing under her skin from the wards she'd shattered above. Every pulse of power left scorched sigils crawling along the walls, like the tower itself was remembering her.

The air was thick—hot with ash, wet with rain leaking through cracked stone. Every step carried her deeper toward the under-transept where she prayed the others had made it.

Guards rounded the corner ahead, shouting over the thunder. She didn't slow. Power flared through her fingers, a snap of blue light that slammed them back into the wall. Stone split. They didn't rise again.

She didn't linger to watch them fall. The distraction only mattered if she stayed one step ahead—if she reached them before Thalen's soldiers sealed the lower halls.

Down two flights, she turned a corner, skidding through debris. Her palms hit the wet stone. Power surged outward in a ring of white-blue fire, rippling down the corridor and blinding the men closing from behind.

"Come on," she hissed under her breath, forcing her legs to move faster.

Through the open arch ahead, lightning from the storm threw her shadow long and sharp. Somewhere above, Vaeronth's roar tore through the clouds again—closer this time, furious and alive.

Hold the upper keep, she sent, breathless.

I am holding everything, came his reply, the words thunder in her skull. *But hurry, Little Flame. They were waiting for us.*

She didn't answer. She couldn't. Her focus narrowed to the stair spiraling down into the dark. The air thickened—less storm, more smoke, more heat.

The lower citadel stank of blood and magic.

By the time she reached the dungeon floor, the world had changed. The gargoyles had been here—their force had ripped the place open. The air still pulsed from it. Half the walls were cracked wide, glowing faintly with bleeding runes.

Eliryn stepped into that fractured light, her boots splashing through shallow puddles and ash. Her hair stuck to her face. Her eyes burned bright enough to shame the torches.

She slowed when she saw movement in the smoke—when she saw *them*.

And then—him.

Garic.

Hunched under the weight of suffering. Wrists raw. Tunic torn and soaked in filth. His hair was matted, his face bruised, one cheek split—but his eyes—gods, his eyes still held fire.

For a heartbeat, she couldn't move. The world narrowed to that single, unbearable truth: he was alive.

Alive.

Her chest hitched for air that tasted like rain and victory and iron. Her magic dimmed, the storm outside pulling away until only her heartbeat filled the space.

Then he lifted his head. The rune-light spilled across his face, and what rose in her wasn't the clash of the trials, but the memory of a quieter bond—the man who had sat with her in silence when grief hollowed her chest, who had slipped her bread and water when she was grieving, who had carried himself through the Trials with a kind of honesty that could not be broken. She had wanted him to win—not only because he was strong, but because he was fair, and because justice would not curdle in his hands. And when the moment came, when Malric's blade hungered for her, Garic had stepped into its path without hesitation. He had known it meant his death. He had chosen it anyway, because giving her the chance to live was worth more to him than keeping his own breath.

Recognition struck his gaze. A spark across dry tinder.

"Eliryn," he rasped. A prayer dragged from the dark.

She stumbled, tripping over her own feet, tears blurring stone into streaks. She hit him like a spent wave. Cold chain bit her forearms. He staggered. Didn't fall. His arms—shaking, scarred, iron-boned—came up and closed around her until the weight of the world found a place to rest.

Time stopped.

There was his heat. The salt of blood and sweat. The rasp of his breath in her hair. The terrible, holy fact of him. Alive.

"You should have stayed away," he whispered into the crown of her head, voice cracked and breaking, and breaking again. "But I am so glad to see that you lived."

Her tears burned clean tracks down her cheeks. "It's only because of you that I'm alive today."

A laugh broke out of him—ragged, disbelieving, a sound that carried both ruin and victory. "Dragonrider... I can't even believe this."

Her runes surged as if answering her title. Light ran living across the walls, silver and bright, shadows fleeing to the cracks like they understood the shape of promise.

Behind them, Meyra wiped her blade in a slow, deliberate stroke and scanned the hall, not blinking, not soft. Druven stood nearby, his chest still heaving from the effort it must have taken to release Garic.

Malric lingered a few paces of; he lowered his head, but not in mockery. It might have been respect.

Vaeronth's roar tore down the spine of the citadel. Not warning. Not rage. A verdict. Stone took it in and shuddered.

Garic's weight sagged into her arms and she steadied him. Meyra was already at his wrists; granite fingers caught chain and parted it like bad thread.

Iron screamed, then gave. Blood welled in grooves the links had left.

"Can you walk?" Eliryn asked, thumb brushing the cut at his cheek like a prayer.

He set his jaw, rolled the stiffness from his shoulders. "I can run," he said, and that was so like him that she almost laughed through the ash in her mouth.

"Good." She forced air in. The world returned in hard detail: tunnel angles, drip cadence, the scuff where a patrol dragged his foot, the distant clamor of an alarm-bell that wasn't the sky-bell. "We go the south stair. Marta and Nim and all the other staff will be gone by now. If they aren't—"

"We warn them," Garic said, hoarse but sure. His gaze snagged on Meyra, her gold-lit veins gleaming faint in the dark, then on Druven's storm-carved bulk behind. His step faltered. "Eliryn…" His voice rasped, torn between disbelief and reverence. "Gargoyles. I thought they were gone. Extinct. Like the dragons."

She didn't break stride. "So did everyone. That was the point. But they weren't gone—they were waiting."

"Waiting?" he echoed, almost breathless.

"For their purpose," she said simply. Her throat worked as the truth pressed close, but she gave him no prophecy, no thread of fate. Not here. Not yet. "To help me save the realm's magic."

Garic blinked hard, the bruises around his eyes tightening. A laugh scraped out of him, raw and half-wild. "Gods' blood. First you return with a drag-on, now you walk beside living stone. No wonder the crown fears you."

But the awe collapsed into something sharper, his gaze cutting toward the man in the shadows. "And him? Why does that viper still walk?"

Eliryn's jaw locked. "Because he knows the citadel's innards better than anyone. Because I'll use every blade, every map, every oath that gets us inside. He is bound. He is nothing else." Her voice was steel, meant for Garic's doubt and Malric's silence both.

Malric only dipped his head, expression unread-able. "Left ahead is trapped," he said, voice flat, giving the route as if it cost him nothing. "A wire at shin height. Old trick—meant to gut men in chain. You won't see it until it sings."

Eliryn's head snapped up, but he kept speaking. "With the guards stirred, it's worse now. Go quiet."

She gave a sharp nod. Not thanks. Never thanks. Her hand found Garic's wrist and squeezed once. "Stay between me and Meyra. When I say down, you go to ground. If anything goes wrong—"

"I'm not going anywhere," Garic rasped, blood cracking at his lip as he tried for a smile. "You should know that."

"Move," Meyra murmured, her sword angled to catch the dim like a held star.

They ran.

The tunnel narrowed and swelled by turns, the old bones of the citadel curling tight around them. Eliryn tasted iron and old rain. Her runes stroked her nerves in warning when wardlines braided overhead—threads of heat singing too high to hear. They ducked the shin-wire trap by a hair's breadth, Malric's clipped "now" saving Garic a scar that would've cost his leg. The pantry floorboards lifted under her palm; Meyra hushed their groan with surgeon's care, and together they slid into a dust-thin crawlspace while the rats fled their passing.

Above them, the world throbbed with war. Dragonfire raged. Garrion's orders sang along the parapet like hammered steel. Vaeronth's joy in ruin thundered through her chest—the sacred, terrible rightness of a dragon at war.

The cistern arch lay ahead, as Malric had promised. Four royal guards already sprawled cooling on the stone, their blood drawn thin into the channel where water trickled. Eliryn swallowed against the taste of iron, against the relief so fierce it threatened to take her knees.

Garic caught her shoulder, squeezed once. "You should have stayed away," he said again, softer now—no rebuke, only the thread back to the moment before time began again.

Eliryn leaned her forehead to his, just for a breath where the world pretended to pause. "And leave you to be made into a story for their crowd?" She huffed a laugh that wasn't a laugh. "Definitely not. Stand or fall, we do it together."

"Together, then," he said.

Footfalls sounded.

Meyra moved before sound fully formed, ghosting to the bend, signaling: patrol. Eliryn shifted Garic behind her without thought. Malric stayed where the dim caught him—hands free, posture easy, expression unreadable. He asked for no blade, no command. But his storm-gray eyes flicked to shadow, to the ripple in a tapestry that betrayed airflow.

The patrol veered down another cut, drawn by Vaeronth's second roar—deeper now, nearer, filled with insult and promise. Light trembled on the walls as some upper parapet gave way, dust snowing down.

Eliryn glanced at Garic. He nodded. They moved again, faster, toward the under-transept stairs that would spill them into shadow near the execution dais. Her magic burned low but steady, the runes on her skin pulsing in time with her breath.

At the stair mouth, she looked once over her shoulder. Meyra's gaze was stone she could step on in flood. Garic's was fire banked hot. Malric's—silent, watching—held a sharpness she refused to unwrap here.

"Up," she breathed.

They climbed.

Behind them, the tunnels exhaled. Lanterns flickered. The citadel listened.

Above, Vaeronth's cry cracked the morning wide open, a sound so vast the fortress itself trembled.

Chapter 27: The Marrow of His Throne

*"When kings grow too greedy for eternity, they harvest
it not from the stars, but from the bones of the living."*
—Fragment of the Broken Codex

The mountain carried war like a drum inside its
ribs.

Every few heartbeats the stone shook—distant
impacts, the smash of parapets, the long rip of fire
across rain. Vaeronth's presence filled the bond, hot

and steady, his breath like bellows driving a forge. He was holding the sky. He was holding her line. He was waiting on her.

Another sound bled through the noise of battle.

Not above. Below.

At first it came like a tremor under her boots. An uneven pulse. A drag. Then a breath—low, wet, pulled through a throat too tired to keep living. Her runes prickled. The glow along her forearms slipped out of time with her heart and fell into step with the thing that moved in the rock.

She stopped so quickly Garic had to catch himself.

"Do you feel that?" she asked.

He listened. The old soldier quiet came over his face. He nodded once, slow. "That isn't the fight."

Meyra's eyes thinned. The light in the gold veining across her stone skin flickered. "It's coming from the bedrock."

Malric angled his head, as if scenting it. "Lower wards. Old ones. He built levels under levels and taught most men to forget them."

"What's down there?" Garic said.

"Whatever he couldn't kill and didn't dare throw away," Malric answered.

Another breath rolled up through the stairwell. The stone under Eliryn's palm flexed and then settled like a tired chest.

"Alive," she said. "He's keeping something alive."

"Many somethings," Malric said quietly.

Eliryn looked to her people—one by one, steadying herself on their faces. Garic, battered and unbowed. Meyra, a pillar that could move. Druven, a weapon. Malric, useful and dangerous and bound. All of them were waiting for her word.

"We go," she said.

They took the downward stair.

The air cooled fast. The torches along the wall burned lower; damp crept in and sucked at the flame. The stone changed underfoot—from cut corridor to older rock, scored and gouged with marks that had nothing to do with chisels.

Garic brushed his knuckles along a groove. "Claws," he said.

Meyra frowned. "Old."

The next landing opened into a narrow hall banded with iron. Letters burned across the metal—three scripts Eliryn didn't know, stacked on top of each other, fighting for the same sentence.

"What does it say?" Garic asked.

Malric studied the strokes. "It says 'sealed,' 'sacred,' and 'do not open.' It also manages to say 'property' if you read it the way Thalen does."

The sound came a third time—longer now. A chain dragged. Somewhere a collar tightened. The runes in Eliryn's skin flared in reflex. Her magic rose like breath she'd been holding too long.

"Careful," Meyra warned softly.

Eliryn nodded. She took one more step down.

The hall ended in a door of fused bone.

It shone dull in the torchlight, slick with damp. Black sigils burned across it, some sharp as fresh cut, others softened by time into bruises. A ridge down the center looked very much like a spine.

"Gods," Garic said.

Malric's face had gone expressionless. "He makes doors out of what resists him," he said. "So walking through reminds you who this house belongs to."

Eliryn put her hand out. The bone flexed under her palm like cartilage.

Her control wavered.

Not because she couldn't break it. Because she wanted to tear it off the hinges and keep tearing until there was nothing left down here that could ever hold breath again.

She breathed instead. In. Out. The way Vaeronth had taught her.

Druven stepped up on her right. Meyra on her left. Garic set himself half a step behind, sword in hand, his weight ready to take the next blow. Malric stayed where he was, eyes on the seam of the door.

Eliryn gathered the power and drove both palms forward.

Blue-white force hit the bone like thunder. The sigils flared, screamed, and popped in a line. The door buckled. Cracks ran through it in a spiderweb. She hit it again, harder. The ridge split. Warm wet smell came through like a wound opening.

On the third strike the door failed.

The sound went down the hall and up the stair-well and into the war above. Dust fell like gray rain. The room beyond exhaled.

They stepped through.

The chamber was huge—big enough for Vaeronth to crouch if he held his wings tight. Chains crossed from pillar to pillar, sunk deep into rock. Cages grew out of the floor as if the mountain had been forced to bear them. Everything pulsed with faint red runes. A low hum pressed against teeth and bone.

The smell hit last. Old blood. Burned fur. Ozone. The air tasted used.

Shapes moved in the cages.

A dragon broke the light first. Smaller than Vaeronth. Thin. Collapsed into itself. Scales dulled to ash. Runes burned along the collar at its throat. Each pulse of red light tugged a shudder from its body.

A unicorn hung half-suspended in a cradle of crystal bars. Its coat had gone from white to gray. The silver blood under it had dried in layers, each ring a story of a day it should not have lived through. Its horn had been cut short and bound in iron.

Garic swore so softly it wasn't really a word.

In the far cell something winged flickered like a lantern about to go out. Feather, smoke, light. It tried to lift its head and the movement killed its own glow.

The air in the chamber thickened until it felt alive. Every breath tasted of metal and rot and old magic.

Meyra stood motionless before a cage, one hand pressed flat to the iron. The light from her veins flickered like a candle about to gutter out. Her voice came rough and raw. "We were made to protect them," she whispered. "Every Kin sworn, every oath written in blood—this was what we were meant to stop."

Druven didn't answer. He turned from cage to cage, claws scraping stone. When he reached the end of the row he stopped, shoulders shaking. A low sound tore out of him—half growl, half grief. His fist hit the floor hard enough to crack it. Dust fell in gray sheets. The creatures didn't even flinch; they were long past reacting to violence.

Garic drifted toward the unicorn's cell. Its chest lifted shallowly, each inhale a fight. He reached through the bars until his fingertips brushed air just above its skin.

"Gods," he murmured. "What did they do to you?"

The unicorn's dull eye rolled toward him, caught the torchlight, and in that reflection Garic saw the truth—awareness still trapped beneath agony. His voice broke. "No one should die this slowly."

Eliryn couldn't move. She saw everything at once—the cages, the chains, the creatures half-living inside them. It was too much. Her runes throbbed under her skin, answering the helpless rage building in her chest.

"How," she breathed. "How could this live under our feet without Vaeronth feeling it?"

Vaeronth stirred in her mind, a flare of alarm through their bond.

Eliryn? What did you—

She slammed her walls up before the question could form. *Not now. Stay with the sky. Please.*

His presence recoiled, uncertain, then steadied—waiting, trusting her silence. She hated the lie that trust had just become.

The dragon closest to her twitched. Its eye—clouded, cracked with pain—fixed on her light. The collar at its throat pulsed once, red against ruined scales. Something in Eliryn snapped. Her knees nearly gave out under the weight of it.

Meyra made a soft, strangled noise beside her. Druven's claws scraped deep furrows in the floor. Garic's breath hitched like he'd taken a blade.

Eliryn stepped forward. The glow along her arms brightened, the air tightening around her. She reached for the bars without thinking, her fingers trembling, her magic answering the pain in the room like a heartbeat calling to another.

"I can't—" she whispered. "I can't look at them and not—"

Her voice cracked. The runes on her skin flared brighter, flooding the cage in trembling blue light.

The others turned toward her—Meyra's hand half-raised, Garic taking a step, Druven's eyes wide—but Eliryn didn't see them. The world had narrowed to the sound of chains straining and the low, broken breath of the creature before her.

The collar pulsed red. Her runes blazed in defiance.

And Eliryn let her magic wash over her.

Interlude 8: Malric

"The worst crimes are not done by the cruel, but by those who closed their eyes and named it peace." —Ancient Kin Proverb

Malric stood just inside the threshold and took the measure of what Thalen's reign rested on.

Chains cabled from ceiling to floor, heavy links sunk into living rock, dark with the oil of years. Cages hewn from the walls bled runes—sickly pulses that crawled at the edge of sight, each throb in time with the shallow, exhausted breathing of whatever lay inside. Conduits ran from the cage sigils into a spine of inscriptions cut down the chamber's heart, vanishing toward the stair that led up—up toward the throne rooms, the ritual dais, the crown. A feed-line. A vein.

He had suspected rot. He had not imagined a marrow like this.

Eliryn moved past him without knowing he'd stepped aside. Her runes threw silver-blue along the rock, and that was the only clean light in the place. Garic's steps scraped behind her, unsteady but unbowed. The big warrior's breath hitched when the smell hit him—old blood, burned hair, the medicinal sour of boiled iron. He swallowed something that might have been a curse or a prayer.

"Don't—" Malric started, but stopped. He had no right to command.

There was a dragon in the nearest pen.

Smaller than Vaeronth by half—young, perhaps, or starved down to a terrible economy of bone—but unmistakably a dragon. Its scales had been the color of stormwater once; now ash dulled them to the matte of a blade left in snow. Iron manacles bit each forelimb and hind, burning at the edges with a sorcerer's glow; a fifth collar circled the throat, welded not only to metal but to the runes in the wall. The creature's sides moved in shallow shudders. One wing lay half-unfolded, membrane torn, the rips mended and re-torn so many times the scar tissue formed a map of refusal.

The dragon's eye opened at the wash of Eliryn's light. It flinched, closed, then opened again. The pupil was blown wide, as if the dark had taught it that cruelty came only with torches; it took a long, pained moment to focus. When it did, it made a sound—nothing like Vaeronth's verdict-roar, nothing like the bright bellow of a creature taking sky. This was a child's question dragged over gravel. Disbelieving. Hungry.

"Dragonrider," it mouthed.

The word landed in Malric's chest like hot iron.

He felt Eliryn tremble more than he saw it. She was a small thing against the cage, her palms flat to iron, silver fire racing up her forearms and into the latticework of the collar that held the dragon's throat. "I'm here," she said. Her voice broke. She tried again, lower, steadier, the way one speaks to a skittish horse or a dying friend. "I'm here. You are not alone anymore. I swear it."

The dragon flinched as if struck—not from her words, but from the light. Even Malric had to squint against it; his eyes, accustomed to dark chambers, prickled and watered. Garic raised a hand to shield his face. In the other cages, shapes stirred, cringing from brightness they hadn't met in years.

"Easy," Garic rasped. "El... you're blinding them."

Eliryn tried to rein the power, to bring it down into her bones the way she must have been trained to do. But grief unbuttoned restraint. It tore, it spilled. He watched her control fray, strand by luminous strand.

There were other cages. Other economies of pain.

A unicorn stood three pens down, knees locked, head swaying in slow arcs. Its horn, once the cleanest line the natural world had conceived, was fissured along its length as if a lightning strike had taken up residence there and refused to leave. Silver blood had crusted where a tube met its vein, a grotesque necklace of collected drips trailing into bowls engraved with language so old he did not recognize even the shapes of its roots. The beast's eyes were glassy. When Eliryn's light reached it, the ears moved—just once—and then the head came up a fraction, and for that fraction it did not look like a thing, but like a person remembering itself.

Beyond that, a sylph hung from the ceiling by six chains that pinned six joints a human would not possess. Its wings—translucent things that should have thrown rainbows—were in tatters, each feather a thin blade frayed to wire. Its mouth was gagged with iron braided through a rune-stiff cloth; breath leaked around the muzzle in a whisper like a flute forced through cracked wood. Its eyes closed against light, tears collecting and trembling but refusing to fall, as if gravity here was too tired to finish its work.

There were others. A thing of living bark that had been trimmed and trimmed until it resembled a flayed sapling; a serpent whose scales had been re-placed in strips by etched plates that hummed with the same sick rhythm as the feeds; a phoenix feather trapped in a glass coffin of runes, ash packed around it as if to smother the idea of beginning. Malric's sol-dier's mind, which had made survival of inventory, rose to count. He throttled it down. Numbers would make this neat, and neatness would be a sin.

Eliryn drew a sharp breath. Her magic surged, and the light burst from her in a single, blinding wave.

Malric shielded his eyes, but still saw it through his fingers—the light flooding every corner, turning chains into fire, turning the air to something that sang. The creatures flinched and went still. For a mo-ment, the whole world stopped.

Then color returned.

The dragon's scales flared bronze. The unicorn lifted its head. The winged shape in the far cage breathed in, light sparking in its veins. Even the air changed—cleaner, sharper, alive again.

Malric stared. "Gods..." It was all he could man-age.

The sylph's bound chest lifted deeper; its tears finally fell. The unicorn's blood stopped its slow drip and settled in its veins with a shiver that rippled hide to hoof. The serpent went still, then began to shed, the etched plates loosening along a seam and falling like bad scales. The phoenix ash in the glass turned from dead gray to faint ember at the edges, as if a very old memory had recalled a song.

And the dragon—gods—its breath stumbled, then steadied. A line in the membrane of its torn wing drew together as if someone had healed it. A scar along the throat softened, the angry red going to sealed pink. The manacle's glow faltered—not enough to free, not yet.

Eliryn's knees buckled. The light pouring from her skin pulsed faster, too much, bleeding into the floor. The wave spread outward, touching each cage in turn—and then, impossibly, reached Garic.

He gasped, his body seizing for a heartbeat, then straightening. The bruises along his ribs faded, the tremor in his hands stilled. Not healed, but steadied. Whole enough to stand.

"Eliryn!" Meyra's voice cut through. "Stop—pull it back!"

Eliryn's eyes glowed white as the light folded inward, collapsing like a tide drawn home. The sound died. The chamber went still.

Druven held her upright as the glow dimmed to a faint shimmer.

For a long moment everyone just breathed in the moment.

"Do you see it?" he heard himself ask. "The conduits."

Eliryn didn't answer. Garic followed Malric's gaze, jaw tightening. The lines carved into the floor had felt like decoration at first, like the old boast of a mason who wanted to sign his name in sigils. Now their intention was clear: they ran from each cage—each life—into a groove that led out through the arch opposite the door. Up. Always up.

Malric imagined the power humming along those channels. He imagined it rising through floors, through prayer rooms and antechambers, through the dais where Thalen liked the sound of his own voice. He imagined it arriving at a crown that thirsted. The ring had given him hunger; the crown had made a diet of it.

"El," Garic said softly, easing close to her shoulder without touching, as if afraid to break something that might have a chance of mending. "We can't... I don't know if we can break these without killing them."

"I know," she said, and the words sounded like a wound. "But we can't leave them either. We can't let this continue one more hour." She lifted her chin toward the dragon as if that alone were a promise. "I won't leave them."

The dragon stared at her. Tears leaked from the outer corners of its eyes—not the dramatic flood of story, but the slow, bewildered response of a body remembering a reflex. "Dragonrider," it said again, and this time the word was not a question. It was a prayer.

Eliryn pressed her brow to the bars, then slid it to the dragon's healed muzzle where it had crept as close as the collar allowed. "I'm here," she whispered again, and every creature in the chamber quieted as if the sentence had halved the rest of their pain. "I will not leave you here."

The dragon closed its eyes and leaned. The sound it made had not been heard in those depths in generations; it was the smallest noise her light would allow, a rumble that was half gratitude and half caution, as if joy were a language the muscles around its heart had forgotten.

Malric stood with his hands bound and watched something he had not thought possible happen without fanfare: power used without hunger.

He had spent years believing there were only two currencies—fear and desire—and that governance was merely the exchange of those in different denominations. He had done things under that math he could count on the sleepless fingers of both hands and still not be done. He had loved that ring because it made the arithmetic simple. Want. Take. Starve. Drink. Repeat.

Shame rose slow and thorough as drowning. He let it.

"I should have looked," he said, and it took him a second to realize he had not thought the words but allowed them out. Garic's head turned, surprise giving way to an appraisal that did not warm. Eliryn did not turn at all; the light went on moving from her into the room as if it had chosen a path and needed no witness. "I heard the sounds," Malric went on, while the part of him that knew how to keep quiet beat its fists against his mouth. "I saw the extra watches. I smelled the magic. I told myself secrets were the price of peace. I liked not knowing. It made my hands feel cleaner than they were."

No one dared comment.

"We need to break the locks," Eliryn said, at last looking back. "Malric—did he booby-trapped the bindings to kill the captives?"

"He did," Malric confirmed.

Garic took a step, fury re-hardening into utility. "How?"

"Kill words braided into the sequence," Malric said, the old precision sliding over his shame not to hide it but to make it do labor. "If you tear iron or cut sigil without quieting the phrase, the collar will read it as attack and complete the circuit."

"And the phrase?" Eliryn asked.

He looked at the collar, trying to see it as a language rather than a fact. "There's no way to know."

Garic tilted his head in the way of men who have learned to live with fury because they cannot afford to let it spend them. "So we find another way."

Interlude 9: Vaeronth, the Endbringer

"Dragons do not rise for glory. They rise because something beneath them forgot to kneel." —Old Kin Proverb

Rain hammered Vaeronth's scales. Wind tore at the scars along his wing-edges. He cut through both and kept his eyes on the citadel.

Below, Vireth spat light. Towers bled ward-fire. Streets crawled with armed men. The outer wall bristled with glass-tipped bolts that hissed when they struck stone. None of it mattered. The sky belonged to him.

He rolled a shoulder and dumped a clutch of archers from a tower crown. Kaelith's wedge came in behind—eight Kin, wings locked, flight-line straight as a spear. They hit the next tower together. Stone burst. The watch bell spun away into the storm.

Hold the east run, Vaeronth sent down the flight-path, not as words but as hard intent that bit through wind and rain. Kaelith felt it, angled, and the wedge split on cue—four to street, four to parapet—clean work, no wasted motion.

He banked once more to read the field.

Garrion's formation rode the crosswind over the southern battlements, shields up, anchor chains trailing like steel vines. They caught three siege frames mid-crank and twisted them to useless iron. Beyond, another squadron dragged a ward-net off a tower cap and flung it into an empty square where it exploded harmlessly. The Kin moved with purpose, old training rising under old instincts. Stone returning to war.

Well done, he sent, and let the satisfaction ripple through them.

Speartips of opposing light cut through the storm—sorcerers on the roofline. Their faces were hidden by hoods lacquered against the rain. Their forearms were wrapped in something pale and ridged. Not metal. Bone.

He knew that taste.

He folded his wings hard and dropped, tail cutting the air to kill his spin. Fire filled his throat in a clean rush, heat drawing from the deep vault behind his heart. He opened his jaw and put a line of heat across the roofline, not wide, not glorious, just enough to take the ground under their feet. Slate boiled. The bone wraps flared, drank, and cracked. One hood fell back, and the man's eyes went stark with shock. He had not expected this fire.

Vaeronth finished it. One exhale, measured, and the roof went to slag around the men who tried to anchor their magic there. Rain hit the melt and hissed white steam into the air.

He felt the city notice him then—the way structures notice when pressure changes. Doors slammed. Bells tried to coordinate and failed. The citadel threw out security measures too late.

It should have felt clean. It did not.

A Kin cry cut across the wind. Not fear. A call: "Kaelith!" A wing had clipped a spire. The flight-line faltered. Vaeronth dropped a wingtip to throw them his wake. They found the slipstream, steadied, and regained height. The broken spire slid off the roof and disintegrated in the street.

He climbed for the higher air. From there, he could see what the storm tried to hide.

The western aqueduct ran like a black tendon across the city. Two of Druven's ground squads had already anchored it with runic nails and started to pry. The structure held. The third nail bit. Stone groaned, then gave. Water hammered into a side street and washed a line of shield-men flat. Garrion shoved his formation through the gap, clean and ruthless.

He should have roared then for the joy of it. He did not. Something in the taste of the wind put iron on his tongue.

He checked the bond.

Eliryn moved below the rooflines, mind bright and focused. Her presence braced him more than any current. It had steadied him through remembering centuries of grief he refused to name out loud. Now it came to him steady as a drummer's hand on a war-board.

Hold the upper keep, she sent across the bond. Nothing ornate. No fear. A message and expectation.

I am holding everything, he returned. He meant it. He stretched himself across the whole field—towers, bastions, alley mouths, gate mouths.

A flare came from the south wall. Not the orange of fire. Green—cold and quick. He tucked, dove, and watched a sheet of color peel off the stone and drift up like an unfurling banner. A wall-spell, designed to blind winged eyes.

He shut his eyelids halfway and let his other senses run the perimeter: pressure, sound, the weight of air moving through microcuts along the stone. The trick had kept him alive in darker skies than this. It kept him alive now. He came out the other side of the green wash and found three roof-magi braced behind shield-men who thought wood could take flame.

It could not. He let the men live and took the roof.

To the west, Kaelith's wedge dove on a tower that had refused to fall. Bolts hissed up. The tips were glass packed with powder that made flesh numb and stone crack shallow. A bad mixture. Easy to defeat if you did not panic. Kaelith did not panic. He rolled his shoulders to catch the first flight on the thickest part of his wing, sent the second through his secondary feathers, and took the third on his shield. The remaining four Kin in his wedge loosed two chains from above and yoked the tower like oxen. The cap tore free. The men under it sprinted for an exit that did not exist.

Vaeronth marked the survivors for ground capture. The Kin would be gentler than he felt.

He pulled up again to take the field's temperature. The east and south walls were no longer coordinated. The north wall tried to improvise, but the command lights on its parapets flickered in different rhythms. He smelled the salt of fear even through the rain.

This should have felt like a turning. Instead it felt like a door opening onto a room he didn't trust.

Across the bond, Eliryn's presence contracted to a narrow thread. He did not push. She was going somewhere tight. He felt the restraint she wrapped around her power and applauded her silently.

Below him, the Kin ground squads broke a gate-house from the inside. The wooden portcullis stuttered upward, then dropped again. Something in the mechanism had been cut. Garrion's voice lifted, carrying because old commanders learn how to put sound where it needs to go. "Second brace! Hook! Pull!" Chains bit. The gate groaned, then jumped, then came up a handspan. That was enough. Kin went under on their bellies, then came up in the courtyard, and men died who had thought themselves safe.

Vaeronth put flame into the courtyard's far corner, just enough to push the defenders into the angle Garrion wanted. The old soldier did not need the help. He took it anyway and turned the pressure into a clean result.

On the paving below, a single Kin met a captain in the king's colors—a thick man braced behind a round shield, a pale ring biting the meat of his trigger hand. Bone. The ring drank the rain and gave back a faint cold shine.

The captain cut high. The Kin took the edge on his forearm, stepped inside the line, and ended the shield with one heel to the rim. Wood split. He chopped the man's throat with the edge of his hand, hooked the wrist with the ring, and wrenched until joints cracked loud. The captain dropped his blade on reflex. The Kin didn't waste the opening—knee to belly, short knife up and under the ribs, twist, done. Efficient. Brutal. No flourish.

The Kin crouched at once, pinning the ruined hand. He pried the bone ring free; it hissed when the rain hit it. No gloat, no war-cry. He thumbed a chalk mark across its inside seam, slid it into a leather satchel at his belt, and stamped the broken fingers once to crush whatever sigil the man had carried in the bone. Not a trophy—containment. The wrong hands would not find it again.

Vaeronth marked the pouch without comment and moved on.

A moving knot along the inner balustrade caught his eye—officers in rain-dark cloaks, heading for the crown stair. He narrowed his focus and caught the mark burned into the leather at one wrist when a hand came free of the cloak for a step. Pale, ridged, faintly luminous. *Bone.*

The same taste he had struck on the roof. The same taste he had once smelled on Malric moments before he made a move to end her life.

He sent the image across the bond—not a word, not a warning, only the flavor of it, that bone-bright, wrong-cold thing. She answered with steel certainty—receipt, not fear—and kept going.

He let the pride move through him without softening him. Pride had no place in this sky. Only work.

He climbed until the wind got clean again, then turned broadside to the storm and gave the Kin his silhouette. They locked onto it as a rally mark and reset their lines. He bled speed into height, kept his tail set, then dropped along the inner curve of the keep, carving a flight-path for everyone to use.

Garrion's squad came up on the left, carrying a chain of runic anchors torn from an old gate. They slung it across a ward-lattice that hung over the south stairs and pulled until the pattern buckled. The stairs lived again as stairs rather than a field designed to eat men. Garrion let himself grin while he worked and then closed his mouth when the next arrow tried for his eye. He would be impossible if he lived to see dawn. Vaeronth hoped he would live to be impossible for a long time.

A half-flight of young Kin tried a fancy dive and came up clean but winded. He gave them his displeasure like a shadow. It cooled them without breaking them. They tucked into Kaelith's slower wedge and learned how the old way keeps wings alive.

A bell deeper in the city began to strike an uneven pattern. He remembered that bell from a different reign. It was rung when the king wanted the streets cleared for parades. Or purges.

Impact along his right flank—two bolts that came out of the dark with no sparkle to give them away. They bit, shallow, and skittered. The men who fired them cheered anyway. He gave them their moment. Then he folded and dropped through the gap between two spires and took the firing platform away with the heel of his wing.

His mind reached without asking permission for Eliryn again. The bond ran a steady line of intent and motion: run, drop, strike, breathe. Then something else moved through it, brief and sharp. Blue rising. Not an attack. Not a shield. *Healing*. The same shape of power that had rolled through the Kin's hall the day she took the first edges off her ruin and made the room stand taller without understanding why.

He flared his wing to catch a gust and caged the startle before it could unseat him.

What are you mending now, Little Flame?

He did not press the bond for an answer. He did not send a question at all.

The citadel tried a clever thing then. A square in the lower city went dark all at once—torchlight doused, shutters slammed, fires smothered. Men rushed into that sudden dark to hide their movement. They did not understand that darkness is a kind of light to a creature who hunts in storms. He rolled his head and watched the way the absence of glow moved. The knot of men turned left, then right, then poured into a stair tunnel that ran up behind the crown tower. He marked them and sent the mark to Kaelith.

The general peeled a wing to handle it. Vaeronth kept the main pressure on the inner wall. If they forced the defenders to commit here and here and here again, the king's officers would run out of hands for their tricks.

Another flare, far south—this time a cup of light on a roof. A focus point. He breathed down it and found a woman with a staff capped in bone, hands spread, face wet with rain and something else. She threw her staff wide and the light on the roof bled sideways instead of upward. It ran into the air and found the nearest Kin wing. The wing stuttered. The Kin lost lift. He cursed her softly on a breath, then banked, came at her from the blind angle, and knocked her clean off the roof with the edge of his foreclaw. She hit the parapet, rolled, and did not get up. The light collapsed. The Kin's wing found its work again.

He tasted glass shards on the wind—shattered ward lanterns. The city would be blind where it trusted glow. He curled along the keep's leeward face, then raked flame across a ballista frame that had managed to survive the first minutes of the assault. The iron bent. The men behind it broke and ran.

A Kin voice lifted from somewhere he could not see. "For our Dragonrider!" It caught the storm like a hook and dragged half a dozen more voices after it. He wanted to tell them she was not a banner. She was a person made of scar and oath. But he let the warriors have their moment and their war cry, and remained silent.

Rain slackened for a breath. In that brief clarity, he saw the broad plan drawn over the city like chalk lines. East wall suppressed. South wall breaking in pieces. North wall making noise without effect. Inner keep holding. Crown tower untouched. The king not visible. Vraxxis not visible. Too clean a map. Too little grit.

He put the unease away without ignoring it. Suspicion kept you alive. Panic could get your Dragonrider killed.

The bond went bright for a heartbeat—blue, clean, bright—then narrowed again. Not an attack. He would have felt it as a sharp line out and back. This was outward, across, downward. A blessing. The word came to him from a religion older than thrones. He did not believe in it. He knew it when he felt it.

Hold, he sent, and let that word mean a hundred things.

Holding, came back across the bond. He let the relief wash him without dulling him. Then he cut across the inner court to put his body between a pocket of Kin and a surge of men who thought numbers could strip stone from the sky.

He hit the men with wind. No fire. Just the force of a wing the size of a roof moving air where air did not want to go. The front line lost their breath. The second line tripped over them. The third line reconsidered. The Kin who had been braced for a last stand found their eyes again and moved.

"Vaeronth!" Garrion's voice. He had found a roof, found a broken horn, found a way to make both carry. "Break that stair mouth and we cut them off!"

The stair mouth he meant was a slit in the inner keep that fed men down and out to the court in a steady stream. Vaeronth had seen it earlier and left it. Now he took it. He put flame into the throat of the stair until stone spalled and timbers went to coals. He stopped before the heat turned the stairwell into a chimney that would feed flame into trapped men. He did not need that death today. He needed the stair unusable.

A new sound rolled out of the tower then—a low, pulsing hum that did not belong to any fire or wind. The south wards. Waking. He felt the way the air changed around their activation—denser, electrical, hungry for spark. He knew what they were designed to do: cut the sky into squares and lock wings inside them.

He climbed hard, straight through the thickest part of the storm, until the world narrowed to rain and breath and the grind of his own muscles. Then he spread wide and let gravity set him for the next pass. Wings that get braced the wrong way in ward-squares tear. He had torn enough of himself on enough human puzzles to learn.

Below, Kin lines adjusted without being told. Garrion's veterans took the angles first, shouldered the newer fliers into safer lanes, and set their bodies as guideposts. Kaelith lifted half a wedge to high guard and let the others do the hard work. This is what you get when stone has time to teach stone. He would take it.

The bond shivered again. Not fear. Strain. Eliryn pushing, then cutting her own force. The pulse scalded his throat with sudden pride. He did not send it. He swallowed it and turned it into a harder dive.

Three magi on a balcony tried to net him with a braided cord that glowed bone-white. He gave them the illusion he meant to take the bait, then dropped his head just enough to let the cord slide over and took the balcony itself with his left shoulder. Load-bearing stones went. The magi fell with the balcony and vanished into the weather. He marked the fall for a ground squad to confirm. He doubted anyone had walked away.

"Report!" Kaelith's bark, carrying.

"East inner wall clear!"

"South inner wall contested!"

"North—" static of battle, then a Kin spitting blood, "—north scattered!"

"Gatehouse—held!"

"Outer districts—burning!"

"Civilian lanes—closing!"

That last was not a celebration. It meant the city elders had started pushing noncombatants into basements and temple halls. It meant the streets would be empty enough for killers to move fast.

He slid through rain and smoke and found the crown tower again. Still no king. Still no Vraxxis.

Every instinct he earned on fields that no longer had names said this was wrong. Kings who think they cannot be killed like to be seen being fearless. Kings who know they can be killed hide. This one was not hiding. He was absent.

A Kin flier shrieked—not a call, not a rally. Pain. He flipped, found the body, found the thing that had caused it: a glass-bolt nest snugged behind a rain-screen. He inhaled and drew a precise line across the screen. Heat and wind took the nest apart. The archer inside tried to draw a second time with burned hands. He respected the will, then he ended the mortal's life.

Movement at the edge of the square pulled his gaze. A knot of cloaked figures moved with purpose where men moved with fear. They ran not to battle but to a door. The door swallowed them. He marked it. A moment later, Malric's scent—cold iron with that wrong sweetness burned low—threaded from that same corridor like a thin smoke. Not the man himself. The places his life had moved through and stained. He scorned the memory, then set it aside. Tools are tools until they cut the hand that holds them. If Eliryn had decided to use this one, he would let her do so until Malric proved to be too dangerous to live.

Another pressure change. The south wards brightened. The ground told him something heavy and arrogant had woken under the citadel, an old mechanism chewing on power that did not want to be chewed. He put that under the same stone in his mind where he stored absence and waited.

He took the next pass low to keep swords off Garrion's backs and gave himself one indulgence: he broke the bronze crown that sat on the square's central plinth. Not a symbol worth heat, but a piece of metal that had watched too many parades. It went to shards. Men shouted. Let them. Pieces on the ground cut bare feet. It would slow reinforcements.

A crack ran up the crown tower's south face. He saw it because he had been watching that stone for the last hour, judging the way rain entered the mortar and the way heat left it. Cracks tell the truth about lies dressed as fortresses. He marked the line, then marked it again. If he had to, he could put his body through that seam and break the tower's ribs.

Kaelith's voice again, hoarse now. "End-bringer—northwest—signal?"

He tasted the wind. An answer lived there, small but real: a flare on a roof far from the main fight, dropped and snuffed immediately, meant for eyes that did not belong to him. Coordinated withdrawal? No. The feel was wrong. Not retreat. Redirection.

"Hold your line," Garrion added. "No pursuit outside the inner ring."

The ground commander was seeing the same map he was.

Three ballista frames became iron knots. Five squads of men decided life might be worth more than loyalty to their corrupt king. The Kin lost two and carried three more who would live if they made it home. He knew every wing by its scars. He added new ones to his mind and kept count.

Then the first drum sounded from beneath the crown tower. He felt it in his bones before he heard it. Slow. Heavy. Old. Not the city's bell. Not a call to arms. A mechanism answering a hand it feared.

His throat filled with heat he did not mean to release. He swallowed once, twice, took the bite of rain into his mouth, and cooled.

He spread wide again and let his shadow cover the square. The Kin rode it into their next positions as if it were a roof. Combat makes families quickly. Fear makes them faster. He wanted them to live long enough for a slow version of both.

West, a squad of city officers tried the bone-light trick again—arms wrapped, rings glimmering on string-thin hands, faces turned up to find the dragon who would give them the power they had been told they deserved. He gave them only heat without flame, hot enough to break concentration, then a downdraft heavy enough to shove them to their knees. When they looked up, Kaelith's wedges were already there. Stone resolved problems the right way.

A final flare along the south wall. Not a trap. A signal. He angled for it and saw exactly what he had feared: no king on the battlements. No Vraxxis in the tower door. Too much room where there should have been pride or theater. He stared at the empty spaces and let the knowledge harden inside him.

This fight had been meant to hold them. Not to beat them. A hand laid on a gameboard to keep a piece busy while another hand moved below the table.

He did not have the luxury of stopping to name it. Naming could come later. Right now, his rider moved under stone. His Kin bled on roof tiles. His old enemy was not where a proper murderer should be.

He took a breath that burned, then sent two commands at once—one down the flight-lines, one across the ground net.

Lock the inner ring. No one leaves without a wing on them.

And to Garrion: *Hold the square and keep eyes on the crown stair. If it opens, you throw everything you have.*

Then he climbed into the storm until the rain became needles and the city was a map of red and gold and shadow below him. He let the roar that lived in his chest loose into the sky—not for fear, not for victory, but to tell the mountain he had heard the drum beneath the tower and he would not look away.

He leveled off, eyes on the crown tower, and waited for the next wrong thing to show itself. The rain came harder. The Kin reset their grips. The enemy drew themselves into fewer, tighter knots. The drum under the tower kept time with a will that did not belong to men.

Something old was waking. He turned his head to feel it better and let a low growl roll through his chest.

Come then, he thought. *Come honest and come now.*

The only reply was the steady pull of his Dragonrider's presence and the sharp, clean hunger in his own lungs as he lined himself up for another pass and bared his fire to a sky that had forgotten its name.

Chapter 28: A New Purpose

"The truest battles are fought where no crowds can see."
—Old Rider's Adage

The chamber held her light desperately; shocked, greedy, and aching.

Eliryn's glow had gentled to a warm, sun-touched hue, but even softened it made the cages flinch and the carved runes waver as if embarrassed to be seen. Breath returned to the room in fits and shivers: the thin whistle through a sylph's gag; the unicorn's long, tremulous exhale; the rattled, sand-dry draw of the chained dragon at her hands. The stink of old blood and boiled iron lay over everything. Beneath it, something sweeter lifted—sap and ash and the clean warmth that followed her healing flare.

She pressed her brow to iron, then to scarred scale. "I'm here," she whispered again, not trusting the strength of her throat. "I'm here."

The dragon's eyes were a lake in drought—black basin, a ring of stormlight at the rim. They watched her the way an abused thing watches a door: hoping, refusing to. When her runes surged it made a sound that might once have been a purr, if the world had been kinder; now it was a bruise of noise, hollow and small.

Eliryn's fingers tightened on the iron where the runes guttered. The heat bit into her palm, but she didn't let go. Her voice shook, but her words were iron.

"Not anymore. Never again."

Garic braced himself against the wall, chest heaving. His eyes raked over the cages, the chains, the blood gone black on stone. His voice cracked like a blade against stone.

"They've been feeding the throne with this. Gods help us."

Eliryn shut her eyes for a heartbeat. A tear burned hot down her cheek. She didn't wipe it away.

"Then we don't break them wrong," she said. "We bring stone and magic enough to tear every word he's written out of this place."

Eliryn turned back to the dragon, pressing her palm against its scarred muzzle. "I'm not leaving you," she whispered. "Not one of you. Not ever. I swear it."

The dragon's head no longer hung like dead weight; it lifted a fraction, eyes clearer, pupils catching her glow. The unicorn's horn no longer cracked with pain at every tremor but hummed faintly, like a string tightened back into tune. Even the sylph's wings twitched, not in despair but in something closer to recognition.

And Garic—though her magic had not been meant for him—drew breath with less raggedness than before. The worst of the tremor had eased from his limbs, and some of the gray drained from his face. He still looked half-broken, but for the first time since she had dragged him from the execution square, he stood without bracing hard on the wall. His eyes met hers, raw gratitude buried under iron stubbornness.

They were not whole. But they were alive. Alive enough to endure a little long

Her runes brightened, bleeding light through the chains until the chamber flinched from it. She pressed inward, into the bond.

Vaeronth?

The dragon's presence hit her like the break of stormclouds—wind, fire, rage, exhaustion, triumph all at once. Images hammered through: torn banners, broken gates, gargoyles falling like meteors into the melee. His voice rolled inside her, old and furious.

The tide is ours. Thalen is held. Vraxxis runs. The field belongs to us, though blood stains it. What do you need, Little Flame?

Eliryn steadied herself, her grief bubbling too close. She hid the worst of it. She showed him only the barest outline: darkness, iron, chains that needed breaking.

We need a little extra time.

I'll see what I can do.

Eliryn didn't want him to know about the horrors they had discovered. Not yet. Not when he was still in battle.

She pushed upright.

She looked up at the vaulted ceiling, at the narrow tunnels yawning back the way they'd come, then back to the dragon's enormous bulk bound in chains thicker than her torso. "Gods," she whispered. "How in all the hells do we move them?"

Garic still leaned against the wall, bruised shoulders rising and falling with every breath. His gaze went from the dragon to the unicorn, then to the serpent coiled like a living river of iron. "We can't walk them out through the same cracks we used. They'd tear themselves apart before they reached daylight."

Garic paused before he continued. "Thalen built the citadel to flaunt power above, but he built the underways to keep secrets buried. A dragon this size does not leave without tearing half the fortress down with it."

Eliryn pressed her palm to the dragon's manacle, the warmth of scale burning through cold iron. Her runes flared, silver-blue. "Then that's what we do. We tear down the entire castle if we need to. I will not leave them behind."

The dragon's vast eyes turned on her, disbelief shivering in molten depths. Its voice was a rasp of ash. "Impossible."

Eliryn met its gaze, her arms blazing brighter until the chamber walls caught her light. "So is surviving centuries in chains. You've already done the impossible. Now it's my turn."

When she spoke, her voice was quiet. Too quiet for a place built on screams. But every word cut like a blade dragged through marrow.

"This castle," she said, her hand pressed to the dragon's muzzle, "these halls, these dungeons—every stone raised on stolen blood, every chain forged on cruelty—they end. Today."

Her eyes rose, meeting Meyra's, then Druven's, then Garic's battered fire. Even Malric's unreadable storm-gray stare could not escape her.

"We are not mending this place," she continued, calm as doom. "We are not patching over rot. We are tearing it down. From the highest spire to the deepest root, this citadel dies with Thalen. And in its ashes, something new will rise—something that will never bow to chains again."

Her runes flared, light spilling like molten silver until it painted every cage, every captive. The unicorn lifted its head fully for the first time, horn gleaming like starlight. The sylph's bound wings strained against iron with a sharp cry. Even the serpent coiled tighter, as though preparing for the strike it had been denied for centuries.

Meyra's blade trembled—not with fear, but with fury too vast for her stone-forged body to contain. "Then say the word," she whispered, gold-veins blazing. "Say it and we'll raze this place to dust."

Druven's claws gouged stone. His rumble shook dust from the ceiling. "Say when."

Eliryn straightened, her glow burning steady, not wild. Not frantic. Inevitable. She raised her hand, light dripping from her skin like judgment.

"Now."

Interlude 10: Thalen

"What fire destroys, grief perfects. Some men bury the ashes. Others build empires from them." —Thalen, Sovereign of Vireth

The first time Thalen saw a unicorn, he begged it for mercy.

His sister had been sick for weeks, her little body burning with fever that no poultice or herb could break. His mother would not move her, even when word came that dragons would battle in the skies nearby. His father refused to abandon them. "Family is not divided," he had said, and Thalen had believed him.

So Thalen had gone into the forest. Only for an hour, no more. Long enough to track the pale shimmer between birch trunks, long enough to chase the myth whispered of in winter tales: a unicorn's horn could heal. He remembered its eyes—silver and bottomless, full of an alien pity. He had begged, voice raw, knees in the snow. But the unicorn only watched.

Then the sky split. The dragons came. Fire rolled across the horizon. The unicorn bolted.

When Thalen stumbled back to his village, the cottage was gone. The house, the fields, the people inside—all ash and bone. His mother clutching his sister's small body. His father's body over them both. They had not run. They had not stood a chance.

The dragons had warned them to leave. That was the apology, given like scraps to dogs. The great war of wings and flame had mattered more than the lives below.

That was the day Thalen's heart changed shape. That was the day he swore dragons—and all who bore their cursed gift—would fall.

Now, years later, he stood in the citadel's high chamber and watched his city buckle under dragonfire. The Endbringer's shadow carved fire across the night sky. Gargoyles dropped from the aqueduct like falling mountains, stone wings catching firelight.

For a moment, Thalen almost laughed. He had not expected the gargoyles. He had thought them long extinct, another myth rotted by time. Yet here they were, answering some ancient oath. His eyes narrowed. *If even one of those relics could be taken alive... if even one could be chained as he had chained the others... the marrow of their power would remake him and the realm anew.*

But he did not give in to the urge to join the fight. He did not command. Not yet. Let them think themselves victorious. Let the beast Vaeronth roar and scorch his towers. Let the gargoyles claim the square. Vraxxis—the new-crowned puppet—would thrash and spit, but that was what Vraxxis was for. A mask, a shield. The true Flame still burned in Thalen's chest, though it strained now, bucked against him, restless in the presence of its true chosen.

He touched the circlet at his brow. Cold metal, hot vein. The Crown of Severance. Dragonbone carved into cruel arcs, inlaid with fragments of relics stolen from centuries of chained beasts—unicorn blood, sylph feathers, basilisk scale, the marrow of things once pure. All bound with his blood. All tuned to one purpose.

The crown did not give power. It *unmade* it.

When Thalen first claimed the Flame, his vengeance was clumsy, wild, and more powerful than he had ever dreamed. He poured every resource into that first strike, hurling the Flame against the dragons who had scorched his home. The magic answered—but it did not confine itself to the sky. It spread outward in a storm, uncontrolled, ripping through dragons and anything else bound to magic's pulse. Unicorns bled silver in their groves. Sylphs fell from air like burnt paper. Forests withered, rivers blackened, and the very fabric of the realm shuddered beneath a rotting wound. Entire bloodlines of creatures vanished, and the air itself seemed thinner for years. Thalen had not intended such collateral ruin, but neither did he mourn it. Magic had always demanded too much; he was content to make it suffer. The price was immense: he burned through reservoirs of power he would spend the next centuries rebuilding, stealing fragment by fragment, feeding on chained beasts to sustain his life and crush every rival. That waste taught him precision. Now, with the Crown of Severance, he did not need to scatter death like salt. He had a weapon honed sharp as a surgeon's knife, able to thread through the marrow of the world and cut exactly what he wished: the sacred bond between dragon and the Last Dragonrider.

She would be the end of him—unless he struck first. Already she was different than the girl who had once stumbled through his citadel, her aura no longer the raw, flame-lit blaze of a half-formed dragonrider but a steadier, silver-blue glow that bled from the runes carved into her skin. Fire had become light. He did not know what had tempered it—or who—but the change unsettled him almost as much as her return.

He watched the battle raging just outside as Vaeronth struck down another bastion, stone crumbling like sand. Gargoyles swept through the streets, unyielding, unbroken. For a moment the citadel shook as though it would belong to them.

And that was when Thalen smiled.

He let his hands rise, steady. He let the crown's runes flare, feeding on every relic it contained. Blood dripped from his temple as the dragonbone cut deeper, greedy, eager.

"It's time, little Dragonrider," he whispered to the dark, savoring the taste of the words. "Time to feel what it is to lose half your soul."

The power surged through him—weight of storm, edge of steel, hunger of centuries—until it burned so sharp it felt like the crown itself was cutting into the marrow of his skull. He loosed it like a spear through the night.

The bond screamed. It wasn't sound, not truly—it was rupture, like the tearing of sinew, like worlds splitting at the seam. Vaeronth's roar answered, but it broke mid-note, shattering into something rawer than agony, a cry that made the air itself convulse. Below, the Dragonrider's light guttered, flared, and faltered, as though someone had plunged their hands into her chest and stolen her lifeforce.

A thunderclap of wings overhead—violent, desperate—before they stuttered and failed. A shadow fell across the citadel as Vaeronth's colossal weight crashed down, striking spires, tearing stone free in an avalanche of ruin. Towers that had stood for generations screamed and folded into dust beneath his fall. The impact shook the foundation of the fortress, and the night swallowed the sound like triumph.

Thalen closed his eyes, drinking in the silence that followed: silence where there had been fire, silence where there had been fighting.

The Dragonrider was lesser again. Broken. Half herself. And now she would learn the cruelty of survival.

Thalen leaned back in his chair, breath steady, eyes cold.

Outside, the citadel was chaos, fire, and ruin. But inside, he had already won.

Chapter 29: The Severing

"When the impossible happens, it does not shatter the world. It shatters you, and the world keeps breathing without you." —The Lament of the First Ride

The citadel shook as if the bones of the world were being wrenched apart. Dust rained down, chains clanged, the very air trembled with Vaeronth's fury—until suddenly, it didn't.

The roar cut off.

The bond tore.

It was like the sudden amputation of a limb she had never known could be taken from her. Pain exploded—raw, impossible, all-consuming—hollowing her chest as though half her soul had been carved away in a single heartbeat. Her breath vanished. Her light guttered.

Eliryn screamed. The sound didn't even feel like hers—it was animal, broken, born of something deeper than body or voice.

And then there was nothing. No warmth at her ribs. No endless thrum of fire steadying her pulse. No heartbeat but her own. The silence inside her was worse than death.

She staggered, collapsed to her knees. Her hands clawed at her chest as if she could dig him back out of the void. "Vaeronth!" The name ripped her throat raw. "Vaeronth!"

But nothing answered.

Garic caught her shoulders, trying to anchor her, his voice hoarse with panic. "Eliryn! Talk to me—what happened?"

She couldn't answer. She was still falling, still screaming inside where no one could hear it. A soul ripped in half. The air around her stung with magic and grief, too sharp to breathe.

Malric had gone very still. His voice was low, muttered almost to himself, but the words carried like a curse.

"That's how the first dragons fell," he whispered, haunted. "Tamper the bond, tear it at the root... Thalen's done it again."

Eliryn's head snapped toward him, fury blazing hot through the hollow. "No." The denial shredded her throat. "No, he's not gone. He can't be—"

The floor shook violently. A thunderous crash reverberated from above, rolling through the stone like the heartbeat of doom. Dust poured from the ceiling. The sound of structures falling.

A dragon's fall collapsing a city.

Eliryn's entire body seized. She doubled over, clutching her stomach as if she'd been stabbed through. Her breath tore out of her in gasps, her sobs raw, unshaped.

"No!" she screamed. "He's alive! He has to be—"

Her words broke, swallowed by grief. She pressed her forehead to the filthy stone, her body shaking so hard her teeth rattled. It felt as if her skin had been peeled away and every nerve exposed.

Meyra dropped her blade, sank to one knee beside Eliryn. Stone-veined arms, unyielding in battle, curved around her with impossible gentleness. She pressed her forehead to Eliryn's crown.

"We are with you," she said, her voice a low grind of rock, steady as bedrock. "Stone and blade. Whatever comes—you will not stand alone."

Druven's growl filled the chamber, a quake rising through the floor, through Eliryn's bones. His claws struck sparks she could hear, not see, the scrape singing against the stone. He moved closer until his presence loomed like a mountain.

"Say the word," he rumbled, thunder cracked open inside his chest. "I will go. Through walls, through sky—I will find him. If Thalen has done this, I will tear him out of his own marrow. Nothing forged by kings can keep me from my bonded."

The chained dragon stirred at that word and Eliryn felt it in her skin: the faint tremor of chains shifting, the sudden rush of heat against her face as its breath deepened. A sound followed, low and ragged, not roar, not sob, but something in between—raw, aching recognition.

The chamber answered.

The unicorn's horn gave a faint thrumming hum she felt in her ribs, a note so steady it rattled her teeth.

The sylph's wings strained, the fetters clinking and ringing like brittle bells.

The serpent dragged scale against iron, a hiss reverberating through the floor like a drawn blade.

Even the dryad shifted, bark creaking, a dustfall whispering across the air like a forest sighing awake.

The sound of straining metal filled her ears.

Eliryn's breath broke on a sob. She clutched at the iron bars, the warmth of scale beneath, the vibration of hope flaring like a wound. She could hardly breathe for the weight of it—the Kin beside her, the captives rising, the silence where Vaeronth had taken up space inside her.

Garic's hand found her shoulder, grounding her left side with scarred, human steadiness. His voice was hoarse but sharp, soldier's steel bared to its edge.

"El," he rasped, "if you still live, so does he. Do you hear me? That bond doesn't end in silence. If you breathe, he breathes somewhere. Hold to that. Hold to him."

Her tears slipped hot, burning her cheeks. She clutched his words like a rope flung across a chasm, Meyra's presence like stone she could kneel upon, Druven's vow like a blade already breaking chains.

And then the chamber shuddered—not with sight, not with light, but with sound and touch: the unicorn's hum swelling, the dragon's body straining against links, the sylph's wings rattling, the serpent's hiss swelling sharp as steel.

It wasn't only her grief filling the room.

It was theirs, too.

They had felt what had been severed. They knew what was missing.

Her sobs hitched, ragged, and she clung to the words like wreckage in a storm.

But the emptiness inside her still screamed louder than any enemy. The silence where Vaeronth had always been was unbearable, unthinkable.

It was only then—amid the sobs, the hollow ache, the aftershocks rattling the floor—that she realized she could not see.

No light. No glow. No shadows. Only black.

Her runes, once bright enough to chase the dark, were dead embers along her skin.

"Eliryn?" Garic's grip tightened as she stiffened.

Her lips parted. The truth landed like a blade to the gut. The grief had been so vast, so annihilating, she hadn't even noticed.

Her sight—gone.

The citadel's silence laughed. Dust drifted from the ruins above like ash on a grave.

And Eliryn, the Last Dragonrider, last hope of her kind, pressed her fists to her ribs and screamed—blind and impossibly broken.

BLIND. BROKEN. UNBOWED.

Blind and hunted, Eliryn runs through a realm unmade by its own king. Her dragon is silent. The Kin are
lost. The realm bleeds starlight and ruin.

To find her dragon, she will have to face the monster
who severed their bond. To end Thalen's reign, she
will have to become something more than mortal.

The gods are waking. The hunt has begun. And only
one will rise from the ruin.

Coming December 2025:
THE WRIT IN RUIN
Book Three of *The Sightless Prophecy Trilogy*
Find updates, teasers, and release info at:
@blacktoppublishing and **@sightlessprophecy**

ABOUT THE AUTHOR:

Jaimie L. Vermette grew up tucked against the edge of the Canadian border, where winter rewrote the world for months at a time and books were the only kind of warmth that lingered.

After earning multiple degrees she doesn't use and working in fields far from fiction, she finally decided to chase the dream she'd shelved for far too long.

The Silent Vow is her second novel and the second book in *The Sightless Prophecy* trilogy—a dark, intimate fantasy of slow-burning obsession, quiet resistance, and the cost of survival.

She writes for the overthinkers, the ones who feel like they're a little too much... and for anyone who's ever fallen so deep into a fictional world, real life felt like the side quest.

And if you know her in real life... no you don't.